BLOOD MUSIC

REMEMBER'D KISSES
by Michael F. Flynn

RECORDING ANGEL
by Ian McDonald

SUNFLOWERS
by Kathleen Ann Goonan

THE LOGIC POOL
by Stephen Baxter

ANY MAJOR DUDE
by Paul Di Filippo

WE WERE OUT OF OUR MINDS WITH JOY
by David Marusek

WILLY IN THE NANO-LAB
a poem by Geoffrey A. Landis

Edited by Jack Dann & Gardner Dozois

UNICORNS!
MAGICATS!
BESTIARY!
MERMAIDS!
SORCERERS!
DEMONS!
DOGTALES!
SEASERPENTS!
DINOSAURS!
LITTLE PEOPLE!
MAGICATS II
UNICORNS II
DRAGONS!
INVADERS!
HORSES!
ANGELS!
HACKERS
TIMEGATES
CLONES
IMMORTALS

Edited by Terri Windling

FAERY!

NANOTECH

EDITED BY
JACK DANN & GARDNER DOZOIS

ACE BOOKS, NEW YORK

This book is an Ace original edition,
and has never been previously published.

NANOTECH

An Ace Book / published by arrangement with
the editors

PRINTING HISTORY
Ace edition / December 1998

Cover art by Doug Struthers.

For information address: The Berkley Publishing Group,
a member of Penguin Putnam Inc.,
375 Hudson Street, New York, NY 10014.

The Penguin Putnam Inc. World Wide Web site address is
http://www.penguinputnam.com

ISBN: 0-441-00585-3

ACE®
Ace Books are published by The Berkley Publishing Group,
a member of Penguin Putnam Inc.,
375 Hudson Street, New York, NY 10014.

PRINTED IN THE UNITED STATES OF AMERICA

10 9 8 7 6 5 4 3 2 1

Acknowledgment is made for permission to reprint the following material:

"Blood Music," by Greg Bear. Copyright © 1988 by Greg Bear. First published in *Analog*, June 1983. Reprinted by permission of the author.

"Margin of Error," by Nancy Kress. Copyright © 1994 by Omni Publication International, Ltd. First published in *Omni*, October 1994. Reprinted by permission of the author.

"Axiomatic," by Greg Egan. Copyright © 1990 by Interzone. First appeared in *Interzone* #41, November 1990. Reprinted by permission of the author.

"Remember'd Kisses," by Michael F. Flynn. Copyright © 1988 by Davis Publications, Inc. First published in *Analog*, December 1988. Reprinted by permission of the author.

"Recording Angel," by Ian McDonald. Copyright © 1996 by Interzone. First published in *Interzone*, February 1996. Reprinted by permission of the author.

"Sunflowers," by Kathleen Ann Goonan. Copyright © 1995 by Interzone. First appeared in *Interzone*, April 1995. Reprinted by permission of the author.

"The Logic Pool," by Stephen Baxter. Copyright © 1994 by Bantam Doubleday Dell Magazines. First published in *Asimov's Science Fiction*, June 1994. Reprinted by permission of the author and the author's agent, Maggie Noach Literary Agency.

"Any Major Dude," by Paul Di Filippo. Copyright © 1991 by Paul Di Filippo. First published in *New Worlds* (Gollancz). Reprinted by permission of the author.

"We Were Out of Our Minds with Joy," by David Marusek. Copyright © 1995 by Bantam Doubleday Dell Magazines. First published in *Asimov's Science Fiction*, November 1995. Reprinted by permission of the author.

"Willy in the Nano-Lab," by Geoffrey A. Landis. Copyright © 1998 by Dell Magazines. First published in *Asimov's Science Fiction*.

CONTENTS

PREFACE

Although stories from way back in the fifties such as Philip K. Dick's "Autofac" and "Second Variety" can be considered to be the aesthetic ancestors of at least one kind of nanotech story (depicting, as they do, self-replicating robot machinery run amok, reproducing unstoppably, and spreading beyond all human control, laying waste to the landscape—basically a variant of what is now known as the "gray goo scenario" in nanotech circles: where out-of-control nanomechanisms eat *everything* in their relentless drive to reproduce more of themselves, turning everything into, well, *gray goo*), "nanotechnology" as such wasn't talked about much in the genre until after the appearance of K. Eric Drexler's extremely influential non-fiction book *Engines of Creation* in 1986.

A speculative look at the eventual possibilities of an emerging future technology—dubbed molecular nanotechnology by Drexler—that might eventually be able to create self-replicating controllable machines, smaller than viruses, that could be used to build or alter almost any structure by directly manipulating atoms or molecules on the nanometer scale, *Engines of Creation* had an enormous impact on the imagination of many of the science fiction writers of the day, perhaps influencing the consensus picture of what the future was going to be like more than any other non-fiction book ever has (with the possible exception of Alvin Toffler's *The Third Wave*, or perhaps of Gordon Rattray Taylor's *The Biological Time-Bomb*, which inspired a subgenre of stories about clones and other marvels of biological technology—and also a flood of stories about the dangers of overpopulation and the destruction of the environment—in the late sixties and seventies).

In the real world, nanotechnology has not yet arrived, although we continue to inch steadily closer with each new breakthrough in microminiature engineering to the day when nanotechnology will be a functional reality—according to *some* scientists, anyway. According to *other* scientists, nanotechnology—of the sort featured in science fiction stories, at least—will never be a practical reality. Only time will tell which of these groups is right. (Perhaps reality will follow a middle course, as it often does, with nanotechnology becoming viable, but proving less all-embracing and omnipotent than some writers have suggested that it will be, perhaps for reasons that have not yet been foreseen. I suspect that if it *is* possible, it's going to turn out to be much more difficult to do than currently expected, and less magically facile of operation—and that its most far-reaching implications for society may be ones that nobody has even *thought* of yet.)

In science fiction, though, nanotechnology is already here, an accepted part of the consensus vision among SF writers as to what the future is going to be like—to the point where, if your future society *doesn't* feature the use of nanotech, you have to explain *why* it doesn't in order to give your future world any credibility at all.

After Drexler, "nanotechnology" became the buzzword of the day, as "virtual reality" and "cyberspace" had been slightly before it, and suddenly every writer with any claim to being *au courant* with the Cutting Edge of science was writing nanotech stories. There were a *lot* of nanotech stories written in the late eighties and all throughout the nineties to date, and, since many of the writers who climbed gladly aboard the nanotech bandwagon had little or no knowledge of science or how technology actually works, nanotech stories quickly became a cliche, overused, just as had happened with overpopulation/Environmental Doom stories by the mid '70s. In some hands, nanotech became merely a Magic Wand, a plot device that enabled you to accomplish anything in a story; no matter how difficult or impossible, the Magic Solution to any problem: Just release your cloud of nanomechanisms at any difficult plot point, and you could turn a mountain into a heap of gold (or into a vast mound of chocolate puddings, for that matter . . . or into anything *else* you could think of), you could instantly reverse aging, bring people back from the dead, change your sex more easily than you can change your socks, turn one character into another, build mile-high skyscrapers in the wink of an eye, effortlessly defeat the villian's Space Fleet in the time it takes you to snap your fingers, and otherwise vault over any corners you may have painted yourself into in the course of telling your story. Needless to say—when *anything* is possible, nothing has much impact—this quickly became dull.

Nevertheless, nanotechnology has not gone away, simply because it was examined in a simplistic fashion by a few writers, any more than the dangers of Environmental Destruction and the potential collapse of the ecosystem have vanished as realworld threats because enough Pollution Stories were written in the '70s that readers became bored with them.

In fact, many of the potential marvels and nightmare threats—and there are some horrifying scenarios that can arise from the use of nanotechnology, including governmental control of thoughts and emotion, as well as the possible total destruction of life on Earth if nanomechanisms should slip out of human control, or be deliberately employed as a Doomsday Weapon—are only now being examined with any sort of real complexity or sophistication, any radical sweep of imagination or intellectual vigor . . . examined by the very writers in the anthology you hold in your hands, among others . . . writers who will take you along to future worlds stranger than you can imagine, but, fortunately for our reading pleasure, no stranger than *they* can imagine!

So turn the page and let these expert dreamers take you to the World of Tomorrow. If you haven't been there lately, you won't *recognize* the place . . .

BLOOD MUSIC

Greg Bear

Born in San Diego, California, Greg Bear made his first sale at the age of fifteen to Robert Lowndes's Famous Science Fiction, *and has subsequently established himself as one of the top professionals in the genre, and seems well on the way to achieving the sort of habitual-bestseller status enjoyed by Arthur C. Clarke. Indeed, he has much in common with Clarke—being, like him, a hard-science writer with a strong streak of the mystic, whose scientifically rigorous scenarios often lead his characters to mysterious transformations and apotheoses beyond the reach of science. He won a Nebula Award for this pyrotechnic novella "Hardfought," a Nebula and Hugo Award for his famous story "Blood Music," which was later expanded into a novel of the same title, and a subsequent Nebula and Hugo for his story "Tangents." His other books include the novels* Hegira, Psychlone, Beyond Heaven's River, Strength of Stones, The Infinity Concerto, The Serpent Mage, Eon, Eternity, The Forge of God, Anvil of Stars, Moving Mars, Heads, Legacy, *and the critically acclaimed* Queen of Angels, *as well as the collections* Wind from a Burning Woman *and* Tangents. *His most recent books are, as editor, the original anthology* New Legends, *and a major new novel called* /(Slash). *He lives with his family just outside of Seattle, Washington.*

Bear has a sweeping, Stapeldonean vision of how different *the future must inevitably be from the present. This vision of the strange, inhuman future to come is featured powerfully in the story that follows, which may be the first true nanotech story, even though it was written several years before the term "nanotechnology" was even coined—a chilling story that warns us that that inhuman future may not be hundreds of years away, or even decades away, but may instead lay waiting for us only next week, or tomorrow, or* today . . .

and that the true frontiers of exploration may not lay Out There, but rather deep inside . . .

There is a principle in nature I don't think anyone has pointed out before. Each hour, a myriad of trillions of little live things—bacteria, microbes, "animalcules"—are born and die, not counting for much except in the bulk of their existence and the accumulation of their tiny effects. They do not perceive deeply. They do not suffer much. A hundred billion, dying, would not begin to have the same importance as a single human death.

Within the ranks of magnitude of all creatures, small as microbes or great as humans, there is an equality of "elan," just as the branches of a tall tree, gathered together, equal the bulk of the limbs below, and all the limbs equal the bulk of the trunk.

That, at least, is the principle. I believe Vergil Ulam was the first to violate it.

It had been two years since I'd last seen Vergil. My memory of him hardly matched the tan, smiling, well-dressed gentleman standing before me. We had made a lunch appointment over the phone the day before, and now faced each other in the wide double doors of the employees' cafeteria at the Mount Freedom Medical Center.

"Vergil?" I asked. "My God, Vergil!"

"Good to see you, Edward." He shook my hand firmly. He had lost ten or twelve kilos and what remained seemed tighter, better proportioned. At university, Vergil had been the pudgy, shock-haired, snaggle-toothed whiz kid who hot-wired doorknobs, gave us punch that turned our piss blue, and never got a date except with Eileen Termagent, who shared many of his physical characteristics.

"You look fantastic," I said. "Spend a summer in Cabo San Lucas?"

We stood in line at the counter and chose our food. "The tan," he said, picking out a carton of chocolate milk, "is from spending three months under a sunlamp. My teeth were straightened just after I last saw you. I'll explain the rest, but we need a place to talk where no one will listen close."

I steered him to the smoker's corner, where three diehard puffers were scattered among six tables.

"Listen, I mean it," I said as we unloaded our trays. "You've changed. You're looking good."

"I've changed more than you know." His tone was motion-picture ominous, and he delivered the line with a theatrical lift of his brows. "How's Gail?"

Gail was doing well, I told him, teaching nursery school. We'd married the year before. His gaze shifted down to his food—pineapple slice and cottage cheese, piece of banana cream pie—and he said, his voice almost cracking, "Notice something else?"

I squinted in concentration. "Uh."

"Look closer."

"I'm not sure. Well, yes, you're not wearing glasses. Contacts?"

"No, I don't need them anymore."

"And you're a snappy dresser. Who's dressing you now? I hope she's as sexy as she is tasteful."

"Candice isn't—wasn't responsible for the improvement in my clothes," he said. "I just got a better job, more money to throw around. My taste in clothes is better than my taste in food, as it happens." He grinned the Vergil self-deprecating grin, but ended it with a peculiar leer. "At any rate, she's left me, I've been fired from my job, I'm living on savings."

"Hold it," I said. "That's a bit crowded. Why not do a linear breakdown? You got a job. Where?"

"Genetron Corp.," he said. "Sixteen months ago."

"I haven't heard of them."

"You will. They're putting out common stock in the next month. It'll shoot off the board. They've broken through with MABs. Medical—"

"I know what MABs are," I interrupted. "At least in theory. Medically Applicable Biochips."

"They have some that work."

"What?" It was my turn to lift my brows.

"Microscopic logic circuits. You inject them into the human body, they set up shop where they're told and troubleshoot. With Dr. Michael Bernard's approval."

That was quite impressive. Bernard's reputation was spotless. Not only was he associated with the genetic engineering biggies, but he had made the news at least once a year in his practice as a neurosurgeon before retiring. Covers on *Time, Mega, Rolling Stone.*

"That's suppose to be secret—stock, breakthrough, Bernard, everything." He looked around and lowered his voice. "But you do whatever the hell you want. I'm through with the bastards."

I whistled. "Make me rich, huh?"

"If that's what you want. Or you can spend some time with me before rushing off to your broker."

"Of course." He hadn't touched the cottage cheese or pie. He had, however, eaten the pineapple slice and drunk the chocolate milk. "So tell me more."

"Well, in med school I was training for lab work. Biochemical research. I've always had a bent for computers, too. So I put myself through my last two years—"

"By selling software packages to Westinghouse," I said.

"It's good my friends remember. That's how I got involved with Genetron, just when they were starting out.

They had big money backers, all the lab facilities I thought anyone would ever need. They hired me, and I advanced rapidly.

"Four months and I was doing my own work. I made some breakthroughs"—he tossed his hand nonchalantly—"then I went off on tangents they thought were premature. I persisted and they took away my lab, handed it over to a certifiable flatworm. I managed to save part of the experiment before they fired me. But I haven't exactly been cautious . . . or judicious. So now it's going on outside the lab."

I'd always regarded Vergil as ambitious, a trifle cracked, and not terribly sensitive. His relations with authority figures had never been smooth. Science, for him, was like the woman you couldn't possibly have, who suddenly opens her arms to you, long before you're ready for mature love—leaving you afraid you'll forever blow the chance, lose the prize. Apparently, he did. "Outside the lab? I don't get you."

"Edward, I want you to examine me. Give me a thorough physical. Maybe a cancer diagnostic. Then I'll explain more."

"You want a five-thousand-dollar exam?"

"Whatever you can do. Ultrasound, NMR, thermogram, everything."

"I don't know if I can get access to all that equipment. NMR full-scan has only been here a month or two. Hell, you couldn't pick a more expensive way—"

"Then ultrasound. That's all you'll need."

"Vergil, I'm an obstetrician, not a glamour-boy lab-tech. OB-GYN, butt of all jokes. If you're turning into a woman, maybe I can help you."

He leaned forward, almost putting his elbow into the pie, but swinging wide at the last instant by scant millimeters. The old Vergil would have hit it square. "Examine me closely and you'll . . ." He narrowed his eyes. "Just examine me."

"So I make an appointment for ultrasound. Who's going to pay?"

"I'm on Blue Shield." He smiled and held up a medical credit card. "I messed with the personnel files at Genetron. Anything up to a hundred thousand dollars medical, they'll never check, never suspect."

He wanted secrecy, so I made arrangements. I filled out his forms myself. As long as everything was billed properly, most of the examination could take place without official notice. I didn't charge for my services. After all, Vergil had turned my piss blue. We were friends.

He came in late one night. I wasn't normally on duty then, but I stayed late, waiting for him on the third floor of what the nurses called the Frankenstein wing. I sat on an orange plastic chair. He arrived, looking olive-colored under the fluorescent lights.

He stripped, and I arranged him on the table. I noticed, first off, that his ankles looked swollen. But they weren't puffy. I felt them several times. They seemed healthy but looked odd. "Hm," I said.

I ran the paddles over him, picking up areas difficult for the big unit to hit, and programmed the data into the imaging system. Then I swung the table around and inserted it into the enameled orifice of the ultrasound diagnostic unit, the hum-hole, so-called by the nurses.

I integrated the data from the hum-hole with that from the paddle sweeps and rolled Vergil out, then set up a video frame. The image took a second to integrate, then flowed into a pattern showing Vergil's skeleton. My jaw fell.

Three seconds of that and it switched to his thoracic organs, then his musculature, and, finally, vascular system and skin.

"How long since the accident?" I asked, trying to take the quiver out of my voice.

"I haven't been in an accident," he said. "It was deliberate."

"Jesus, they beat you to keep secrets?"

"You don't understand me, Edward. Look at the images again. I'm not damaged."

"Look, there's thickening here"—I indicated the ankles—"and your ribs—that crazy zigzag pattern of interlocks. Broken sometime, obviously. And—"

"Look at my spine," he said. I rotated the image in the video frame.

Buckminster Fuller, I thought. It was fantastic. A cage of triangular projection, all interlocking in ways I couldn't begin to follow, much less understand. I reached around and tried to feel his spine with my fingers. He lifted his arms and looked off at the ceiling.

"I can't find it," I said. "It's all smooth back there." I let go of him and looked at his chest, then prodded his ribs. They were sheathed in something tough and flexible. The harder I pressed, the tougher it became. Then I noticed another change.

"Hey," I said. "You don't have any nipples." There were tiny pigment patches, but no nipple formations at all.

"See?" Vergil asked, shrugging on the white robe, "I'm being rebuilt from the inside out."

In my reconstruction of those hours, I fancy myself saying, "So tell me about it." Perhaps mercifully, I don't remember what I actually said.

He explained with his characteristic circumlocutions. Listening was like trying to get to the meat of a newspaper article through a forest of sidebars and graphic embellishments.

I simplify and condense.

Genetron had assigned him to manufacturing prototype biochips, tiny circuits made out of protein molecules. Some were hooked up to silicon chips little more than a micrometer in size, then went through rat arteries to chemically keyed locations, to make connections with the rat tissue and attempt to monitor and even control lab-induced pathologies.

"*That* was something," he said.

"We recovered the most complex microchip by sacrificing the rat, then debriefed it—hooked the silicon portion up to an imaging system. The computer gave us bar graphs, then a diagram of the chemical characteristics of about eleven centimeters of blood vessels . . . then put it all together to make a picture. We zoomed down eleven centimeters of rat artery. You never saw so many scientists jumping up and down, hugging each other, drinking buckets of bug juice." Bug juice was lab ethanol mixed with Dr. Pepper.

Eventually, the silicon elements were eliminated completely in favor of nucleoproteins. He seemed reluctant to explain in detail, but I gathered they found ways to make huge molecules—as large as DNA, and even more complex—into electrochemical computers, using ribosome-like structures as "encoders" and "readers" and RNA as "tape." Vergil was able to mimic reproductive separation and reassembly in his nucleoproteins, incorporating program changes at key points by switching nucleotide pairs. "Genetron wanted me to switch over to supergene engineering, since that was the coming thing everywhere else. Make all kind of critters, some out of our imagination. But I had different ideas." He twiddled his finger around his ear and made theremin sounds. "Mad scientist time, right?" He laughed, then sobered. "I injected my best nucleoproteins into bacteria to make duplication and compounding easier. Then I started to leave them inside, so the circuits could interact with the cells. They were heuristically programmed; they taught themselves. The cells fed chemically coded information to the computers, the computers processed it and made decisions, the cells became smart. I mean, smart as planaria, for starters. Imagine an *E. coli* as smart as a planarian worm!"

I nodded. "I'm imagining."

"Then I really went off on my own. We had the equipment, the techniques; and I knew the molecular language. I could make really dense, really complicated biochips by compounding the nucleoproteins, making them into little brains. I did some research into how far I could go, theoretically. Sticking with bacteria, I could make a biochip with the computing capacity of a sparrow's brain. Imagine how jazzed I was! Then I saw a way to increase the complexity a thousandfold, by using something we regarded as a nuisance—quantum chit-chat between the fixed elements of the circuits. Down that small, even the slightest change could bomb a biochip. But I developed a program that actually predicted and took advantage of electron tunneling. Emphasized the heuristic aspects of the computer, used the chit-chat as a method of increasing complexity."

"You're losing me," I said.

"I took advantage of randomness. The circuits could repair themselves, compare memories, and correct faulty elements. I gave them basic instructions: Go forth and multiply. Improve. By God, you should have seen some of the cultures a week later! It was amazing. They were evolving all on their own, like little cities. I destroyed them all, I think one of the petri dishes would have grown legs and walked out of the incubator if I'd kept feeding it."

"You're kidding." I looked at him. "You're not kidding."

"Man, they *knew* what it was like to improve! They knew

where they had to go, but they were just so limited, being in bacteria bodies, with so few resources."

"How smart were they?"

"I couldn't be sure. They were associating in clusters of a hundred to two hundred cells, each cluster behaving like an autonomous unit. Each cluster might have been as smart as a rhesus monkey. They exchanged information through their pili, passed on bits of memory, and compared notes. Their organization was obviously different from a group of monkeys. Their world was so much simpler, for one thing. With their abilities they were masters of the petri dishes. I put phages in with them; the phages didn't have a chance. They used every option available to change and grow."

"How is that possible?"

"What?" He seemed surprised I wasn't accepting everything a face value.

"Cramming so much into so little. A rhesus monkey is not your simple little calculator, Vergil."

"I haven't made myself clear," he said, obviously irritated. "I was using nucleoprotein computers. They're like DNA, but all the information can interact. Do you know how many nucleotide pairs there are in the DNA of a single bacteria?"

It had been a long time since my last biochemistry lesson. I shook my head.

"About two million. Add in the modified ribosome structures—fifteen thousand of them, each with a molecular weight of about three million—and consider the combinations and permutations. The RNA is arranged like a continuous loop paper tape, surrounded by ribosomes ticking off instructions and manufacturing protein chains . . ." His eyes were bright and slightly moist. "Besides, I'm not saying every cell was a distinct entity. They cooperated."

"How many bacteria in the dishes you destroyed?"

"Billions. I don't know." He smirked. "You got it, Edward. Whole planetsful of *E. coli.*"

"But Genetron didn't fire you then?"

"No. They didn't know what was going on, for one thing. I kept compounding the molecules, increasing their size complexity. When bacteria were too limited, I took blood from myself, separated out white cells, and injected them with the new biochips. I watched them, put them through mazes and little chemical problems. They were whizzes. Time is a lot faster at that level—so little distance for the messages to cross, and the environment is much simpler. Then I forgot to store a file under my secret code in the lab computers. Some managers found it and guessed what I was up to. Everybody panicked. They thought we'd have every social watchdog in the country on our backs because of what I'd done. They started to destroy my work and wipe my programs. Ordered me to sterilize my white cells. Christ." He pulled the white robe off and started to get dressed. "I only had a day or two. I separated out the most complex cells—"

"How complex?"

"They were clustering in hundred-cell groups, like the bacteria. Each group as smart as a four-year-old kid, maybe." He studied my face for a moment. "Still doubting? Want me to run through how many nucleotide pairs there are in a mammalian cell? I tailored my computers to take advantage of the white cells' capacity. Four billion nucleotide pairs, Edward. And they don't have a huge body to worry about, taking up most of their thinking time."

"Okay," I said. "I'm convinced. What did you do?"

"I mixed the cells back into a cylinder of whole blood and injected myself with it." He buttoned the top of his shirt and smiled thinly at me. "I'd programmed them with every drive I could, talked as high a level as I could using just enzymes and such. After that, they were on their own."

"You programmed them to go forth and multiply, improve?" I repeated.

"I think they developed some characteristics picked up by the biochips in their *E. coli* phases. The white cells could talk to each other with extruded memories. They found ways to ingest other types of cells and alter them without killing them."

"You're crazy."

"You can see the screen! Edward, I haven't been sick since. I used to get colds all the time. I've never felt better."

"They're inside you, finding things, changing them."

"And by now, each cluster is as smart as you or I."

"You're absolutely nuts."

He shrugged. "Genetron fired me. They thought I was going to take revenge for what they did to my work. They ordered me out of the labs, and I haven't had a real chance to see what's been going on inside me until now. Three months."

"So . . ." My mind was racing. "You lost weight because they improved your fat metabolism. Your bones are stronger, your spine has been completely rebuilt—"

"No more backaches even if I sleep on my old mattress."

"Your heart looks different."

"I didn't know about the heart," he said, examining the frame image more closely. "As for the fat—I was thinking about that. They could increase my brown cells, fix up the metabolism. I haven't been as hungry lately. I haven't changed my eating habits that much—I still want the same old junk—but somehow I get around to eating only what I need. I don't think they know what my brain is yet. Sure, they've got all the glandular stuff—but they don't have the *big* picture, if you see what I mean. They don't know *I'm* in here. But boy, they sure did figure out what my reproductive organs are."

I glanced at the image and shifted my eyes away.

"Oh, they look pretty normal." he said, hefting his scrotum obscenely. He snickered. "But how else do you think I'd land a real looker like Candice? She was just after a one-night stand with a techie. I looked okay then, no tan but trim, with good clothes. She'd never screwed a techie before. Joke time, right? But my little geniuses kept us up half the night. I think they made improvement each time. I felt like I had a goddamned fever."

His smile vanished. "But then one night my skin started to crawl. It really scared me. I though things were getting out of hand. I wondered what they'd do when they crossed the blood-brain barrier and found out about *me*—about the brain's real function. So I began a campaign to keep them under control. I figured, the reason they wanted to get into the skin was the simplicity of running circuits across a surface. Much easier than trying to maintain chains of communication in and around muscles, organs, vessels. The skin was much more direct. So I bought a quartz lamp." He caught my puzzled expression. "In the lab, we'd break down the protein in biochip cells by exposing them to ultraviolet light. I alternated sunlamp with quartz treatments. Keeps them out of my skin and gives me a nice tan."

"Give you skin cancer, too," I commented.

"They'll probably take care of that. Like police."

"Okay. I've examined you, you've told me a story I still find hard to believe . . . what do you want me to do?"

"I'm not as nonchalant as I act, Edward. I'm worried. I'd like to find some way to control them before they find out about my brain. I mean, think of it, they're in the trillions by now, each one smart. They're cooperating to some extent. I'm probably the smartest thing on the planet, and they haven't even begun to get their act together. I don't really want them to take over." He laughed unpleasantly. "Steal my soul, you know? So think of some treatment to block them. Maybe we can starve the little buggers. Just think on it." He buttoned his shirt. "Give me a call." He handed me a slip of paper with his address and phone number. Then he went to the keyboard and erased the image on the frame, dumping the memory of the examination. "Just you," he said. "Nobody else for now. And please . . . hurry."

It was three o'clock in the morning when Vergil walked out of the examination room. He'd allowed me to take blood samples, then shaken my hand—his palm was damp, nervous—and cautioned me against ingesting anything from the specimens.

Before I went home, I put the blood through a series of tests. The results were ready the next day.

I picked them up during my lunch break in the afternoon, then destroyed all of the samples. I did it like a robot. It took me five days and nearly sleepless nights to accept what I'd seen. His blood was normal enough, though the machines diagnosed the patient as having an infection. High levels of leukocytes—white blood cells—and histamines. On the fifth day, I believed.

Gail came home before I did, but it was my turn to fix dinner. She slipped one of the school's disks into the home system and showed me video art her nursery kids had been creating. I watched quietly, ate with her in silence.

I had two dreams, part of my final acceptance. In the first, that evening, I witnessed the destruction of the planet Krypton, Superman's home world. Billions of superhuman geniuses went screaming off in walls of fire. I related the destruction to my sterilizing the samples of Vergil's blood.

The second dream was worse. I dreamed that New York City was raping a woman. By the end of the dream, she gave birth to little embryo cities, all wrapped up in translucent sacs, soaked with blood from the difficult labor.

I called him on the morning of the sixth day. He answered on the fourth ring. "I have some results," I said. "Nothing conclusive. But I want to talk with you. In person."

"Sure," he said. "I'm staying inside for the time being." His voice was strained; he sounded tired.

Vergil's apartment was in a fancy high-rise near the lake shore. I took the elevator up, listening to little advertising jingles and watching dancing holograms display products, empty apartments for rent, the building's hostess discussing social activities for the week.

Vergil opened the door and motioned me in. He wore a checked robe with long sleeves and carpet slippers. He clutched an unlit pipe in one hand, his fingers twisting it back and forth as he walked away from me and sat down, saying nothing.

"You have an infection," I said.

"Oh?"

"That's all the blood analyses tell me. I don't have access to the electron microscopes."

"I don't think it's really an infection," he said. "After all, they're my own cells. Probably something else . . . some sign of their presence, of the change. We can't expect to understand everything that's happening."

I removed my coat. "Listen," I said, "you really have me worried now." The expression on his face stopped me: a kind of frantic beatitude. He squinted at the ceiling and pursed his lips.

"Are you stoned?" I asked.

He stood his head, then nodded once, very slowly. "Listening," he said.

"To what?"

"I don't know. Not sounds . . . exactly. Like music. The heart, all the blood vessels, friction of blood along the arteries, veins. Activity. Music in the blood." He looked at me plaintively. "Why aren't you at work?"

"My day off. Gail's working."

"Can you stay?"

I shrugged. "I suppose." I sounded suspicious. I glanced

around the apartment, looking for ashtrays, pack of papers.

"I'm not stoned, Edward," he said. "I may be wrong, but I think something big is happening. I think they're finding out who I am."

I sat down across from Vergil, staring at him intently. He didn't seem to notice. Some inner process involved him. When I asked for a cup of coffee, he motioned to the kitchen. I boiled a pot of water and took a jar of instant from the cabinet. With cup in hand, I returned to my seat. He twisted his head back and forth, eyes open. "You always knew what you wanted to be, didn't you?" he asked.

"More or less."

"A gynecologist. Smart moves. Never false moves. I was different. I had goals, but no direction. Like a map without roads, just places to be. I didn't give a shit for anything, anyone but myself. Even science. Just a means. I'm surprised I got so far. I even hated my folks."

He gripped his chair arms.

"Something wrong?" I asked.

"They're talking to me," he said. He shut his eyes.

For an hour he seemed to be asleep. I checked his pulse, which was strong and steady, felt his forehead—slightly cool—and made myself more coffee. I was looking through a magazine, at a loss what to do, when he opened his eyes again. "Hard to figure exactly what time is like for them," he said. "It's taken them maybe three, four days to figure out language, key human concepts. Now they're on to it. On to me. Right now."

"How's that?"

He claimed there were thousands of researchers hooked up to his neurons. He couldn't give details. "They're damned efficient, you know," he said. "They haven't screwed me up yet."

"We should get you into the hospital now."

"What in hell could other doctors do? Did *you* figure out any way to control them? I mean, they're my own cells."

"I've been thinking. We could starve them. Find out what metabolic differences—"

"I'm not sure I want to be rid of them," Vergil said. "They're not doing any harm."

"How do you know?"

He shook his head and held up one finger. "Wait. They're trying to figure out what space is. That's tough for them: They break distances down into concentrations of chemicals. For them, space is like intensity of taste."

"Vergil—"

"Listen! Think, Edward!" His tone was excited but even. "Something big is happening inside me. They talk to each other across the fluid, through membranes. They tailor something—viruses?—to carry data stored in nucleic acid chains. I think they're saying 'RNA.' That makes sense. That's one way I programmed them. But plasmidlike structures, too. Maybe that's what your machines think is a sign of infection—all their chattering in my blood, packets of data. Tastes of other individuals. Peers. Superiors. Subordinates."

"Vergil, I still think you should be in a hospital."

"This is my show, Edward," he said. "I'm their universe. They're amazed by the new scale." He was quiet again for a time. I squatted by his chair and pulled up the sleeve to his robe. His arm was crisscrossed with white lines. I was about to go to the phone when he stood and stretched. "Do you realize," he said, "how many body cells we kill each time we move?"

"I'm going to call for an ambulance." I said.

"No, you aren't." His tone stopped me. "I told you, I'm not sick, this is my show. Do you know what they'd do to me in a hospital? They'd be like cavemen trying to fix a computer. It would be a farce."

"Then what the hell I doing here?" I asked, getting angry. "I can't do anything. I'm one of those cavemen."

"You're a friend," Vergil said, fixing his eyes on me. I had the impression I was being watched by more than just Vergil. "I want you here to keep me company." He laughed. "But I'm not exactly alone."

He walked around the apartment for two hours, fingering things, looking out windows, slowly and methodically fixing himself lunch. "You know, they can actually feel their own thoughts," he said about noon. "I mean the cytoplasm seems to have a will of its own, a kind of subconscious life counter to the rationality they've only recently acquired. They hear the chemical 'noise' of the molecules fitting and unfitting inside."

At two o'clock, I called Gail to tell her I would be late. I was almost sick with tension, but I tried to keep my voice level. "Remember Vergil Ulam? I'm talking with him right now."

"Everything okay?" she asked.

Was it? Decidedly not. "Fine," I said.

"Culture!" Vergil said, peering around the kitchen wall at me. I said good-bye and hung up the phone. "They're always swimming in that bath of information. Contributing to it. It's kind of gestalt thing. The hierarchy is absolute. They send tailored phages after cells that don't interact properly. Viruses specified to individuals or groups. No escape. A rogue cell gets pierced by the virus, the cell blebs outward, it explodes and dissolves. But it's not just a dictatorship. I think they effectively have more freedom than in a democracy. I mean, they vary so differently from individual to individual. Does that make sense? They vary different ways than we do."

"Hold it," I said, gripping his shoulders. "Vergil, you're pushing me to the edge. I can't take this much longer. I don't understand. I'm not sure I believe—"

"Not even now?"

"Okay, let's say you're giving me the right interpretation. Giving it to me straight. Have you bothered to figure out the consequences yet? What all this means, where it might lead?"

He walked into the kitchen and drew a glass of water from the tap, then returned and stood next to me. His expression had changed from childish absorption to sober concern. "I've never been very good at that."

"Are you afraid?"

"I was. Now, I'm not sure." He fingered the tie of his robe. "Look, I don't want you to think I went around you, over your head or something. But I met with Michael Bernard yesterday. He put me through his private clinic, took specimens. Told me to quit the lamp treatments. He says it all checks out. And he asked me not to tell anybody." He paused and his expression became dreamy again. "Cities of cells," he continued. "Edward, they push tubes through the tissues, spread information—"

"Stop it!" I shouted. "Checks out? What checks out?"

"As Bernard puts it, I have 'severely enlarged macrophages' throughout my system. And he concurs on the anatomical changes."

"What does he plan to do?"

"I don't know. I think he'll probably convince Genetron to reopen the lab."

"Is that what you want?"

"It's not just having the lab again. I want to show you. Since I stopped the lamp treatments, I'm still changing." He undid his robe and let it slide to the floor. All over his body, his skin was crisscrossed with white lines. Along his back, the lines were starting to form ridges.

"My God," I said.

"I'm not going to be much good anywhere else but the lab

soon. I won't be able to go out in public. Hospitals wouldn't know what to do, as I said."

"You're . . . you can talk to them, tell them to slow down," I said, aware how ridiculous that sounded.

"Yes, indeed I can, but they don't necessarily listen."

"I thought you were their god or something."

"The ones hooked up to my neurons aren't the big wheels. They're researchers, or at least serve the same function. They know I'm here, what I am, but that doesn't mean they've convinced the upper levels of the hierarchy."

"They're disputing?"

"Something like that. It's not all that bad, anyway. If the lab is reopened, I have a home, a place to work." He glanced out the window, as if looking for someone. "I don't have anything left but them. They aren't afraid, Edward. I've never felt so close to anything before." The beatific smile again. "I'm responsible for them. Mother to them all."

"You have no way of knowing what they're going to do."

He shook his head.

"No, I mean it. You say they're like a civilization—"

"Like a thousand civilizations."

"Yes, and civilizations have been known to screw up. Warfare, the environment—"

I was grasping at straws, trying to restrain a growing panic. I wasn't competent to handle the enormity of what was happening. Neither was Vergil. He was the last person I would have called insightful and wise about large issues.

"But I'm the only one at risk."

"You don't know that. Jesus, Vergil, look what they're *doing* to you!"

"To me, all to me!" he said. "Nobody else."

I shook my head and held up my hands in a gesture of defeat. "Okay, so Bernard gets them to reopen the lab, you move in, become a guinea pig. What then?"

"They treat me right. I'm more than just good old Vergil Ulam now. I'm goddamned galaxy, a super-mother."

"Super-host, you mean." He conceded the point with a shrug.

I couldn't take any more. I made my exit with a few flimsy excuses, then sat in the lobby of the apartment building, trying to calm down. Somebody had to talk some sense into him. Who would he listen to? He had gone to Bernard . . .

And it sounded as if Bernard was not only convinced, but very interested. People of Bernard's stature didn't coax the Vergil Ulams of the world along unless they felt it was to their advantage.

I had a hunch, and I decided to play it. I went to a pay phone, slipped in my credit card, and called Genetron.

"I'd like you to page Dr. Michael Bernard," I told the receptionist.

"Who's calling, please?"

"This is his answering service. We have an emergency call and his beeper doesn't seem to be working."

A few anxious minutes later, Bernard came on the line. "Who in the hell is this?" he asked. "I don't have an answering service."

"My name is Edward Milligan. I'm a friend of Vergil Ulam's. I think we have some problems to discuss."

We made an appointment to talk the next morning.

I went home and tried to think of excuses to keep me off the next day's hospital shift. I couldn't concentrate on medicine, couldn't give my patients anywhere near the attention they deserved.

Guilty, angry, afraid.

That was how Gail found me. I slipped on a mask of calm and we fixed dinner together. After eating, holding onto each other, we watched the city lights come on in late twilight through the bayside window. Winter starlings pecked at the yellow lawn in the last few minutes of light, then flew away with a rising wind which made the windows rattle.

"Somethings's wrong," Gail said softly. "Are you going to tell me, or just act like everything's normal?"

"It's just me," I said. "Nervous. Work at the hospital."

"Oh, lord," she said, sitting up. "You're going to divorce me for that Baker woman." Mrs. Baker weighed three hundred and sixty pounds and hadn't known she was pregnant until her fifth month.

"No," I said, listless.

"Rapturous relief," Gail said, touching my forehead lightly. "You know this kind of introspection drives me crazy."

"Well, it's nothing I can talk about yet, so . . ." I patted her hand.

"That's disgustingly patronizing," she said, getting up. "I'm going to make some tea. Want some?" Now she was miffed, and I was tense with not telling.

Why not just reveal all? I asked myself. An old friend was turning himself into a galaxy.

I cleared away the table instead. That night, unable to sleep, I looked down on Gail in bed from my sitting position, pillow against the wall, and tried to determine what I knew was real, and what wasn't.

I'm a doctor, I told myself. A technical, scientific profession. I'm suppose to be immune to things like future shock.

Vergil Ulam was turning into a galaxy.

How would it feel to be topped off with a trillion Chinese? I grinned in the dark and almost cried at the same time. What Vergil had inside him was unimaginably stranger than Chinese. Stranger than anything I—or Vergil—could easily understand. Perhaps ever understand.

But I knew what was real. The bedroom, the city lights

faint through gauze curtains. Gail sleeping. Very important. Gail in bed, sleeping.

The dream returned. This time the city came in through the window and attacked Gail. It was a great, spiky lighted-up prowler, and it growled in a language I couldn't understand, made up of auto horns, crowd noises, construction bedlam. I tried to fight it off, but it got to her—and turned into a drift of stars, sprinkling all over the bed, all over everything. I jerked awake and stayed up until dawn, dressed with Gail, kissed her, savored the reality of her human, unviolated lips.

I went to meet with Bernard. He had been loaned a suite in a big downtown hospital; I rode the elevator to the sixth floor, and saw what fame and fortune could mean.

The suite was tastefully furnished, fine serigraphs on wood-paneled walls, chrome and glass furniture, cream-colored carpet, Chinese brass, and wormwood-grain cabinets and tables.

He offered me a cup of coffee, and I accepted. He took a seat in the breakfast nook, and I sat across from him, cradling my cup in moist palms. He wore a dapper gray suit and had graying hair and a sharp profile. He was in his mid sixties and he looked quite a bit like Leonard Bernstein.

"About our mutual acquaintance," he said. "Mr. Ulam. Brilliant. And, I won't hesitate to say, courageous."

"He's my friend. I'm worried about him."

Bernard held up one finger. "Courageous—and a bloody damned fool. What's happening to him should never have been allowed. He may have done it under duress, but that's no excuse. Still, what's done is done. He's talked to you, I take it."

I nodded. "He wants to return to Genetron."

"Of course. That's where all his equipment is. Where his home probably will be while we sort this out."

"Sort it out—how? Why?" I wasn't thinking too clearly. I had a slight headache.

"I can think of a large number of uses for small, superdense computer elements with a biological base. Can't you? Genetron has already made breakthroughs, but this is something else again."

"What do you envision?"

Bernard smiled. "I'm not really at liberty to say. It'll be revolutionary. We'll have to get him in lab conditions. Animal experiments have to be conducted. We'll start from scratch, of course. Vergil's . . . um . . . colonies can't be transferred. They're based on his own white blood cells. So we have to develop colonies that won't trigger immune reactions in other animals."

"Like an infection?" I asked.

"I suppose there are comparisons. But Vergil is not infected."

"My test indicate he is."

"That's probably the bits of data floating around in his blood, don't you think?"

"I don't know."

"Listen, I'd like you to come down to the lab after Vergil is settled in. Your expertise might be useful to us."

Us. He was working with Genetron hand in glove. Could he be objective? "How will you benefit from all this?"

"Edward, I have always been at the forefront of my profession. I see no reason why I shouldn't be helping here. With my knowledge of brain and nerve functions, and the research I've been conducting in neurophysiology—"

"You could help Genetron hold off an investigation by the government," I said.

"That's being very blunt. Too blunt, and unfair."

"Perhaps. Anyway, yes: I'd like to visit the lab when Vergil's settled in. If I'm still welcome, bluntness and all."

He looked at me sharply. I wouldn't be playing on *his* team; for a moment, his thoughts were almost nakedly apparent.

"Of course," Bernard said, rising with me. He reached out to shake my hand. His palm was damp. He was as nervous as I was, even if he didn't look it.

I returned to my apartment and stayed there until noon, reading, trying to sort things out. Reach a decision. What was real, what I needed to protect.

There is only so much change anyone can stand: innovation, yes, but slow application. Don't force. Everyone has the right to stay the same until they decide otherwise.

The greatest thing in science since . . .

And Bernard would force it. Genetron would force it. I couldn't handle the thought. "Neo-Luddite," I said to myself. A filthy accusation.

When I pressed Vergil's number on the building security panel, Vergil answered almost immediately. "Yeah," he said. He sounded exhilarated. "Come on up. I'll be in the bathroom. Door's unlocked."

I entered his apartment and walked through the hallway to the bathroom. Vergil lay in the tub, up to his neck in pinkish water. He smiled vaguely and splashed his hands. "Looks like I slit my wrists, doesn't it?" he said softly. "Don't worry. Everything's fine now. Genetron's going to take me back. Bernard just called." He pointed to the bathroom phone and intercom.

I sat on the toilet and noticed the sunlamp fixture standing unplugged nest to the linen cabinets. The blubs sat in a row on the edge of the sink counter. "You're sure that's what you want," I said, my shoulders slumping.

"Yeah, I think so," he said. "They can take better care of me. I'm getting cleaned up, going over there this evening. Bernard's picking me up in his limo. Style. From here on in, everything's style."

The pinkish color in the water didn't look like soap. "Is that bubble bath?" I asked. Some of it came to me in a rush then and I felt a little weaker; what had occurred to me was just one more obvious and necessary insanity.

"No," Vergil said. I knew that already.

"No," he repeated, "it's coming from my skin. They're not telling me everything, but I think they're sending out scouts. Astronauts." He looked at me with an expression that didn't quite equal concern; more like curiosity as to how I'd take it.

The confirmation made my stomach muscles tighten as if waiting for a punch. I had never even considered the possibility until now, perhaps because I had been concentrating on other aspects. "Is this the first time?" I asked.

"Yeah," he said. He laughed. "I've half a mind to let the little buggers down the drain. Let them find out what the world's really about."

"They'd go everywhere," I said.

"Sure enough."

"How . . . how are you feeling?"

"I'm feeling pretty good now. Must be billions of them." More splashing with his hands. "What do you think? Should I let the buggers out?"

Quickly, hardly thinking, I knelt down beside the tub. My fingers went for the cord on the sunlamp and I plugged it in. He had hot-wired doorknobs, turned my piss blue, played a thousand dumb practical jokes and never grown up, never grown mature enough to understand that he was sufficiently brilliant to transform the world; he would never learn caution.

He reached for the drain knob. "You know, Edward, I—"

He never finished. I picked up the fixture and dropped it into the tub, jumping back at the flash of steam and sparks. Vergil screamed and thrashed and jerked and then everything was still, except for the low, steady sizzle and the smoke wafting from his hair.

I lifted the toilet lid and vomited. Then I clenched my nose and went into the living room. My legs went out from under me and I sat abruptly on the couch.

After an hour, I searched through Vergil's kitchen and found bleach, ammonia, and a bottle of Jack Daniel's. I returned to the bathroom, keeping the center of my gaze away from Vergil. I poured first the booze, then the bleach, then the ammonia into the water. Chlorine started bubbling up and I left, closing the door behind me.

The phone was ringing when I got home. I didn't answer. It could have been the hospital. It could have been Bernard. Or the police. I could envision having to explain everything to the police. Genetron would stonewall; Bernard would be unavailable.

I was exhausted, all my muscles knotted with tension and whatever name one can give to the feelings one has after—

Committing genocide?

That certainly didn't seem real. I could not believe I had just murdered a hundred trillion intelligent beings. Snuffed a galaxy. It was laughable. But I didn't laugh.

It was easy to believe that I had just killed one human being, a friend. The smoke, the melted lamp rods, the drooping electrical outlet and smoking cord.

Vergil.

I had dunked the lamp into the tub with Vergil.

I felt sick. Dreams, cities raping Gail (and what about his girlfriend, Candice?). Letting the water filled with them out. Galaxies sprinkling over us all. What horror. Then again, what potential beauty—a new kind of life, symbiosis and transformation.

Had I been thorough enough to kill them all? I had a moment of panic. Tomorrow, I thought, I will sterilize his apartment. Somehow, I didn't even think of Bernard.

When Gail came in the door, I was asleep on the couch. I came to, groggy, and she looked down at me.

"You feeling okay?" she asked, perching on the edge of the couch. I nodded.

"What are you planning for dinner?" My mouth didn't work properly. The words were mushy. She felt my forehead.

"Edward, you have a fever," she said. "A very high fever."

I stumbled into the bathroom and looked in the mirror. Gail was close behind me. "What is it?" she asked.

There were lines under my collar, around my neck. White lines, like freeways. They had already been in me a long time, days.

"Damp palms," I said. So obvious.

I think we nearly died. I struggled at first, but in minutes I was too weak to move. Gail was just as sick within an hour.

I lay on the carpet in the living room, drenched in sweat. Gail lay on the couch, her face the color of talcum, eyes closed, like a corpse in an embalming parlor. For a time I thought she was dead. Sick as I was, I raged—hated, felt tremendous guilt at my weakness, my slowness to understand all the possibilities. Then I no longer cared. I was too weak to blink, so I closed my eyes and waited.

There was a rhythm in my arms, my legs. With each pulse of blood, a kind of sound welled up within me, like an orchestra thousands strong, but not playing in unison; playing whole seasons of symphonies at once. Music in the blood. The sound became harsher, but more coordinated, wave-trains finally canceling into silence, then separating into harmonic beats.

The beats seemed to melt into me, into the sound of my own heart.

First, they subdued our immune responses. The war—

and it was a war, on a scale never before known on Earth, with trillions of combatants—lasted perhaps two days.

By the time I regained enough strength to get to the kitchen faucet, I could feel them working on my brain, trying to crack the code and find the god within the protoplasm. I drank until I was sick, then drank more moderately and took a glass to Gail. She sipped at it. Her lips were cracked, her eyes bloodshot and ringed with yellowish crumbs. There was some color in her skin. Minutes later, we were eating feebly in the kitchen.

"What in the hell is happening?" was the first thing she asked. I didn't have the strength to explain. I peeled an orange and shared it with her. "We should call a doctor," she said. But I knew we wouldn't. I was already receiving messages; it was becoming apparent that any sensation of freedom we experienced was illusory.

The messages were simple at first. Memories of commands, rather than the commands themselves, manifested themselves in my thoughts. We were not to leave the apartment—a concept which seemed quite abstract to those in control, even if undesirable—and we were not to have contact with others. We would be allowed to eat certain foods and drink tap water for the time being.

With the subsidence of the fevers, the transformations were quick and drastic. Almost simultaneously, Gail and I were immobilized. She was sitting at the table, I was kneeling on floor. I was able barely to see her in the corner of my eye.

Her arm developed pronounced ridges.

They had learned inside Vergil; their tactics within the two of us were very different. I itched all over for about two hours—two hours in hell—before they made the breakthrough and found me. The effort of ages on their timescale paid off and they communicated smoothly and directly with this great, clumsy intelligence who had once controlled their universe.

They were not cruel. When the concept of discomfort and its undesirability was made clear, they worked to alleviate it. They worked too effectively. For another hour, I was in a sea of bliss, out of all contact with them.

With dawn the next day, they gave us freedom to move again; specifically, to go to the bathroom. There were certain waste products they could not deal with. I voided those—my urine was purple—and Gail followed suit. We looked at each other vacantly in the bathroom. Then she managed a slight smile. "Are they talking to you?" she asked. I nodded. "Then I'm not crazy."

For the next twelve hours, control seemed to loosen on some levels. I suspect there was another kind of war going on in me. Gail was capable of limited motion, but no more.

When full control resumed, we were instructed to hold each other. We did not hesitate.

"Eddie . . ." she whispered. My name was the last sound I ever heard from outside.

Standing, we grew together. In hours, our legs expanded and spread out. Then extensions grew to the windows to take sunlight, and to the kitchen to take water from the sink. Filaments soon reached to all corners of the room, stripping paint and plaster from the walls, fabric and stuffing from the furniture.

By the next dawn, the transformation was complete.

I no longer have any clear view of what we look like. I suspect we resemble cells—large, flat, and filamented cells, draped purposefully across most of the apartment. The great shall mimic the small.

Our intelligence fluctuates daily as we are absorbed into the minds within. Each day, out individuality declines. We are, indeed, great clumsy dinosaurs. Our memories have been taken over by billions of them, and our personalities have been spread through the transformed blood.

Soon there will be no need for centralization.

Already the plumbing has been invaded. People throughout the building are undergoing transformation.

Within the old time frame of weeks, we will reach the lakes, rivers, and seas in force.

I can barely begin to guess the results. Every square inch of the planet will teem with thought. Years from now, perhaps much sooner, they will subdue their own individuality—what there is of it.

New creatures will come, then. The immensity of their capacity for thought will be inconceivable.

All my hatred and fear is gone now.

I leave them—us—with only one question.

How many times has this happened, elsewhere? Travelers never came through space to visit the Earth. They had no need.

They had found universes in grains of sand.

MARGIN OF ERROR

Nancy Kress

Born in Buffalo, New York, Nancy Kress now lives in Brockport, New York. She began selling her elegant and incisive stories in the mid-seventies, and has since become a frequent contributor to Asimov's Science Fiction, The Magazine of Fantasy and Science Fiction, Omni, *and elsewhere. Her books include the novels* The Prince Of Morning Bells, The Golden Glove, The White Pipes, An Alien Light, *and* Brain Rose, *the collection* Trinity And Other Stories, *the novel version of her Hugo and Nebula-winning story,* Beggars in Spain, *and a sequel,* Beggars and Choosers. *Her most recent books include a new collection,* The Aliens of Earth, *and a new novel,* Oaths & Miracles. *She has also won a Nebula Award for her story "Out of All Them Bright Stars."*

In the chilling little story that follows, she reaffirms the truth of that old saying about revenge. It is *a dish best served cold.*

Paula came back in a blaze of glory, her institute uniform with its pseudomilitary medals crisp and bright, her spine straight as an engineered diamond-fiber rod. I heard her heels clicking on the sidewalk and I looked up from the bottom porch step, a child on my lap. Paula's face was genemod now, the blemishes gone, the skin fine-pored, the cheekbones chiseled under green eyes. But I would have known that face anywhere. No matter what she did to it.

"Karen?" Her voice held disbelief.

"Paula," I said.

"Karen?" This time I didn't answer. The child, my oldest, twisted in my arms to eye the visitor.

It was the kind of neighborhood where women sat all morning on porches or stoops, watching children play on the sidewalk. Steps sagged; paint peeled; small front lawns were scraped bare by feet and tricycles and plastic wading pools. Women lived a few doors down from their mothers, both of them growing heavier every year. There were few men. The ones there were didn't seem to stay long.

I said, "How did you find me?"

"It wasn't hard," Paula said, and I knew she didn't understand my smile. Of course it wasn't hard. I had never intended it should be. This was undoubtedly the first time in nearly five years that Paula had looked.

She lowered her perfect body onto the porch steps. My little girl, Lollie, gazed at her from my lap. Then Lollie opened her cupped hands and smiled. "See my frog, lady?"

"Very nice," Paula said. She was trying hard to hide her contempt, but I could see it. For the sad imprisoned frog, for Lollie's dirty face, for the worn yard, for the way I looked.

"Karen," Paula said, "I'm here because there's a problem. With the project. More specifically with the initial formulas, we think. With a portion of the nanoassembler code from five years ago, when you were . . . still with us."

"A problem," I repeated. Inside the house, a baby wailed. "Just a minute."

I set Lollie down and went inside. Lori cried in her crib. Her diaper reeked. I put a pacifier in her mouth and cradled her in my left arm. With the right arm I scooped Timmy from his crib. When he didn't wake, I jostled him a little. I carried both babies back to the porch, deposited Timmy in the portacrib, and sat down next to Paula.

"Lollie, go get me a diaper, honey. And wipes. You can carry your frog inside to get them."

Lollie went; she's a sweet-natured kid. Paula stared incredulously at the twins. I unwrapped Lori's diaper and Paula grimaced and slid father away.

"Karen . . . . are you listening to me? This is *important*!"

"I'm listening."

"The nanocomputer instructions are off, somehow. The major results check out, obviously . . ." *Obviously*. The media had spent five years exclaiming over the major results. ". . . but there are some odd foldings in the proteins of the twelfth-generation nanoassemblers." Twelfth generation. The nanocomputer attached to each assembler replicates itself every six months. That was one of the project's checks and balances on the margin of error. It had been five and a half years. Twelfth generation was about right.

"Also," Paula continued, and I heard the strain in her voice, "there are some unforeseen macrolevel developments. We're not sure yet that they're tied to the nanocomputer protein folds. What we're trying to do now is cover all the variables."

"You must be working on fairly remote variables if you're reduced to asking me."

"Well, yes, we are. Karen, do you have to do that *now*?"

"Yes." I scraped the shit off Lori with one edge of the soiled diaper. Lollie danced out of the house with a clean one. She sat beside me, whispering to her frog. Paula said, "What I need . . . what the project needs . . ."

I said, "Do you remember the summer we collected frogs? We were maybe eight and ten. You'd become fascinated reading about that experiment where they threw a frog in boiling water but it jumped out, and then they put a frog in cool water and gradually increased the temperature to boiling until the stupid frog just sat there and died. Remember?"

"Karen . . ."

"I collected sixteen frogs for you, and when I found out what you were going to do with them, I cried and tried to let them go. But you boiled eight of them anyway. The other eight were controls. I'll give you that—proper scientific method. To reduce the margin of error, you said."

"Karen . . . we were just kids . . ."

I put the clean diaper on Lori. "Not all kids behave like that. Lollie doesn't. But you wouldn't know that, would you? Nobody in your set has children. You should have had a baby, Paula." She barely hid her shudder. But then, most of the people we knew felt the same way. She said, "What the project needs is for you to come back and work on the same small area you did originally. Looking for something—anything—you might have missed in the proteincoded instructions to successive generations of nanoassemblers."

"No," I said.

"It's not really a matter of choice. The macrolevel problems—I'll be frank, Karen. It looks like a new form of cancer. Unregulated replication of some very weird cells."

"So take the cellular nanomachinery out." I crumpled the stinking diaper and set it out of the baby's reach. Closer to Paula.

"You know we can't do that! The project's irreversible!"

"Many things are irreversible," I said. Lori started to fuss. I picked her up, opened my blouse, and gave her the breast. She sucked greedily. Paula glanced away. She has had nanomachinery in her perfect body, making it perfect, for five years now. Her breasts will never look swollen, blue-veined, sagging.

"Karen, listen . . ."

"No . . . you listen," I said quietly. "Eight years ago you convinced Zweigler I was only a minor member of the research team, included only because I was your sister. I've always wondered, by the way, how you did that—were you sleeping with him, too? Seven years ago you got me shunted off into the minor area of the project's effect on female gametes—which nobody cared about because it was already clear there was no way around sterility as a side effect. Nobody thought it was too high a price for a perfect, self-repairing body, did they? Except me." Paula didn't answer. Lollie carried her frog to the wading pool and set it carefully in the water. I said, "I didn't mind working on female gametes, even if it was a backwater, even if you got star billing. I was used to it, after all. As kids, you were always the cowboy; I got to be the horse. You were the astronaut, I was the alien you conquered. Remember? One Christmas you used up all the chemicals in your first chemistry set and then stole mine."

"I don't think trivial childhood incidents matter in . . ."

"Of course you don't. And I never minded. But I did mind when five years ago you made copies of all my notes and presented them as yours, while I was so sick during my pregnancy with Lollie. You claimed *my* work. Stole it. Just like the chemistry set. And then you eased me off the project."

"What you did was so minor . . ."

"If it was so minor, why are you here asking for my help now? And why would you imagine for half a second I'd give it to you?" She stared at me, calculating. I stared back coolly. Paula wasn't used to me cool. I'd always been the excitable one. Excitable, flighty, unstable—that's what she told Zweigler. A security risk.

Timmy fussed in his portacrib. I stood up, still nursing Lori, and scooped him up with my free arm. Back on the steps, I juggled Timmy to lie across Lori on my lap, pulled back my blouse, and gave him the other breast. This time Paula didn't permit herself a grimace.

She said, "Karen, what I did was wrong. I know that now. But for the sake of the project, not for me, you have to . . ."

"You *are* the project. You have been from the first moment you grabbed the headlines away from Zweigler and the others who gave their life to that work. 'Lovely Young

Scientist Injects Self with Perfect-Cell Drug!' 'No Sacrifice Too Great to Circumvent FDA Shortsightedness, Heroic Researcher Declares.'"

Paula said flatly, "You jealous. You're obscure and I'm famous. You're a mess and I'm beautiful. You're . . ."

"A milk cow? While you're a brilliant researcher? Then solve your own research problems."

"This was your area . . ."

"Oh, Paula, they were *all* my areas. I did more of the basic research than you did, and you know it. But you knew how to position yourself with Zweigler, to present key findings at key moments, to cultivate the right connections. And, of course, I was still under the delusion we were partners. I just didn't realize it was a barracuda partnering a goldfish."

From the wading pool Lollie watched us with big eyes. "Mommy . . ."

"It's okay, honey. Mommy's not mad at you. Look, better catch your frog—he's hopping away."

She shrieked happily and dove for the frog. Paula said softly, "I had no idea you were so angry after all this time. You've changed, Karen."

"But I'm not angry. Not any more. And you never knew what I was like before. You never bothered to know."

"I knew you never wanted a scientific life. Not the way I did. You always wanted kids. Wanted . . . *this.*" She waved her arm around the shabby yard. David left eighteen months ago. He sends money. It's never enough.

"I wanted a scientific establishment that would let me have both. And I wanted credit for my work. I wanted what was mine. How did you do it, Paula—end up with what was yours and what was mine, too?"

"Because you were distracted by baby shit and frogs!" Paula yelled, and I saw how scared she really was. Paula didn't make admissions like that. A tactical error. I watched her stab desperately for a way to retain the advantage. A way to seize the offensive. I seized it first. "You should have left David alone. You already had Zweigler; you should have left me David. Our marriage was never the same after that."

She said, "I'm dying, Karen."

I turned my head from the nursing babies to look at her.

"It's true. My cellular machinery is running wild. The nanoassemblers are creating weird structures, destructive enzymes. For five years they replicated perfectly and now . . . For five years it all performed *exactly* as it was programmed to . . ."

I said, "It still does."

Paula sat very still. Lori had fallen asleep. I juggled her into the portacrib and nestled Timmy more comfortably on my lap. Lollie chased her frog around the wading pool. I squinted to see if Lollie's lips were blue.

Paula choked out, "You programmed the assembler machinery in the ovaries to . . ."

"Nobody much cares about women's ovaries. Only fourteen percent of college-educated women want to muck up their lives with kids. Recent survey result. Less than one percent margin of error."

". . . you actually sabotaged . . . hundreds of women have been injected by now, maybe *thousands* . . ."

"Oh, there's a reverser enzyme," I said. "Completely effective if you take it before the twelfth-generation replication. You're the only person that's been injected that long. I just discovered the reverser a few months ago, tinkering with my old notes for something to do in what your friends probably call my idle domestic prison. That's provable, incidentally. All my notes are computer-dated."

Paula whispered, "Scientists don't *do* this . . ."

"Too bad you wouldn't let me be one."

"Karen . . ."

"Don't you want to know what the reverser is, Paula? It's engineered from human chorionic gonadotropin. The pregnancy hormone. Too bad you never wanted a baby."

She went on staring at me. Lollie shrieked and splashed with her frog. Her lips *were* turning blue. I stood up, laid Timmy next to Lori in the portacrib, and buttoned my blouse.

"You made an experimental error twenty-five years ago," I said to Paula. "Too small a sample population. Sometimes a frog jumps out."

I went to lift my daughter from the wading pool.

AXIOMATIC

Greg Egan

Today it's everyone's prerogative to change their minds, but enjoy that freedom while you can—in the nanotech-dominated world of the future, you might not only not be able *to change your mind, you might not even be able to* want *to change it . . .*

Only a bit over halfway through the decade, it's already a fairly safe bet to predict that Australian writer Greg Egan is going to come to be recognized (if indeed he hasn't already *been so recognized) as being one of the Big New Names to emerge in SF in the nineties. In the last few years, he has become a frequent contributor to* Interzone *and* Asimov's Science Fiction, *and has made sales as well as to* Pulphouse, Analog, Aurealis, Eidolon, *and elsewhere; many of his stories have also appeared in various "Best of the Year" series, and he was on the Hugo Final Ballot in 1995 for his story "Cocoon," which won the Ditmar Award and the* Asimov's *Readers Award. His first novel,* Quarantine, *appeared in 1992, to wide critical acclaim, and was followed by a second novel in 1994,* Permutation City, *which won the John W. Campbell Memorial Award. His most recent books are a collection of his short fiction,* Axiomatic, *and two new novels,* Distress *and* Diaspora.

". . . *like your brain* has been frozen in liquid nitrogen, and then smashed into a thousand shards!"

I squeezed my way past the teenagers who lounged outside the entrance to The Implant Store, no doubt fervently hoping for a holovision news team to roll up and ask them why they weren't in school. They mimed throwing up as I passed, as if the state of not being pubescent and dressed like a member of Binary Search was so disgusting to contemplate that it made them physically ill.

Well, maybe it did.

Inside, the place was almost deserted. The interior reminded me of a video ROM shop; the display racks were virtually identical, and many of the distributors' logos were the same. Each rack was labelled: PSYCHEDELIA. MEDITATION AND HEALING. MOTIVATION AND SUCCESS. LANGUAGES AND TECHNICAL SKILLS. Each implant, although itself less than half a millimetre across, came in a package the size of an old-style book, bearing gaudy illustrations and a few lines of stale hyperbole from a marketing thesaurus or some rent-an-endorsement celebrity. "*Become* God! *Become* the Universe!" "The Ultimate Insight! The Ultimate Knowledge! The Ultimate Trip!" Even the perennial "This implant changed my life!"

I picked up the carton of *You Are Great!*—its transparent protective wrapper glistening with sweaty fingerprints—and thought numbly: If I bought this thing and used it, I would actually believe that. No amount of evidence to the contrary would be *physically able* to change my mind. I put it back on the shelf, next to *Love Yourself A Billion* and *Instant Willpower, Instant Wealth.*

I knew exactly what I'd come for, and I knew that it wouldn't be on display, but I browsed a while longer, partly out of genuine curiosity, partly just to give myself time. Time to think through the implications once again. Time to come to my senses and flee.

The cover of *Synaesthesia* showed a blissed-out man with a rainbow striking his tongue and musical staves piercing his eyeballs. Beside it, *Alien Mind-Fuck* boasted "a mental state so bizarre that even as you experience it, you won't know what it's like!" Implant technology was originally developed to provide instant language skills for business people and tourists, but after disappointing sales and a takeover by an entertainment conglomerate, the first mass-market implants appeared: a cross between video games and hallucinogenic drugs. Over the years, the range of confusion and dysfunction on offer grew wider, but there's only so far you can take that trend; beyond a certain point, scrambling the neural connections doesn't leave anyone *there* to be entertained by the strangeness, and the user, once restored to normalcy, remembers almost nothing.

The first of the next generation of implants—the so-called axiomatics—were all sexual in nature; apparently that was the technically simplest place to start. I walked over to the Erotica section, to see what was available—or at least, what could legally be displayed. Homosexuality, heterosexuality, autoerotism. An assortment of harmless fetishes. Eroticisation of various unlikely parts of the body. Why, I wondered, would anyone choose to have their brain rewired to make them crave a sexual practice they otherwise would have found abhorrent, or ludicrous, or just plain boring? To comply with a partner's demands? Maybe, although such extreme submissiveness was hard to imagine, and could scarcely be sufficiently widespread to explain the size of the market. To enable a part of their own sexual identity, which, unaided, would have merely nagged and festered, to triumph over their inhibitions, their ambivalence, their revulsion? Everyone has conflicting desires, and people can grow tired of both wanting and not wanting the very same thing. I understood *that*, perfectly.

The next rack contained a selection of religions, everything from Amish to Zen. (Gaining the Amish disapproval of technology this way apparently posed no problem; virtually every religious implant enabled the user to embrace far stranger contradictions.) There was even an implant called *Secular Humanist* ("You WILL hold these truths to be self-evident!"). No *Vacillating Agnostic*, though; apparently there was no market for doubt.

For a minute or two, I lingered. For a mere fifty dollars, I could have bought back my childhood Catholicism, even if the Church would not have approved. (At least, not officially; it would have been interesting to know exactly who was subsidising the product.) In the end, though, I had to admit that I wasn't really tempted. Perhaps it would have solved my problem, but not in the way that I wanted it solved—and after all, getting my own way was the whole point of coming here. Using an implant wouldn't rob me of my free will; on the contrary, it was going to help me to assert it.

Finally, I steeled myself and approached the sales counter.

"How can I help you, sir?" The young man smiled at me brightly, radiating sincerity, as if he really enjoyed his work. I mean, really, *really*.

"I've come to pick up a special order."

"Your name, please, sir?"

"Carver. Mark."

He reached under the counter and emerged with a parcel, mercifully already wrapped in anonymous brown. I paid in cash, I'd brought the exact change: $399.95. It was all over in twenty seconds.

I left the store, sick with relief, triumphant, exhausted. At least I'd finally bought the fucking thing; it was in my hands now, no one else was involved, and all I had to do was decide whether or not to use it.

After walking a few blocks towards the train station, I tossed the parcel into a bin, but I turned back almost at once and retrieved it. I passed a pair of armoured cops, and I pictured their eyes boring into me from behind their mirrored faceplates, but what I was carrying was perfectly legal. How could the Government ban a device which did no more than engender, in those who *freely chose* to use it, a particular set of beliefs—without also arresting everyone who shared those beliefs naturally? Very easily, actually, since the law didn't have to be consistent, but the implant manufacturers had succeeded in convincing the public that restricting their products would be paving the way for the Thought Police.

By the time I got home, I was shaking uncontrollably. I put the parcel on the kitchen table, and started pacing.

This wasn't for Amy. I had to admit that. Just because I still loved her, and still mourned her, didn't mean I was doing this for *her*. I wouldn't soil her memory with that lie.

In fact, I was doing it to free myself from her. After five years, I wanted my pointless love, my useless grief, to finally stop ruling my life. Nobody could blame me for that.

She had died in an armed hold-up, in a bank. The security cameras had been disabled, and everyone apart from the robbers had spent most of the time face-down on the floor, so I never found out the whole story. She must have moved, fidgeted, looked up, she must have done *something*; even at the peaks of my hatred, I couldn't believe that she'd been killed on a whim, for no comprehensible reason at all.

I knew who had squeezed the trigger, though. It hadn't come out at the trial; a clerk in the Police Department had sold me the information. The killer's name was Patrick Anderson, and by turning prosecution witness, he'd put his accomplices away for life, and reduced his own sentence to seven years.

I went to the media. A loathsome crime-show personality had taken the story and ranted about it on the airwaves for a week, diluting the facts with self-serving rhetoric, then grown bored and moved on to something else.

Five years later, Anderson had been out on parole for nine months.

OK. *So what?* It happens all the time. If someone had

come to me with such a story, I would have been sympathetic, but firm. "Forget her, she's dead. Forget him, he's garbage. Get on with your life."

I didn't forget her, and I didn't forget her killer. I had loved her, whatever that meant, and while the rational part of me had swallowed the fact of her death, the rest kept twitching like a decapitated snake. Someone else in the same state might have turned the house into a shrine, covered every wall and mantelpiece with photographs and memorabilia, put fresh flowers on her grave every day, and spent every night getting drunk watching old home movies. I didn't do that, I couldn't. It would have been grotesque and utterly false; sentimentality had always made both of us violently ill. I kept a single photo. We hadn't made home movies. I visited her grave once a year.

Yet for all of this outward restraint, inside my head my obsession with Amy's death simply kept on growing. I didn't *want* it, I didn't *choose* it, I didn't feed it or encourage it in any way. I kept no electronic scrapbook of the trial. If people raised the subject, I walked away. I buried myself in my work; in my spare time I read, or went to the movies, alone. I thought about searching for someone new, but I never did anything about it, always putting it off until that time in the indefinite future when I would be human again.

Every night, the details of the incident circled in my brain. I thought of a thousand things I "might have done" to have prevented her death, from not marrying her in the first place (we'd moved to Sydney because of my job), to magically arriving at the bank as her killer took aim, tackling him to the ground and beating him senseless, or worse. I knew these fantasies were futile and self-indulgent, but that knowledge was no cure. If I took sleeping pills, the whole thing simply shifted to the daylight hours, and I was literally unable to work. (The computers that help us are slightly less appalling every year, but air-traffic controllers *can't* daydream.)

I had to do something.

Revenge? Revenge was for the morally retarded. Me, I'd signed petitions to the UN, calling for the worldwide, unconditional abolition of capital punishment. I'd meant it then, and I still meant it. Taking human life was *wrong*; I'd believed that, passionately, since childhood. Maybe it started out as religious dogma, but when I grew up and shed all the ludicrous claptrap, the sanctity of life was one of the few beliefs I judged to be worth keeping. Aside from any pragmatic reasons, human consciousness had always seemed to me the most astonishing, miraculous, *sacred* thing in the universe. Blame my upbringing, blame my genes; I could no more devalue it than believe that one plus one equalled zero.

Tell some people you're a pacifist, and in ten seconds flat they'll invent a situation in which millions of people will die in unspeakable agony, and all your loved ones will be raped and tortured, if you don't blow someone's brains out. (There's always a contrived reason why you can't merely *wound* the omnipotent, genocidal madman.) The amusing thing is, they seem to hold you in even greater contempt when you admit that, yes, you'd do it, you'd kill under those conditions.

Anderson, however, clearly was not an omnipotent, genocidal madman. I had no idea whether or not he was likely to kill again. As for his capacity for reform, his abused childhood, or the caring and compassionate alter ego that may have been hiding behind the façade of his brutal exterior, I really didn't give a shit, but nonetheless I was convinced that it would be wrong for me to kill him.

I bought the gun first. That was easy, and perfectly legal; perhaps the computers simply failed to correlate my permit application with the release of my wife's killer, or perhaps the link was detected, but judged irrelevant.

I joined a "sports" club full of people who spent three hours a week doing nothing but shooting at moving, human-shaped targets. A recreational activity, harmless as fencing; I practised saying that with a straight face.

Buying the anonymous ammunition from a fellow club member *was* illegal; bullets that vaporised on impact, leaving no ballistics evidence linking them to a specific weapon. I scanned the court records; the average sentence for possessing such things was a five-hundred-dollar fine. The silencer was illegal, too; the penalties for ownership were similar.

Every night, I thought it through. Every night, I came to the same conclusion: despite my elaborate preparations, I wasn't going to kill anyone. Part of me wanted to, part of me didn't, but I knew perfectly well which was strongest. I'd spend the rest of my life dreaming about it, safe in the knowledge that no amount of hatred or grief or desperation would ever be enough to make me act against my nature.

I unwrapped the parcel. I was expecting a garish cover—sneering body builder toting sub-machine-gun—but the packaging was unadorned, plain grey with no markings except for the product code, and the name of the distributor, Clockwork Orchard.

I'd ordered the thing through an on-line catalogue, accessed via a coin-driven public terminal, and I'd specified collection by "Mark Carver" at a branch of The Implant Store in Chatswood, far from my home. All of which was paranoid nonsense, since the implant was legal—and all of which was perfectly reasonable, because I felt far more nervous and guilty about buying it than I did about buying the gun and ammunition.

The description in the catalogue had begun with the statement *Life is cheap!* then had waffled on for several lines in the same vein: *People are meat. They're nothing, they're worthless.* The exact words weren't important, though; they weren't a part of the implant itself. It wouldn't be a matter of a voice in my head, reciting some badly written spiel which I could choose to ridicule or ignore; nor would it be a kind of mental legislative decree, which I could evade by means of semantic quibbling. Axiomatic implants were derived from analysis of actual neural structures in real people's brains, they weren't based on the expression of the axioms in language. The spirit, not the letter, of the law would prevail.

I opened up the carton. There was an instruction leaflet, in seventeen languages. A programmer. An applicator. A pair of tweezers. Sealed in a plastic bubble labelled STERILE IF UNBROKEN, the implant itself. It looked like a tiny piece of gravel.

I had never used one before, but I'd seen it done a thousand times on holovision. You placed the thing in the programmer, "woke it up", and told it how long you wanted to be active. The applicator was strictly for tyros; the jaded cognoscenti balanced the implant on the tip of their little finger, and daintily poked it up the nostril of their choice.

The implant burrowed into the brain, sent out a swarm of nanomachines to explore, and forge links with, the relevant neural systems, and then went into active mode for the predetermined time—anything from an hour to infinity—doing whatever it was designed to do. Enabling multiple orgasms of the left kneecap. Making the colour blue taste like the long-lost memory of mother's milk. Or, hard-wiring a premise: *I will succeed. I am happy in my job. There is life after death. Nobody died in Belsen. Four legs good, two legs bad . . .*

I packed everything back into the carton, put it in a drawer, took three sleeping pills, and went to bed.

Perhaps it was a matter of laziness. I've always been biased towards those options which spare me from facing the very same set of choices again in the future; it seems so *inefficient* to go through the same agonies of conscience more than once. To *not* use the implant would have meant having to reaffirm that decision, day after day, for the rest of my life.

Or perhaps I never really believed that the preposterous toy would work. Perhaps I hoped to prove that my convictions—unlike other people's—were engraved on some metaphysical tablet that hovered in a spiritual dimension unreachable by any mere machine.

Or perhaps I just wanted a moral alibi—a way to kill Anderson while still believing it was something that the *real* me could never have done.

At least I'm sure of one thing. I didn't do it for Amy.

I woke around dawn the next day, although I didn't need to get up at all; I was on annual leave for a month. I dressed, ate breakfast, then unpacked the implant again and carefully read the instructions.

With no great sense of occasion, I broke open the sterile bubble and, with the tweezers, dropped the speck into its cavity in the programmer.

The programmer said, "Do you speak English?" The voice reminded me of one of the control towers at work; deep but somehow genderless, businesslike without being crudely robotic—and yet, unmistakably inhuman.

"Yes."

"Do you want to program this implant?"

"Yes."

"Please specify the active period."

"Three days." Three days would be enough, surely; if not, I'd call the whole thing off.

"This implant is to remain active for three days after insertion. Is that correct?"

"Yes."

"This implant is ready for use. The time is seven forty-three a.m. Please insert the implant before eight forty-three a.m., or it will deactivate itself and reprogramming will be required. Please enjoy this product and dispose of the packaging thoughtfully."

I placed the implant in the applicator, then hesitated, but not for long. This wasn't the time to agonise; I'd agonised for months, and I was sick of it. Any more indecisiveness and I'd need to buy a second implant to convince me to use the first. I wasn't committing a crime; I wasn't even coming close to guaranteeing that I would commit one. Millions of people held the belief that human life was nothing special, but how many of them were murderers? The next three days would simply reveal how *I* reacted to that belief, and although the attitude would be hard-wired, the consequences were far from certain.

I put the applicator in my left nostril, and pushed the release button. There was a brief stinging sensation, nothing more.

I thought, *Amy would have despised me for this.* That shook me, but only for a moment. Amy was dead, which made her hypothetical feelings irrelevant. Nothing I did could hurt her now, and thinking any other way was crazy.

I tried to monitor the progress of the change, but that was a joke; you can't check your moral precepts by introspection every thirty seconds. After all, my assessment of myself as being unable to kill had been based on decades of observation (much of it probably out of date). What's more, that assessment, that self-image, had come to be as much a *cause* of my actions and attitudes as a reflection of them—and apart from the direct changes the implant was making to my brain, it was breaking that feedback loop by providing a rationalisation for me to act in a way I'd convinced myself was impossible.

After a while, I decided to get drunk, to distract myself from the vision of microscopic robots crawling around in my skull. It was a big mistake; alcohol makes me paranoid. I don't recall much of what followed, except for catching sight of myself in the bathroom mirror, screaming, "HAL's breaking First law! HAL's breaking First Law!" before vomiting copiously.

I woke just after midnight, on the bathroom floor. I took an anti-hangover pill, and in five minutes my headache and nausea were gone. I showered and put on fresh clothes. I'd bought a jacket especially for the occasion, with an inside pocket for the gun.

It was still impossible to tell if the thing had done anything to me that went beyond the placebo effect; I asked myself, out loud, "Is human life sacred? Is it wrong to kill?" but I couldn't concentrate on the question, and I found it hard to believe that I ever had in the past; the whole idea seemed obscure and difficult, like some esoteric mathematical theorem. The prospect of going ahead with my plans made my stomach churn, but that was simple fear, not moral outrage; the implant wasn't meant to make me brave, or calm, or resolute. I could have bought those qualities too, but that would have been cheating.

I'd had Anderson checked out by a private investigator. He worked every night but Sunday, as a bouncer in a Surry Hills nightclub; he lived nearby, and usually arrived home, on foot, at around four in the morning. I'd driven past his terrace house several times, I'd have no trouble finding it. He lived alone; he had a lover, but they always met at her place, in the afternoon or early evening.

I loaded the gun and put it in my jacket, then spent half an hour staring in the mirror, trying to decide if the bulge was visible. I wanted a drink, but I restrained myself. I switched on the radio and wandered through the house, trying to become less agitated. Perhaps taking a life was now no big deal to me, but I could still end up dead, or in prison, and the implant apparently hadn't rendered me uninterested in my own fate.

I left too early, and had to drive by a circuitous route to kill time; even then, it was only a quarter past three when I parked, a kilometre from Anderson's house. A few cars and taxis passed me as I walked the rest of the way, and I'm sure I was trying so hard to look at ease that my body language radiated guilt and paranoia—but no ordinary driver would have noticed or cared, and I didn't see a single patrol car.

When I reached the place, there was nowhere to hide—no gardens, no trees, no fences—but I'd known that in advance. I chose a house across the street, not quite opposite Anderson's, and sat on the front step. If the occupant appeared, I'd feign drunkenness and stagger away.

I sat and waited. It was a warm, still, ordinary night; the sky was clear, but grey and starless thanks to the lights of the city. I kept reminding myself: *You don't have to do this, you don't have to go through with it.* So why did I stay? The hope of being liberated from my sleepless nights? The idea was laughable; I had no doubt that if I killed Anderson, it would torture me as much as my helplessness over Amy's death.

Why did I stay? It was nothing to do with the implant; at most, that was neutralising my qualms; it wasn't forcing me to *do* anything.

Why, then? In the end, I think I saw it as a matter of honesty. I had to accept the unpleasant fact that I honestly wanted to kill Anderson, and however much I had also been repelled by the notion, to be true to myself I had to do it—anything less would have been hypocrisy and self-deception.

At five to four, I heard footsteps echoing down the street. As I turned, I hoped it would be someone else, or that he would be with a friend, but it was him, and he was alone. I waited until he was as far from his front door as I was, then I started walking. He glanced my way briefly, then ignored me. I felt a shock of pure fear—I hadn't seen him in the flesh since the trial, and I'd forgotten how physically imposing he was.

I had to force myself to slow down, and even then I passed him sooner than I'd meant to. I was wearing light, rubber-soled shoes, he was in heavy boots, but when I crossed the street and did a U-turn towards him, I couldn't believe he couldn't hear my heartbeat, or smell the stench of my sweat. Metres from the door, just as I finished pulling out the gun, he looked over his shoulder with an expression of bland curiosity, as if he might have been expecting a dog or a piece of windblown litter. He turned around to face me, frowning. I just stood there, pointing the gun at him, unable to speak. Eventually he said, "What the fuck do you want? I've got two hundred dollars in my wallet. Back pocket."

I shook my head. "Unlock the front door, then put your hands on your head and kick it open. Don't try closing it on me."

He hesitated, then complied.

"Now walk in. Keep your hands on your head. Five steps, that's all. Count them out loud. I'll be right behind you."

I reached the light switch for the hall as he counted four, then I slammed the door behind me, and flinched at the sound. Anderson was right in front of me, and I suddenly felt trapped. The man was a vicious killer; *I* hadn't even thrown a punch since I was eight years old. Did I really believe the gun would protect me? With his hands on his head, the muscles of his arms and shoulders bulged against his shirt. I should have shot him right then, in the back of the head. This was an execution, not a duel; if I'd wanted some quaint idea of honour, I would have come without a gun and let him take me to pieces.

I said, "Turn left." Left was the living room. I followed

him in, switched on the light. "Sit." I stood in the doorway, he sat in the room's only chair. For a moment, I felt dizzy and my vision seemed to tilt, but I don't think I moved, I don't think I sagged or swayed; if I had, he probably would have rushed me.

"What do you want?" he asked.

I had to give that a lot of thought. I'd fantasised this situation a thousand times, but I could no longer remember the details—although I did recall that I'd usually assumed that Anderson would recognise me, and start volunteering excuses and explanations straight away.

Finally, I said, "I want you to tell me why you killed my wife."

"I didn't kill your wife. Miller killed your wife."

I shook my head. "That's not true. I *know*. The cops told me. Don't bother lying, because I *know*."

He stared at me blandly. I wanted to lose my temper and scream, but I had a feeling that, in spite of the gun, that would have been more comical than intimidating. I could have pistol-whipped him, but the truth is I was afraid to go near him.

So I shot him in the foot. He yelped and swore, then leant over to inspect the damage. "Fuck you!" he hissed. "Fuck you!" He rocked back and forth, holding his foot. "I'll break your fucking neck! I'll fucking kill you!" The wound bled a little through the hole in his boot, but it was nothing compared to the movies. I'd heard that the vaporising ammunition had a cauterising effect.

I said, "Tell me why you killed my wife."

He looked far more angry and disgusted than afraid, but he dropped his pretence of innocence. "It just happened," he said. "It was just one of those things that happens."

I shook my head, annoyed. "No. *Why?* Why did it happen?"

He moved as if to take off his boot, then thought better of

it. "Things were going wrong. There was a time lock, there was hardly any cash, everything was just a big fuck-up. I didn't mean to do it. It just happened."

I shook my head again, unable to decide if he was a moron, or if he was stalling. "Don't tell me 'it just happened'. *Why* did it happen? Why did you do it?"

The frustration was mutual; he ran a hand through his hair and scowled at me. He was sweating now, but I couldn't tell if it was from pain or from fear. "What do you want me to say? I lost my temper, all right? Things were going badly, and I lost my fucking temper, and there she was, all right?"

The dizziness struck me again, but this time it didn't subside. I understood now; he wasn't being obtuse, he was telling the entire truth. I'd smashed the occasional coffee cup during a tense situation at work. I'd even, to my shame, kicked our dog once, after a fight with Amy. Why? *I'd lost my fucking temper, and there she was.*

I stared at Anderson, and felt myself grinning stupidly. It was all so clear now. I understood. I understood the absurdity of everything I'd ever felt for Amy—my "love", my "grief". It had all been a joke. She was meat, she was nothing. All the pain of the past five years evaporated; I was drunk with relief. I raised my arms and spun around slowly. Anderson leapt up and sprung towards me; I shot him in the chest until I ran out of bullets, then I knelt down beside him. He was dead.

I put my gun in my jacket. The barrel was warm. I remembered to use my handkerchief to open the front door. I half expected to find a crowd outside, but of course the shots had been inaudible, and Anderson's threats and curses were not likely to have attracted attention.

A block from the house, a patrol car appeared around a corner. It slowed almost to a halt as it approached me. I kept my eyes straight ahead as it passed. I heard the engine idle. Then stop. I kept on walking, waiting for a shouted command, thinking: if they search me and find the gun, I'll confess; there's no point in prolonging the agony.

The engine spluttered, revved noisily, and the car roared away.

Perhaps I'm *not* the number-one most obvious suspect. I don't know what Anderson was involved in since he got out; maybe there are hundreds of other people who had far better reasons for wanting him dead, and perhaps when the cops have finished with them, they'll get around to asking me what I was doing that night. A month seems an awfully long time, though. Anyone would think they didn't care.

The same teenagers as before are gathered around the entrance, and again the mere sight of me seems to disgust them. I wonder if the taste in fashion and music tattooed on their brains is set to fade in a year or two, or if they have sworn lifelong allegiance. It doesn't bear contemplating.

This time, I don't browse. I approach the sales counter without hesitation.

This time, I know exactly what I want.

What I want is what I felt that night: the unshakeable conviction that Amy's death—let alone Anderson's—simply didn't matter, any more than the death of a fly or an amoeba, any more than breaking a coffee cup or kicking a dog.

My one mistake was thinking that the insight I gained would simply vanish when the implant cut out. It hasn't. It's been clouded with doubts and reservations, it's been undermined, to some degree, by my whole ridiculous panoply of beliefs and superstitions, but I can still recall the peace it gave me, I can still recall that flood of joy and relief, and *I want it back*. Not for three days; for the rest of my life.

Killing Anderson *wasn't* honest, it wasn't "being true to myself." Being true to myself would have meant living with all my contradictory urges, suffering the multitude of voices in my head, accepting confusion and doubt. It's too late for that now; having tasted the freedom of certainty, I find I can't live without it.

"How can I help you, sir?" The salesman smiles from the bottom of his heart.

Part of me, of course, still finds the prospect of what I am about to do totally repugnant.

No matter. That won't last.

REMEMBER'D KISSES

Michael F. Flynn

Born in Easton, Pennsylvania, Michael F. Flynn has a BA in math from La Salle College and an MS for work in topology from Marquette University, and works as an industrial quality engineer and statistician. Since his first sale there in 1984, Flynn has become a mainstay of Analog, *and one of their most frequent contributors. He has also made sales to* The Magazine of Fantasy and Science Fiction, Asimov's Science Fiction, *and elsewhere, and is thought of as one of the best of the crop of new "hard science" writers. His first novel was the well-received* In the Country of the Blind. *It was followed by* Fallen Angels, *a novel written in collaboration with Larry Niven and Jerry Pournelle, and a solo novel* The Nanotech Chronicles. *His most recent book is a collection,* The Forest of Time and Other Stories. *He now lives in Edison, N.J.*

Flynn has written frequently about the promise and the dangers of nanotechnology, in nanotech-oriented stories such as "Soul of the City," "The Washer at the Ford," "The Laughing Clone," and "The Blood Upon the Rose." In the unsettling story that follows, he suggests that sometimes, even after the most grievous of loses, even with the most-advanced of technology at your disposal, you really should leave well-enough alone . . .

Click.

A mechanical sound. A relay, perhaps. A flip-flop switch or maybe a butterfly valve. Very soft. Almost muffled.

Sigh.

And that was hydraulics. Escape gas bleeding off. Pressure relief. Again, a muted sound, not particularly obtrusive.

Click.

It was a metronome. A syncopation. If you focused all your attention on it, it could become—

Sigh.

—quite relaxing. Hypnotic even. It would be easy to lose oneself in its rhythm.

Click!

The sudden hand on his shoulder made him start.

"Mr. Carter?"

Sigh.

He turned, unwilling; guided by the gentle but persistent pressure of the hand on his shoulder. His vision rotated, camera-like. Away from the equipment; along the tubing, hanging in catenary loops; past the blinking monitors; toward the sight that he had been avoiding ever since he had stepped into the room.

Click.

"Yes, Doctor?" His voice was listless, uninterested. He heard it as if he were a spectator at a very bad play.

"We did all we could, Mr. Carter. The medics stabilized her as soon as the police cut her out of the car. But I'm afraid there was little else they could do."

Sigh.

He looked at the doctor, turning his head quickly, so that the bed itself flicked across his vision without registering. But his subconscious saw the subliminal afterimage and began sending messages of pain and fear.

Click.

"I understand, Doctor. . . ." He glanced at the name tag pinned to the white uniform, trying not to notice the little splashes of red on the sleeves and on the chest. "I understand, Doctor Lapointe. I'm sure you did everything possible."

"If we had gotten to her sooner, or if the trauma had been

less severe, we might have been able to repair the damage. There have been incredible advances in tissue repair nanomachines in the last several years. . . ."

Sigh.

Henry Norris Carter wondered if the doctor thought he was being comforting. Tell me more, he thought. Tell me all the different ways you might have saved her. If only. If only this advance had been made; if only that had been done sooner. If only. If only.

Well, take it as he meant it. "Yes, Doctor Lapointe, but I'm sure you understand that such speculations cannot make me feel any better about what's happened." (And a part of his mind curled up and gibbered, *Nothing's happened! Nothing's happened!*) "I'm quite aware of the advances in nanotechnology. My wife and I both work—" He suddenly realized he had used the present tense and stopped, confused. "—no, worked—" But that wasn't right, either. Not yet. "I mean we were both genetic engineers at SingerLabs over in New Jersey. We both donated DNA to the cell library there. As long as we're talking 'if only's,' if only I had her cell samples with me—"

"No, Mr. Carter, you mustn't think that. As I said, the trauma was too severe. Even the most advanced nanomachines are still too slow to have saved your wife before irreversible brain damage set in."

So. Finally. He forced himself to look directly at the figure on the bed. The maze of tubing crawled snake-like around it. Encircling it; binding it; piercing it. Up nose. Down throat. Into vein and groin. Pushing the fluids and the gasses in and sucking them out, because the body itself had given up the task. The click/sigh of the respirator faded into the background.

The contours of the sheet were not quite right; as if parts of what was under it were missing. The doctors, he supposed, had cobbled the body back together as best they could, but their hearts hadn't been entirely in it. The whole left side of her face was an ugly purple bruise. And the symmetry of her nose and cheekbones and jaw was irretrievably lost. The right eye was closed, as if sleeping; and the left—The left eye was hidden under a mass of bandages. *If it's there at all.* Judging by the extent of the damage on that side, it was doubtful that the eye had remained in its socket.

He wanted to scream and his stomach gave a queer flip-flop and his knees felt suddenly weak. He trembled all over. Don't think about that. Think about anything else. Think about—

Quiet evenings at home. She, reading her favorite Tennyson in a circle of soft light cast by the goose-neck lamp; while he pretended to read, but watched her secretly over the lip of his book and she knew he was watching her and was waiting for just the right moment to—

Running through the rainstorm down 82nd Street from the Met, his trenchcoat an umbrella over both their heads. Laughing because it was so silly to get caught unprepared like that and they were soaked to the skin already and—

Hiking the Appalachian Trail where it lost itself in the granite mountains of New England and stopping to examine the wildflowers by the edge of the path and wondering why on earth the stems would always branch in just exactly that way and—

Four-wheeling over Red Cone that summer in Colorado and how he had froze at the wheel because all he could see out either side of the Bronco was sky because the road ran up a ridge only a little wider than the car itself and how could anyone expect to drive over a knob of rock that steep? And how the sign on the other side, by Montezuma, had said dangerous road travel at your own risk and wasn't that a hell of a place to put it and—

Her eyes had been a most lovely shade of hazel.

"Pardon me?"

Henry looked at the doctor and blinked away the memories that had blurred his vision. "I said her eyes were hazel."

"Oh."

He turned and looked again at his wife. The doctor seemed at a loss for what to say and for a crazy instant Henry felt sorry for *him*. The doctor wanted to say something, anything to pierce Henry's shell of misery; but there was nothing that anyone could ever say or do that would make the slightest particle of difference in how he felt.

He felt . . . Nothing. He was numb. He refused to accept what he saw.

"Barbara."

"She can't hear you. She's far too deep in coma for that."

He ignored the doctor's comment. It was patently absurd. Voices made sound waves; and soundwaves vibrated eardrums; and eardrums made nerve impulses; and somewhere, somewhere deep inside that dying body there had to be a tiny, glimmering spark, wondering why everything was growing so much dimmer and fainter, and he would be *damned* before he let that spark flicker out all alone in silence.

He drifted toward the bed; and the doctor, sensing his intention, guided him toward her relatively uninjured right side. The doctor lifted the sheet, exposing her hand and Carter took it in both of his. He noticed the mole on her right side, just above the curve of the hip, and touched it briefly with his forefinger.

"The other driver," the doctor said, "the one who ran the red light, was killed instantly. An eighteen-year-old kid and dead drunk. Now he's just dead."

Henry shook his head. Did the doctor think that that thought would comfort him? He felt a brief regret that the drunk hadn't suffered; and a second regret that he would wish such a thing of anyone; and then he felt nothing once more.

"Barbry, I'm here. I came as soon as they called." He stroked her hand gently, fingertips on palm, and let his palm run under her limp fingertips; and was embarrassed to notice how his body, for a brief instant, responded to the remembered touch.

He began telling her about his day, because there wasn't much of anything else he could think of to talk about. (And why had she taken the day off to shop for his birthday? They should have been together in the lab, safe. Instead—)

Instead, he told her how he and Bill Canazetti had finally made some progress on the Barnsleyformer; because the trick wasn't in the morphogenesis after all, but in the fractal geometry of the genes. They had gotten a brief, tantalizing glimpse of a simple and elegant recursion formula and would have continued to work on it well after quitting time except the phone call had come from the hospital and—

And the traffic at the tunnel ramp had been terrible. Backed up all the way around halfway to the turnpike gate. Wasn't it always that way when you were in a hurry?

At any rate, he told her, 'Dolph Kavin was doing a slow burn because he'd been passed over for project leader on the cloning team. Old Lady Peeler had picked Amanda Jacobs and 'Dolph had complained bitterly to anyone who would listen (and there weren't that many) how women always stuck together; but you know how it is with office politics. And he said it was probably a lot different in the old days before Singer had died and the Lab was run on a more personal level.

And—

"She's gone, Mr. Carter."

He jerked for the second time at the unexpected touch;

and looked from the hand tentatively laid on his wrist, up the arm to the doctor's sympathetic face.

"What?"

"She's gone. All brain activity has ceased. I—" He broke off, looked uncomfortable, mustered his resolve. "If you would sign a few forms, please. Many of her organs can still be saved, if we act quickly." The doctor looked at him in mute appeal. Your wife is dead, his eyes seemed to say; but we can still save others if you help.

Others.

Strangers.

And why should he care about strangers?

Donate organs. A nice way of saying, let's cut up your wife's body into little chunks and sew them into other people. Intellectually, he and Barbara had always supported the organ donor movement; but it was different when the actual time came. And what the hell did it matter? Barbry didn't live there any more.

"Yes," he said; and his voice came out in a sort of croak. "Yes," he repeated. "Go ahead. It's what she would have wanted."

"You're doing the right thing," the doctor assured him. "Your wife may be dead, but part of her will go on living through others."

Click.

The most awful thing about the whole business, Henry decided as he rose shakily from the chair, was the way the respirator continued to pump air and the way in which the sheets continued to rise and fall. As if the person beneath them had only fallen into a deep slumber and would awaken when the morning came.

Sigh.

Of course, they insisted that he stay and rest. They gave him a mild sedative and they made him lie down for an hour or so. He closed his eyes, but his mind wouldn't shut down. It kept spinning and spinning, trying to find a way out of accepting what had happened. When he arose only a short while later, he was unrested and unrefreshed.

It was the early morning pre-dawn hours when he left Roosevelt Hospital and made his way down Ninth Avenue toward the Lincoln Tunnel entrances. There was a mist off the Hudson that gave the West Side a ghostly and unreal appearance. Sounds echoed as if on a damp and abandoned stage set. His was the only car on Ninth Avenue and in the distance a single pair of headlights drifted crosstown. If New York was The City That Never Slept, during these hours it at least dozed fitfully.

Some part of him had taken over from the gibbering, helpless personality crouching in the back of his head. It was a part of him that felt nothing and thought nothing. It was an automaton that made his body do all the right things, like some faithful robot dutifully carrying home its injured master.

The neighborhood north of the tunnel ramps had once been called Hell's Kitchen; but the new yuppy-fied city was a little ashamed of its rough-necked, blue-collar past, so they called it Chelsea North now. They could call it what they damn well pleased, but some things never change. It was still Hell's Kitchen and if the police no longer walked the beat in squads of five as they once did, it was because they seldom left their patrol cars.

If Henry had been entirely himself, he would never have made the wrong turn. But automatons do make mistakes and the sign with the arrow pointing toward the tunnel was placed ambiguously. He meant to turn right at the *next* corner; but his eyes saw the sign and his hands spun the wheel, and there he was.

He realized his error almost immediately. He cursed for a moment or two and checked the street sign at the next intersection to get his bearings. He turned, and turned again, and then he saw her.

The streetlight was a stage spot highlighting a tableau. Brown, ratted hair hanging low around familiar eyes and nose; her body wrapped in a tattered pea jacket, and huddled over a heating grate; hugging a tattered shopping bag to her. Three men—two black, one white—loomed over her, laughing, giving her little shoves, while her eyes darted like mice eyes back and forth, looking for escape.

"Barbry!"

Henry hit the brakes, twisted and grabbed the jack handle from the floor in the back. He burst from the car. "You! You, there! Leave that woman alone!"

The men laughed and turned on him and the laughter died. If Henry had been entirely himself, they would have pounced without a thought, like any wolf pack. But he was not entirely himself, and he had a jack handle in his hand, and there was something in his eyes. A flame. They used to call it the berserker look. It was the look that said that, whatever came, life or death, he would accept it gladly.

The three liked long odds in their favor. Three strong young males against a lone woman, that was acceptable. But against a crazy man with the berserker look? No. You couldn't win against a man who didn't give a damn. They might walk out of it, but maybe not all three, and certainly not all whole. So they sought the better part and walked away, throwing obscene words and gestures after them to show they hadn't been afraid after all, not really.

Henry walked to the woman on the grate and took her by the hands and raised her to her feet. She looked at him with fear in her eyes.

"Barbry?"

And she didn't really look like Barbara at all, and that broke the spell. Henry blinked and his surroundings came crashing down around him. Hell's Kitchen? My God! How had he gotten here? He could remember nothing since lying down at the hospital. And who was this woman?

She looked like—But, no. Her hair was brown, like Barbara's; but it was a shade darker. The face had the same shape; but the cheekbones sat lower. And there was a scar that ran from under the right eye, across the cheek toward the ear. She stank: of sweat and booze and excrement. Whoever it was, it wasn't Barbara. And why on earth would he ever have thought that?

"Who are you?" he asked.

She didn't answer and tried to pull her hands from his. Henry remembered leaping from the car, and looked around with sudden alarm. Those three punks might come back any moment. He began to shake as he realized what he had done.

He turned back to his car, remembered the woman, and hesitated. He couldn't just drive off and leave her here. If those punks came back, she'd be worse off than if he had never stopped.

"Come on," he said. "Get in the car."

She looked at him doubtfully and backed away a step, holding her shopping bag like Hector's shield. Henry pulled open the passenger's door. "Get in," he repeated. "They might come back."

That seemed to get through to her. She glanced down the street in the direction her tormentors had gone, then looked back at Henry's Town Car. Her tongue swept out and around her lips. She looked at him again. Then she made up her mind and darted into the safety of the automobile.

Henry slammed the door, ran around to the driver's side, and slid behind the wheel. He hit the door lock and all four doors snapped at once. The sound startled the woman who jerked around anxiously. She tried the door and it wouldn't open; so she slid across the seat from him as far as she could go, putting her bag between them and clutching it to her.

• • •

He took her with him back to Short Hills because he didn't know what else to do and it was easier to make no decisions than to decide anything. Once home, he hustled her inside his house, glancing over his shoulder while he did so, to see if—despite the hour—any of the neighbors were watching.

In the kitchen, she pulled away from him and ran to the farthest corner and crouched there, making small sounds in her throat. Henry wondered how much human being was left imprisoned within her skull. There but for the grace of God. . . . Barbry and this bag lady looked somewhat alike, enough to be taken for sisters if not for twins; yet, Barbry had lived here, in comfort if not in luxury, while this woman had lived on a heating vent in Hell's Kitchen. How easily it might have happened the other way. What trauma might have been enough?

"Now that I've got you," Henry told the woman, "what do I do with you?"

She seemed to shrink within himself and Henry held out what he meant to be placating hands. "Don't worry. I won't hurt you. If you want, you can have a shower and a meal. And a change of clothes." The thought of giving this woman one of Barbry's dresses was distressing. He wasn't ready to part with anything of hers, not yet. But there was a trunk in the attic, with some cast-offs that she had meant to donate to charity anyway.

He took the bag lady by the hand, noticing as he did so the track of needlemarks up the inside of her arm, and showed her the shower in the bathroom. He gave her a washrag and towels and one of Barbara's old housecoats and told her to leave her dirty clothing for disposal. The woman glared at him suspiciously, so he shrugged and walked away.

In the kitchen, he opened a can of beef broth into a pot and turned on the heat. Something not too taxing for her system. As the odor filled the room he realized he was hungry, too, and he added a second can to the pot. After it had come to a boil, he reduced the heat to simmer and walked to the kitchen window.

The kitchen faced on a woods protected by "greenbelt" legislation from development. No danger of ticky-tacking working class homes depressing the property values. The canopy of the trees looked like a silhouette cut from black construction paper, the false dawn providing an eerie backlighting.

He still didn't know her name. He had asked twice on the drive back, but she had remained silent, staring at him with ferret eyes, and he began to wonder if she even realized what was happening to her. Probably not much intelligence left. Etched away by years on the streets and a constant drip-drip-drip of heroin on the brain cells. Odd, how much—and how little—she looked like Bar—Like Barb—

He squeezed his eyes shut and willed himself not to think of her. The sound of her voice. A wisp of perfume. Remembered kisses.

After a while, he realized that he couldn't hear the shower running upstairs. What was that bag lady doing?

When he checked the bathroom she wasn't there, so he searched from room to room until he found her. She was hiding in the closet in the guest bedroom. She had taken the few odd garments hanging there and made a sort of nest of them. The wire hangers swung and tinkled like Japanese wind chimes. She looked at him with those ferret eyes; expecting anything, surprised at nothing.

Somewhere, she had found an old bag of salted peanuts. A relic of some airline flight Henry had long forgotten. She had poured the nuts into her palm and was gnawing at them. When she saw Henry at the closet door, she clutched the foil bag to her, as if she expected him to try to take it away.

• • •

Eventually, she did eat. Not the peanut bag, but the soup Henry had prepared. She wolfed it in greedy gulps, her left arm encircling the bowl, and her right wielding the soup spoon like a shovel. She kept her eye fixed warily on him the whole time, except when she darted quick looks around her, like an animal guarding its prey.

When she was done he took the bowl, which she released only reluctantly; and this time when he led her to the shower she seemed to understand. She grabbed the towels from his hands and stared at them. Then she stared at him.

"Go on," he said gruffly. "You shower now. I'll go up to the attic and see if I can find some old clothes for you."

When he returned from the attic with an armful of clothing, Henry found the woman in the library, sitting in Barbry's favorite reading chair. Showered and scrubbed, she seemed like a different person. Certainly, she smelled different: fresh and clean. From the rear, in the soft light and wearing Barbry's bathrobe, she looked enough like Barbara to make Henry's heart freeze for a moment. The dresses fell from his arms and he braced himself against the back of his own reading chair.

And the illusion vanished. All he saw was a bag lady holding the portrait photograph that Barbara and he had had taken only eight months before.

"That was my wife," he said, and she jumped a little and turned and looked at him. Her eyes were childlike. Green, he saw, and not hazel. They didn't look at all like the suspicious ferret eyes he had seen earlier. "My wife, Barbara," he explained, pointing to the photo. "She was— she was killed today in an automobile accident."

There. He had said it out loud. Now it was true. All of a sudden, he couldn't look at the photograph. The bag lady looked from the portrait to him and back to the portrait.

Then she stroked Barbara's face gently. She nodded her head up and down in a slow cadence and made a low keening sound. Henry dropped into his chair, crushing the dresses he had laid there. He covered his face with his hands and time went by.

When he looked up again, he saw that the woman had gone to the mirror by the bookshelves and was staring at her own face. She was holding the photograph in her right hand so she could see both herself and Barbara side-by-side. With her left, she held the front of the housecoat gathered together.

"Yes, you do look a little like her," Henry said. "Not much, but that's what made me stop there on the street. I—" He suddenly realized he had as much as said he wouldn't have stopped otherwise.

But the bag lady seemed not to have noticed, or, if noticed, not to have cared. "I'm Sadie," she said and Henry jerked his head in surprise at hearing her speak. "Sadie the Lady. That's me." She said it in a kind of sing-song voice. She returned her attention to the study of herself and the photograph.

Henry stood up and walked behind her so he could see the two faces from the same angle. "Yes. You know, if you did your hair up the same way, you would look even more like her." Barbry had always worn her hair piled up.

Sadie the Lady smiled, showing an incisor missing on the upper right. She put the photograph down and reached with both her hands to gather her hair into a rough approximation of Barbara's. She primped for the mirror, turning this way and that. Henry, watching her reflection, blushed. He should have known she would need new underwear, too.

The tableau in the cemetery seemed unreal. As if he were watching it from far away. Voices buzzed. Puppet figures stood around. He felt things only as if through layers of cotton. People he knew kept coming up to him and gripping his arm and telling him how sorry they were. He couldn't understand why they were so sorry, but he smiled and said everything was going to be all right.

Bill Canazetti, his lab partner, told him it was all right to cry. That he shouldn't hold it in. But Henry just shook his head. Later he would do that for Her. Just now, he couldn't.

There was a preacher. Barbara had been a church-goer, High Church, and Henry had sometimes gone with Her. He wished now he had gone more often. It was a portion of Her life that he could no longer share.

The preacher (Priest, he supposed. There was a difference.) The priest spoke of comforting impossibilities. Eternal life. The immortal soul. Barbara had gone to a better world. She had left behind this vale of tears. Henry listened. He wanted to believe it. He tried to believe it. It was better to believe such things than to believe that there was no Barbara at all, anywhere. Death was the Great Proselytizer.

"Most of all," the man in the funny collar said to the assembled group, "Barbara lives on in the hearts and minds of those of us who knew and loved her. We carry some piece of her with us always. . . ."

Now, that was certainly true. At least, since he had donated Her organs. There was no doubt several people already carried a piece of Her with them. And there was the DNA sample at the lab. Under proper conditions it should last nearly forever. Immortality of a sort, though he doubted that that was what the priest had meant.

Henry decided that, if Barbry did live somehow in his memories, the first thing he should do when he got home was to record those memories on tape. Everything about Her. That way he could never forget.

He had kept Her clothes and other things. He couldn't bear to part with them just yet. They were memories, too, in a way; and he wasn't quite ready to cast them out. In fact (and it would shame him if it ever got out), he slept at night with one of Her slips tucked beneath his pillow.

And then there was Sadie the Lady.

Henry had talked her into staying. He didn't know why. He had put her up in the guest bedroom and let her wear Barbara's old things. Suspicious at first, she had gradually loosened up. She spoke now, at least once or twice a day; and had wandered off to her closet nest only once. She was still hoarding food, Henry discovered, in several caches around the house, which Henry left undisturbed. It seemed . . . right that she should be in the house.

The worst part had been the heroin withdrawal. Henry hadn't believed that such agony was possible. Sadie had moaned and sweated and begged him to find her connection. But her connection was in Manhattan and Henry had not allowed her out of the house, despite her pleading, her tears, and her threats. At times, he had to restrain her, physically; and found that, for her condition, she was surprisingly strong. Together, they had finally weathered the crisis; and when it was over they were both drained.

Afterwards she had begun to show more interest in herself. She bathed more regularly, and brushed and combed her hair. She became a kind of housekeeper, doing odd chores around the house. Cleaning. Cooking his meals. Sometimes mumbling to herself. Once or twice saying a few words out loud. Perhaps it was gratitude. Her way of repaying him for what he had done for her that night on the streets. Or perhaps she was trying to help him through his bereavement. Henry didn't know.

Sometimes when he saw Sadie in the hall or in the kitchen, Henry squinted his eyes and pretended to himself that she was actually Barbara. The mental novocaine was wearing off and Henry was starting to feel the pain of Barbara's loss. His little game with Sadie helped numb the pain, at least for a little while. It was a harmless bit of self-deception.

And it was only a game, of course. He knew when he did it that he was only pretending.

It was two weeks before he returned to work.

No one else was in the lab yet. Henry had come to work early on purpose. His cubicle was at the far end of the common room, farthest from the door, and he hadn't wanted to face the others, to run the gauntlet of their pity. Not right away. He had wanted some time alone, with Barbara, in the cell library.

She really was there, in a way. The culture dish contained all the information that was Barbara. Everything, that is, except the experiences and memories that had made Her a *person* rather than an organism. He told Her how much he missed Her, but mostly he was just silent, remembering things. Then he noticed the time and slipped hastily out of the cell library before anyone could see him there. People wouldn't understand and might think him a little odd.

He returned to his cubicle and looked around vaguely, as if he were in a strange country. He fiddled with the clutter on his desk and wondered how far Bill had gotten on their project. Bill hadn't been idle, he was sure. The guy was a certified workaholic. The two of them worked well together. The tortoise and the hare. Bill was a great one for leaping ahead in flashes of intuition; while Henry was the plodder who filled in the details and proved whether Bill's gut feeling was something more than what he had eaten for breakfast.

Well, he couldn't sit here all day looking like a zombie. Lord knows what the others would read into that. He activated the terminal screen and began studying the log-book. Minutes went by.

"Henry!"

He turned and saw his partner, Bill Canazetti shrugging out of his jacket. Was it 0800 already? Canazetti laid a hand on Henry's shoulders, a heavy hand that was supposed to be reassuring. "I was so sorry to hear about Barbara," he murmured. "We all were. She was the best."

Henry took a deep breath. He had been dreading this ritual all morning. Everyone would feel obligated to say something to him. Something to remind him of what he only wanted to forget. The fact that most of them had already done so at the funeral wouldn't stop them. Perhaps it satisfied some inner need; a need to participate in another's grief. Certainly, it did nothing for Henry except pick at the psychic scab. But he could face their awful sympathy now. He really could.

"Never mind that," he told Canazetti, more gruffly than he had intended. Bill looked hurt, so he added, "it's over with. And besides, Barbry's not really gone. She's still with me. Now it's time to get on with life."

"Yes, I suppose." Canazetti looked uncomfortable. "Is there—well, anything I can get you?" He was like all the others; eager to help where no help was possible.

"A cup of decaf would be nice," Henry told him. "I do need to catch up on our project. Let me just read the notes here and then you can fill me in on the details."

Canazetti nodded slowly. "All right." He left and Henry immersed himself in the notes on the Barnsleyformer.

He and Bill had been working to improve SingerLabs' line of cell repair nanomachines. To achieve the elusive goal of Whole-Body Repair.

C/R nannies had changed the face of medicine over the last ten years, ever since Singer had created the first one. Repairing damage to tissues was easy now. All the doctor had to do was inject a dose of microscopic machines into the affected tissue. The nannies would visit each cell; compare it to the blueprints stored in the nucleus; disassemble any proteins not to spec; and reassemble them properly.

The problem was that, if multiple trauma was involved, only one tissue at a time could be treated. Each nanny was designed specifically for a certain tissue; and, if two nannies were introduced into the body at the same time, each would perceive the other as a foreign body and engage in a war of mutual extermination.

The information load was the limiting factor. The nannies were controlled by microscopic processors, dubbed Big NIM, that compared DNA strands in triplicate and directed the myriads of C/R machines. But even a single tissue complex involved an incredible amount of data. As Carl Sagan might have put it: Billions and Billions of Bits. There were hundreds of different proteins: enzymes and hormones. There were mitochondria, granules, and countless other cellular structures; each with a detailed set of "drawings" that described what it should look like. The limit seemed to be one tissue per nanny. Whole Body Repair seemed out of reach. There was just too much data to store and process. Big NIM always ran out of memory, no matter how much they stretched its capacity.

Bill and he had been ready to quit at one point. They had gone to see Old Lady Peeler to tell her it was impossible. There was a natural barrier, they had said, like the speed of light. Information bits must be carried on matter-energy "markers," and that set a lower limit on the scale for information processors. The machine could not be smaller than its information content. So, there was no way nanoscale processors could ever handle the data load for an entire organism, at least for an organism at the human level of complexity.

Dr. Peeler had listened to them in silence. Then she stared thoughtfully into the distance, working her lips. Finally, she had shaken her head and muttered, as if to herself, "I wonder how genes manage to do it."

And of course she was right.

Genes were natural nanomachines; yet they managed to build an entire complex organism from a single, undifferentiated cell. Morphogenesis, the biologists called it. The "unfolding" of structure from simplicity. Somehow, a zygote managed to contain all the information needed to grow a complete adult.

And that was a paradox.

Because the genes really weren't big enough to handle the information load. There just wasn't room for a complete set of elaborate blueprints in such a small space. Yet there had to be. Finally, in frustration, Henry had blurted out, "Maybe there aren't any blueprints at all!"

And that had reminded Bill of something. A dimly recalled oddity of the early 1980s. Michael Barnsley, an early chaotist, had discovered that random inputs to certain recursion formulas always generated the same precise shape. Take a simple random process, like tossing a coin, and define a positioning rule for each outcome. If the coin lands "heads," move a specified distance and direction from the current position. If "tails," a different distance and direction. Then start somewhere—anywhere!—on a grid and flip a coin. After the first fifty moves or so, start marking the positions where your random process takes you. Eventually, the recorded points will accumulate into a definite shape—the "limit shape." Iterate the process thousands of times. The limit shape is always the same, regardless of the actual sequence of coin tosses.

Somehow, the end result was encoded in the formula itself, irrespective of the input. It was like a magical machine that always produced the same product, no matter what raw material it was fed.

One set of Barnsley's recursion formulas generated a

drawing of a fern leaf. The same leaf appeared every time he ran the simulation, regardless of the particular random inputs. That led him to suggest that the genes contained information, not on how the leaf was shaped, but on how to run the recursion formulas. With that information in hand, random chance took care of all the rest.

Many biologists, and even some other chaos scientists, had objected. There is no room for randomness in biology, they had argued. In biology, randomness is death.

Which was true, but they had missed the point. Randomness was built into the universe. The physicists had shown long ago that randomness underlay all phenomena. It impinged constantly upon biological growth and evolution. Yet, individuals within a species always matured into the same basic shape. Sometimes, two people, unrelated to each other, even wore the same face. And species living in similar ecological niches evolved into similar forms. There had been sabre-tooth cats in Pleistocene North America. There had been sabre-tooth marsupial "cats" in Pleistocene South America. Everywhere the same shapes asserted themselves. The stems of a flower species always branched precisely so. Every flower.

Once again, science had shown that there were always simple answers to complex questions. Barnsley's algorithm was a transformer. Like an electrical transformer, it changed one thing into another. In this case, it transformed random causes into deterministic results. Bill had dubbed the mechanism a Barnsleyformer, but Henry had his own private name.

He called it the Template of God.

Thus far, their work on that fatal Thursday, two weeks ago, Bill and he had learned how recursion formulas generated structure; but they had been stuck on the inverse process. Generating the structure from the formulas was one thing.

Deducing the recursion formulas from the structure was more difficult. Now Henry saw that Canazetti had found a promising solution and he followed the reasoning closely in the log. Bill had decided that the recursion formulas worked the way they did because certain creatures of the generated structures were "fractal." That is, they were invariant under changes of magnitude. He had developed a technique he called "tyling," in which the structure was tyled with smaller and smaller replicates of itself. In this way he was able to create inductively the generating equations.

"The trick," he said in Henry's ear, "was getting the number of dimensions right."

Canazetti's unexpected voice made him jerk and he looked around over his shoulder.

"Sorry," said Canazetti, handing him his coffee.

Henry frowned and sipped the brew. He grimaced and looked at the cup. It was as bad as he remembered. He set it aside. "Dimensions," he prompted.

"Right." Canazetti pulled out his desk chair and rolled it under his backside. "A coin toss gives you a Barnsleyformer with up to two dimensions, a plane. But how many do we actually need?"

"Three," Henry replied. But he suspected he was wrong. Otherwise, why would Bill have asked him?

"Wrong." Canazetti shook his head emphatically. "And, once again, the physicists have been there ahead of us. Damned mechanics. Every time a bioscientist rolls over a new rock, he finds a physicist underneath it. No, Henry, there are actually eleven dimensions." Henry looked skeptical, and Canazetti shrugged. "Take my word for it." He held up his fingers. "Three gross spatial dimensions," he said, counting them off. "Length, height, and breadth. Seven quantum hypo-dimensions rolled up in what they call subspace. And . . ." He had run out of fingers and he looked blankly at his hands for a moment before shrugging.

"And time. I've logged the references in there." He pointed at the disc drive.

Henry decided he would review the literature later. It sounded bizarre to him, but then, most of modern physics did. "Then Barnsleyformers must generate biological structure in all eleven dimensions," he murmured. "Son of a bitch. The morphogenesis must be incredibly more complex than we thought. No wonder our three dimensional models—Hey, wait a minute!" His head shot up.

"What?"

"*All* the dimensions? Including time? That can't be."

"Oh? Why not?"

"Because the time dimension of an organism is its lifespan. How can the gene know ahead of time how long the organism will live?"

Canazetti shrugged again. "I don't know. It's a hunch. Did you ever read Heinlein's story, *Lifeline*? But I suspect that the time dimension of the structure only specifies endogenous death. You know, from internal causes, like old age or birth defects. Exogenous death comes from outside the organism. Accidents, like being hit with a virus or an automo—" He cut off abruptly and looked embarrassed. "Sorry."

Henry was more upset by Canazetti's circumspection than by any reference to Barbara's death; but he kept his silence. What did happen to the morphogenetic pattern when death came from the outside? Eleven dimensions. Might not some part of the pattern survive the truncation, at least for a while longer. At least until the original time span was reached? The Egyptians had believed something of the sort. That the spirit lived on—but only for a while—somewhere beyond our normal senses. There were, after all, those seven other dimensions Canazetti had mentioned. Subspace. Might the "soul" live there?

A thought began to form in the back of his head.

Something nebulous and disturbing, that made his chest tremble inside. He ignored it. "Have you begun *in vivo* experimentation?" he asked.

"Just last week. I reprogrammed a scyphozoan cell-repair machine with recursion formulas tyled from its own DNA."

"A jellyfish?"

Canazetti waved his hand the way only an Italian could. "I wanted something simple enough for a first try, but complex enough to be interesting."

"And?"

Canazetti reached past Henry and pressed a few buttons on the computer terminal. A damaged molecular chain appeared on the screen. A phosphorus group was missing entirely and several carbon rings were broken. "These are the scans recorded through the digital microscope," he told him. "Watch."

Something crawled across the molecules. It looked to Henry like a slime mold; or like tarnish growing at high speed across a set of copper Tinker-Toys. The colloidal agar for the cell repair nano-machines. After a few moments, it faded and the molecules underneath reappeared. Henry whistled.

"Like brand new," he said. "And fast."

Fast. What if it had been available two weeks ago? Would it have been fast enough? Henry refused to let himself think about that.

"Yeah." Canazetti's voice was less than ecstatic and Henry looked a question at him. Canazetti waved his hand in frustrated loops. "There're still a couple of stumbling blocks," he admitted. "For one thin, if you program the nanny with the DNA of one jellyfish, it doesn't work so well on other jellyfish."

"How so?"

"Well, every jellyfish carries the basic 'I-am-a-jellyfish' information, but it also carries information that individualizes it: 'I-am-Joe-the-jellyfish.' So, if you use it on a different individual, the nanny tries to restructure it as well as repair it."

Canazetti called up another visual on the terminal. "The jellyfish on the left," he said, "was repaired with nannies grown from the DNA of the one on the right."

Henry inspected the two cell diagrams. "How close is the match?"

"Eighty-seven percent."

"Nearly complete." Henry's own voice sounded far away. He could hear the rush of his blood in his ears. He felt light-headed. Nearly complete.

"Only if the donor and recipient are the same species," said Canazetti's voice. "Otherwise it doesn't work at all. Rejection sets in. Even within a species, I suppose the greater the initial similarity, the better it would work. That's just a hunch. But it doesn't help the doctors any. We want to repair cells, not rearrange them."

Henry tapped the screen with a fingernail. "Then why not clone the nannies from the patient's own cells; tailor them individually for each patient?

"That would be fine, except for stumbling block number two. It takes time to style the material and to deduce the recursion equations. Remember, there are eleven dimensions to consider. And then it takes more time to grow the nannies. What's the patient doing in the meantime?"

Dying, obviously.

We could have saved her, if only—

If only—

If only—

Henry felt faint. He sagged in his chair and Canazetti's hairy Italian arms reached out and braced him.

"Easy there. Are you all right?"

"Yes," Henry told him after a moment. He rubbed his face with his hand. "Yes, I'm all right."

• • •

"Easy there. Are you all right?"

"Yes," Sadie told him after a moment. She rubbed her face with her hand. "Yes, I'm all right."

It was Friday evening and he was seated at the kitchen table, eating the late supper that Sadie had prepared for him. Setting the pot back on the stove, she had staggered and slumped, almost spilling the pot. Henry wiped his lips with his napkin and pushed himself from the table. He went to Sadie and took her by the arm. He felt her forehead.

"You look flushed. Why don't you go upstairs and lie down. I'll bring you some medicine."

"No. 'M a burden, me. Too good to ol' Sadie. Time t' move on."

"Nonsense. You go upstairs. You've been working too hard these last two months. Maybe you've picked up a flu bug, or something."

He watched her leave and waited for her footsteps to die away. Then he went to his briefcase on the table in the hallway and opened it.

The zip-locked baggie lay on top of everything else. He picked it up and held it. There were three gelatin capsules inside. One was a specific against the flu bug that he had given Sadie. The other two— He began to open the bag but found that his hands were shaking too badly to break the seal. He set it down and leaned with both his hands on the table. He closed his eyes and breathed several long slow breaths.

". . . *the nanny tries to restructure as well as repair.*"

She's only a bag lady, after all, and an addict. It's for her own good.

"I suppose the greater the initial similarity, the better it would work. . . ."

She'll just find her way back to the streets again. I can't

baby-sit her forever. She'll find her connection again. An addict's need never really dies.

"*. . . the time variable only specifies endogenous death. . . . Exogenous death comes from outside the organism . . . there are eleven dimensions to consider.*"

And what kind of life was it, living from a shopping bag on a heating grate? She'll be much happier.

When he felt calmer, he picked the bag up and pulled it open. He poured the three capsules into his hand. He looked at them and rolled them back and forth in his palm. They felt cold and heavy, like stones; but he knew that was only his imagination.

Before he could think about it, he turned and climbed the stairs, two at a time. He stopped in the washroom and filled a glass of water and took it with him to the guest room.

Sadie the Lady was lying in the bed. She hadn't bothered to take her clothes off. She seldom did. Henry still had to remind her to bathe about once a week. She was propped up on the pillows, but her eyes were closed and her breathing was shallow.

"Sadie?" he asked. She had to be conscious to swallow pills.

The bag lady opened her eyes and mumbled something incoherent.

"It's only an autumn cold," he told her. "Here. Take these." He thrust his hand out. The capsules seemed to have grown warmer. They were like small coals in his palm. "Take them," he said again. And his voice trembled.

Sadie reached out her arm and Henry saw the tracks of the needlemarks lining the inside. Small red circles. Craters left from years of meteoric bombardment. "Here. Take these pills." And the words came more easily this time; and the capsules had ceased to burn his skin.

She plucked them from his outstretched hand and placed them one at a time in her mouth, following each one with a swallow of water. Her throat worked and they went down. She gave him back the glass. "T'anks."

The glass rattled when he set it on the end table. He waited. The minutes dragged out. Sadie's breath came more and more slowly, until finally a light snore told Henry that she was asleep.

For a few minutes he stood there, clenching and unclenching his hands. Finally, he nerved himself and reached down and lifted her in his arms. He was surprised to discover how light she was.

He carried her to the master bedroom and laid her down on Barbara's side of the bed. He pulled off her shoes, and adjusted the sheets around her. Then he went to the stereo in the wall unit and fumbled a cassette into the tape deck. He hit play.

The voice that issued from the speakers was his own. He turned the volume down low, so the words were barely audible. The speakers whispered. Memories of Barbara. Her family; her history; how they had met; her life with him. Henry listened for a few minutes, but after a while he couldn't take any more, so he tip-toed out of the bedroom and eased the door shut. Behind him, memories played into sleeping ears.

The next morning, he began calling her "Barbry."

The first couple of times earned him curious glances, but the bag lady seemed just to shrug it off. She seemed to accept everything he did with an odd mixture of blank fatalism and a pathetic eagerness to please. Henry dug out the old photo albums and spent all day Saturday showing the pictures to her. This is Barbry when She was six. This is the house She grew up in; and those are Her parents. Sadie nodded and grinned her gap-tooth grin. Once, passing a photograph back and forth, their hands touched and Henry was caught between a sudden desire to clasp her hand and an equally sudden desire to pull away.

She studied the pictures carefully, holding them close to her eyes, squinting, as if something had gone wrong with her vision. As if her eyes were not what they had been the previous night.

Henry peered at her face. Did it already look a little different? Were the cheekbones a little higher? The hair a little lighter? The scar a little fainter?

Or his imagination a little wilder?

A human body was more complex than a jellyfish's; and the process should take a good deal longer. But Bill Canazetti's tyling algorithm was wonderfully simple; and growing a Barnsleyformer from Barbara's DNA had taken more time than brilliance. For three weeks, Henry had remained at work, after the others had gone for the day. Bill had given him some quizzical stares over the extra hours but seemed to assume that Henry was using the work as a way of dealing with his grief.

And, in a way, of course, he was right.

Henry thought he had covered his tracks pretty thoroughly. The recorded weights of the specimens in the cell library would still tally. All the reagents and other supplies were properly accounted for. There was nothing out of place that they could trace to him. Not even the flu virus. Certainly not Barbara's cell samples.

"You must have loved her very much."

He emerged, startled, from his reverie. Sadie the Lady was holding out a snapshot. It was a picture of him and Barbara, taken during their vacation in the Rockies. There they stood, his arm around Her waist; both of them smiling foolishly, waving to the stranger who had held their camera. They were posing in front of their rented Bronco on the old railroad trestle on the Corona Pass Road. Behind them, the Devil's Slide fell a thousand feet into the forest below.

Barbry was pointing back toward the Needle's Eye Tunnel that they had just negotiated. A frozen moment of happiness.

Henry remembered every detail of that day. The bite of the insects. The sawtooth sound of their chirping. How the sun had beat down on them, and how, despite that, it had been chillingly cold at the summit. Corona Pass was not a real road, but the remains of a narrow-gage railroad bed that switch-backed up the sheer side of a mountain. It was one lane wide, which made for interesting decisions when upslope and downslope traffic met. The Needle's Eye, a hole pierced through solid rock, had once been closed for several years by a rockslide, and the trestle over the Devil's Slide did not inspire great confidence, despite its solid timbers. The ruins of the old train depot lay astride the Continental Divide, and Barbry and he had found a secluded spot off the nature trail there, and had necked up a storm as if they had been teenagers.

"Yes. Very much," he said. "I miss her." More than anything else in the world, he wanted her back. "I love you very much, Barbry." And he looked Sadie straight in the eye when he said that.

Fear danced in her eyes, and then something else. "I lo—"

The snapshot flicked from her fingers and floated like an autumn leaf to the carpet. Sadie's left cheek twitched and she stood and trembled like a fawn. "Don't feel good," she said.

Henry caught her before she fell and carried her back to the bedroom. "You're still sick, Barbry," he told her. *(Yes, her hair was definitely lighter now.)* He laid her down on the bed. "Rest up. Everything will be all right in a little while. A couple of days, at the most."

The cheek was twitching constantly now. It tugged at the nose and the corners of the mouth and eyes. Henry could swear he saw the cheekbone beneath it *flow*. He pulled a chair up next to the bed and sat there rubbing first one hand then the other.

Sadie began to pant, short gasps, bitten off. Her eyes bulged and sweat rolled off her forehead staining the pillowcase. She arched her back and her eyes rolled up in her head. Her hands clenched into fists that twisted and wrung the sheets. A scream trickled through her tightened throat.

Henry saw a tremendous spasm run through her right thigh muscle. It jerked once, twice, three times. Then Sadie collapsed. Her mouth hanging slack and her fingers curling and uncurling. Her breathing became long and shallow, as if she had just finished a long race.

Henry could not move. *The nanny will try to restructure as well as repair.* But, dear Lord, he had never imagined that it would *hurt*. How long will this go on, he wondered? He bit into his knuckles and drew blood.

Her breathing began to quicken again, rasping like a saw through pine, and Henry saw the tension build in her muscles. It was like childbirth, almost. Worse than childbirth. She began moaning and the moaning increased in pitch and tempo and would have ended in a scream except that nothing but a whine escaped. Her whole body jerked this time and she rolled halfway onto her side.

I can't take this, Henry thought and he pushed himself from the chair to go.

But her eyes snapped open and pinned him there, like a butterfly to a board. She spoke; and the timbre of the voice was more than Sadie, but not quite Barbara, and there was pain and hurt in it. "What are you doing to me?" he cried. And she spoke again; and again there was pain and hurt, but of a different kind. "*Why* are you doing this to me?"

The scream, when it finally came, was Henry's.

• • •

For the next three days, Henry avoided the room except to bring meals, which she did not touch; and pain-killers, which she did; and to reset and play the tapes that he had made. Through the door, he would hear cries; cries that were weeping as often as they were screaming. They were muffled and Henry knew that that was because she would thrust her face into the pillows to stifle the sound of it.

Barbara had been like that. She hated to cry and always tried to hide it.

He did not linger when he heard the crying, but fled instead to the quiet of the kitchen and, once, to the solitude of the greenbelt behind the house.

He got no sleep that weekend and when Monday came, he called in sick. Bill Canazetti took the call and Henry wanted to tell him that Barbry wasn't feeling well so he was staying home to take care of her. But he said nothing, because Bill might not have understood.

Or perhaps, he might have understood too well.

Late Monday afternoon a hammering sound brought him running up the stairs. He burst into the room and found Barbara/Sadie banging her head against the headboard of the bed. She would lean forward and then throw her head back hard against the carved wood. There were dark stains there.

His heart dropped like a stone. He bounded to her side and wrapped his arms around her to hold her back. "What are you doing?" he cried.

She grabbed her head in both her hands. "Make it stop!" she sobbed. "It hurts so much! Please make it stop!"

The brain, he thought. The nannies have reached the brain and are restructuring it to look more like Barbara's brain. Synapses and neurons were being rewired. Network configuration was changing. *It shouldn't hurt,* he told himself. *It wasn't supposed to hurt.* He held on to her more tightly and she buried her face in his shoulder, making small, animal sounds.

And what will happen now? Wasn't memory stored in the arrangement of synapses? In the network? No one really knew. No one understood how the brain worked. And there were always those seven "ghost" dimensions in Barbara's DNA.

He tried giving her headache medicine; but that didn't seem to work; so he tried a sedative and that at least stopped the whimpering, although in her sleep she continued to moan and toss.

And then, after a very long while, it was Tuesday. . . .

He was in the kitchen, drinking breakfast. Bourbon, neat. An anaesthetic to dull his own pain. He had not showered nor changed his clothes since Friday and they were stained at the collar, at the armpits, at the small of the back, in the crotch; and smelled of sweat and fear. Four days of stubble had made sandpaper of his face. His eyes were rimmed with red. He had not slept since Sunday.

A footstep in the hall.

He jerked his head up. She stood there, unsteady, leaning against the doorpost from the hallway, her jeans and blouse as filthy and disarrayed as his. More so, since she had been unable to visit the bathroom during her ordeal. Her hair, dirty from sweat and oil, was ratted and tangled. It was as if she had never left the heating grate in Hell's Kitchen.

He put his shot glass down so hard that the amber liquid splashed onto his hand. He half-rose from his chair. "Barbara?"

She stared at him vacantly. After a few moments, she shook her head. "No, I—Henry?"

He stood and walked around the table to her. "You've had a bad accident," he told her. "Amnesia."

As he got closer to her he began to see more clearly that

she was not quite Barbara. The facial scar was gone; but a faint line remained. The missing incisor was still missing. There were other, more subtle differences; but differences that thirteen years of marriage had made plain.

He took her hands in his but stopped short of embracing her.

"How do you feel."

"Bad as you look," she replied. "I—" A pause. A grimace. "Twinges, time to time." Her face tightened and she looked at him hard. "Y'gimme somethin', dincha? Some kinda pill."

"It was medicine. You were sick."

"I never been sick."

Henry swallowed. "Yes, you were. Five years ago. We took you to St. Barnabas. Don't you remember?"

She pulled her hands away. "Don't! Yer crazy, you." She turned, took one step, and stopped. Three heartbeats went by; then she looked back over her right shoulder. "Bright pastels," she said. "The room was painted in bright pastels. The TV set was broken and you made them replace it."

"Yes."

"No!" She put her hands to her head. "Never happened. I'se in Rochester, me. Five years 'go I'se'n Rochester!" Her hands dropped slowly. "I think I was. I—" She began to cry. "'M confused. So confused. Henry? Help me."

He led her back upstairs to the shower and gave her Barbry's favorite baby doll pajamas. While she washed up, he stripped the bedsheets and replaced them with fresh linens. He took the soiled sheets to the laundry in the basement, but he remembered in time not to start the load while the shower was running.

While he waited for the water to stop he gradually became aware of his own condition. He rubbed a hand over the stubble on his jaw and caught a good whiff of his own odor. *I need a shower, too,* he thought. *And a shave.*

• • •

The shower felt good, and it relaxed him to the point where his lost sleep caught up with him. He decided to take a nap, so he wrapped himself in a towel and went to the master bedroom to find a pair of pajamas.

And Sadie was in the bed, asleep.

Henry stopped short and wondered why that should surprise him. After all, he had been putting her there himself. But, this was the first time she had done so on her own. She had finished showering and then come to this bed, as if it were the most natural thing in the world.

His mouth twitched and he tiptoed to his dresser, where he reached around the bottom drawer for a pair of pajamas. Her breathing behind him was soft and regular. Relaxed, even; although a slight nasal blockage made a clicking sound whenever she breathed in.

He straightened and turned and looked at her. She was lying atop the sheets, her back to him. The rust-colored camisole top had ridden up to reveal her matching panties and a small, dark mole on the lower right side of her back.

He stared at the mole for a long time. He knew that mole. Even in the dark, he could have pointed to its exact location. It was not possible for two people to have that same mole.

He dropped the pajamas, and the towel, and crept gently into the bed. When he put his arms around her from the back, he felt her stiffen; but he stroked her gently, along the flank, and up and down the back—with a light touch, the way She always liked it—and, after a little while she relaxed and began making contented sounds in her throat.

Gradually, his hand widened its area of search. Up. Around. Here. There. Her breathing quickened and she twisted to face him. Her eyes were still closed, as if she were still asleep; but her mouth sought his and they embraced.

A quiet and desperate urgency followed, with quickly breathed assurances of love and pleasure. The baby dolls joined his towel.

"Barbry," he said. "Oh, Barbry."

And she stiffened again; but only for a moment. "Oh, Henry. I've missed you."

In the morning, he and Barbry lay contentedly side-by-side. The remnants of some bad dream nibbled at the edges of his mind; but he could not remember what it was. Something terrible. Something too distressing to be borne. He felt like a swimmer who had been sucked under by a sinking ship; who had kicked desperately toward the shining surface above until, lungs bursting, he had broken through into the cool, pure air.

Everything was going to be all right now.

Barbry was still asleep and Henry watched her silently for a while, admiring the smoothness of her body, the peacefulness of her face, the way her breasts rose and fell. He kept thinking that there was something he was supposed to do for her. Something important that he had forgotten. Well, it would come to him.

He eased out of bed and put his housecoat on. Then he slipped out of the room to the kitchen, where he made breakfast for the two of them. He felt like he was on his honeymoon, but that was ridiculous. Barbry and he had been married for donkey's years. He put the breakfasts on a tray and carried them back to the bedroom.

Barbry was awake when he entered, just beginning to get out of bed. She saw he was bringing her breakfast and laughed. "Breakfast in bed? Oh, Henry. No one ever done that for me." She put herself back under the covers, sitting up against the pillows.

Henry knew that the accident had given her partial amnesia, so he didn't make an issue of how often they had done this in the past. He opened the legs of the tray and set it across her, then he crawled in next to her.

She explored her breakfast with her fork. "What's this?" she asked.

"Poached eggs. Just the way you like them."

"Just the way— Course. Forgot."

While they ate, Henry noticed her giving him sidelong glances out of the corners of her eyes. She was watching him. Waiting for him, to do what? Henry took a bite of his toast and chewed. When he glanced back at her, he noticed a tear had worked its way down the side of her right cheek.

"Barbry! What's wrong? Why are you crying?"

"Nothing." She shook her head. "Nothing. Someone's died, is all."

"Died?" An unaccountable shiver ran through him. "Who?"

She looked at him and he saw there were tears in both her eyes. Tiny tears. She seemed more wistfully sad than bereaved. She shook her head again. "No one you ever knew," she said. "No one you ever knew."

She was in the library, sitting in her chair, but with her legs pulled up under her. She had a book open and she was reading it intently. A frown creased her brows and her lips moved silently as she followed the words across the page. He came up behind her and leaned on the back of the chair.

"What are you reading?" he asked.

"The poems of Tennyson," she replied. "Tennyson was h—Tennyson is my favorite poet, but I don't remember any of his poems."

He rubbed her shoulders with his hands. "It was a bad accident," he told her. "It will take a long time to remember everything. The doctors didn't have much hope for you, you know. But we showed them, didn't we?"

She twisted and looked at him. She patted his hand. "Yes,

we showed them. You'll play the tapes for me again tonight, won't you, dear?"

"Of course."

"Good. Meanwhile . . ." She turned back and reopened her book. She found her place and ran her finger down the page. "This poem. Could you explain what it means? It's called 'Tears, Idle Tears.' I'll read it to you."

She hefted the book and cleared her throat. Then she began to recite:

'Dear as remember'd kisses after death,
And sweet as those by hopeless fancy feign'd
On lips that are for others; deep as love,
Deep as first love, and wild with all regret;
O Death in Life, the days that are no more.'

He felt it rise in his throat. A feeling of intense longing and loneliness. There was no question about it. The old Brit knew how to string words together. But why should those words affect him so?

He felt the tears warm his cheeks. He tried to excuse himself to Barbry, but no words came out, only uncontrollable sobbing. It was embarrassing. He was crying like a baby. He had not cried like this since . . . since . . .

There was something that was supposed to have made him cry like this, but he had forgotten what it was. Forgotten when it was. Forgotten everything, except that he was supposed to have cried; and that now the crying may have come too late.

Bill Canazetti fidgetted nervously by the front door, waiting for . . . her to get his coat. Dinner had been uncomfortable. A mostly silent affair, broken only by the tink of glasses and silverware. Afterwards, a few awkward sallies into conversation. Then he had made his excuses to leave.

She brought his coat to him and helped him into it. "Now, be sure to button up, Bill. It's chilly outside. The leaves are all off the trees. It's a lot colder here than where we used to live. It's too bad we don't get together more often."

"It's a long trip to Morristown," he agreed. He only wanted to leave. To get away from this place. To forget everything he had seen.

When he looked at his hostess, he saw Barbara Carter, smiling, waiting. He had always kissed her when leaving their house. A quick pass across the lips and a murmured quip about her husband finding out. It was a little game they had played between themselves; but there was no way this woman would know about it. Henry's theories about the seven hidden dimensions holding a person's soul and memories were just so much nonsense. Weren't they?

He put his hand on the doorknob and twisted. The chill autumn air swirled in around him. He hesitated. He had to know.

"Barbara," he said, turning around. "Tell me one thing." He searched her eyes. "*Are* you Barbara?"

Changes chased themselves across her eyes. Surprise. Curiosity. Wonder. Perhaps, wistfulness. "Most of the time," she said. "More and more nowadays."

"But—"

"But am I really her?" She laughed and shook her head. "No. I'm just an old junkie bag lady, me. He gave me something. A nano—"

"Nanomachine."

"Yes, thank you. A nanomachine. It rebuilt my body. It rewired my brain. I remember Sadie, but it's faint, like an old dream. And I remember some other things. Things that happened to Barbry. They're faint, too. Did they come from the tapes? Or from somewhere else? I don't know. And there are other odd memories. Things that never happened at all, either to Barbry or Sadie."

Canazetti's throat felt tight. "Sadie's memories patched onto different circuits. They're hallucinatory, those memories."

"Maybe. Still. I know who I am. Most of the time, anyway."

"Then why do you do it? Why do you stay with him and pretend? I've done some experimental work. With frogs. The nerves. When they change. It—" He didn't know how to put it. "It must have been painful," he said, not looking at her.

"Yes. Yes, it was. Very painful. But Henry saw me through it."

He turned to her. "He might have killed you," he blurted out. "He didn't know enough to try it. We *still* don't know enough to try it. Dammit, he had no right to do what he did to you!"

"Bill, do you know what my life was like before he rescued me?"

He shook his head.

"How can I explain it? I can go to sleep and not be afraid that I'll freeze to death before morning, or that some kids will set me on fire just for the hell of it. And my new body, it's healthy. It doesn't *need* snow or crack like my old body did. And I can see and understand so much that I couldn't before, because my brain has been de-toxed."

Canazetti looked past her shoulder, down the hallway, into the kitchen where he saw Henry carrying dinner dishes to the sink. He was humming to himself.

"Do you love him, then?"

"Yes. Both of us do."

His head jerked and he looked at her.

"When I'm Barbry," she explained, "I love him for Barbry's sake. But Sadie loved him, too. Because he had saved her life. Because he took care of her. He's given her more than she ever dared to dream about. Except for one thing."

Canazetti's voice was choked. "What's that?"

"He never told Sadie that he loved her. He never saw her."

"Damn him!"

"No, don't say that."

"But, what he did to you. What he put you through. The selfishness."

"He couldn't love anyone else. He loved Her. He wasn't rational. What would you have done in his place?"

"I feel responsible, you know. It was my invention."

She put a hand on his arm. "Don't blame yourself for that, Bill. He would have tried something, even without your nano. I don't know. Brainwashing, maybe."

"I just can't help thinking that he did something wicked. A crime. And he should be punished."

She turned and watched Henry through the kitchen doorway while he rinsed the dishes and put them in the dishwasher. He noticed them watching him and grinned and waved.

"He is being punished," she said. "The worst punishment of all. He thinks he's happy."

RECORDING ANGEL

Ian McDonald

If we *can invent nanotechnology, perhaps* aliens *can as well, and the uses to which they* put *that technology might be, well*—alien. *Beyond our human understanding. Here's a look at a vivid and terrifying future where something enigmatic and implacable is* eating *Africa, and the people in the way are just going to have to come to terms with it—however they can.*

British author Ian McDonald is an ambitious and daring writer with a wide range and an impressive amount of talent. His first story was published in 1982, and since then he has appeared with some frequency in Interzone, Asimov's Science Fiction, New Worlds, Zenith, Other Edens, Amazing, *and elsewhere. He was nominated for the John W. Campbell Award in 1985, and in 1989 he won the* Locus *"Best First Novel" Award for his novel* Desolation Road. *He won the Philip K. Dick Award in 1992 for his novel* King of Morning, Queen of Day. *His other books include the novels* Out On Blue Six *and* Hearts, Hands and Voices, *and two collections of his short fiction,* Empire Dreams *and* Speaking In Tongues. *His most recent books include the well-received new novel* Evolution's Shore, *as well as several graphic novels, and he is at work on another new novel, tentatively entitled* Necroville. *Born in Manchester, England, in 1960, McDonald has spent most of his life in Northern Ireland, and now lives and works in Belfast.*

For the last ten miles she drove past refugees from the xenoforming. Some were in their own vehicles. Many rode town buses that had been commandeered to take the people south, or the grubby white trucks of the UNHCR. Most walked, pushing the things they had saved from the advancing Chaga on handcarts or barrows, or laden on the heads and backs of women and children. That has always been the way of it, the woman thought as she drove past the unbroken file of people. The world ends, the women and children must carry it, and the United Nations sends its soldiers to make sure they do not drop it. And the news corporations send their journalists to make sure that the world sees without being unduly disturbed. After all, they are only Africans. A continent is being devoured by some thing from the stars, and I am sent to write the obituary of a hotel.

"I don't do gossip," she had told T. P. Costello, SkyNet's Nairobi station chief when he told her of the international celebrities who were coming to the deathparty of the famous Treehouse Hotel. "I didn't come to this country to cream myself over who's wearing which designer dress or who's having an affair with or getting from whom."

"I know, I know," T. P. Costello had said. "You came to Kenya to be a player in Earth's first contact with the alien. Everyone did. That's why I'm sending you. Who cares what Brad Pitt thinks about the Gas Cloud theory versus the Little Gray Men theory? Angles are what I want. You can get angles, Gaby. What can you get?"

"Angles, T. P.," she had replied, wearily, to her editor's now-familiar litany.

"That's correct. And you'll be up there with it, right on terminum. That's what you want, isn't it?"

That's correct, T. P., she thought. Three months in Kenya and all she had seen of the Chaga had been a distant line of color, like surf on a far reef, under the clouded shadow of Kilimanjaro, advancing imperceptibly but inexorably across the Amboseli plain. The spectator's view. Up there, on the highlands around Kirinyaga where the latest biological package had come down, she would be within touching distance of it. The player's view.

There was a checkpoint up at Nanyuki. The South African soldiers in blue UN helmets at first did not know how to treat her, thinking that with her green eyes and long mahogany hair she might be another movie star or television celebrity. When her papers identified her as Gaby McAslan, on-line multimedia journalist with SkyNet East Africa, they stopped being respectful. A woman they could flirt with, a journalist they could touch for bribes. Gaby endured their flirtations and gave their commanding officer three of the dwindling stock of duty-free Swatches she had bought expressly for the purpose of petty corruption. In return she was given a map of the approved route to the hotel. If she stayed on it she would be safe. The bush patrols had orders to shoot suspected looters or loiterers.

Beyond the checkpoint there were no more refugees. The only vehicles were carrying celebrities to the party at the end of the world, and the news corporations following them. The Kikuyu *shambas* on either side of the road had been long abandoned. Wild Africa was reclaiming them. For a while, then something else would reclaim them from wild Africa. Reverse terraforming, she thought. Instead of making an alien world into Earth, Earth is made into an alien world. In her open-top SkyNet 4x4, Gaby could sense the Chaga behind the screen of heavy high-country timber, and edgy presence of the alien, and electric tingle of anticipation. She had never been this close before.

When the first biological package came down on the summit of Kilimanjaro, she had known, in SkyNet Multimedia News's UK office among the towers of London's Docklands, that this fallen star had her name written on it. The stuff that had come out of it, that looked a little like rain forest and a little like drained coral reef but mostly like nothing anyone had ever seen before, that disassembled terrestrial vegetation into its component molecules and incorporated them into its own matrix at an unstoppable fifty meters every day, confirmed her holy business. The others that came down in the Bismarck Archipelago, the Ruwenzori, in Ecuador and Papua New Guinea and the Maldives, these were only memos from the star gods. It's here, it's waiting for you. Hurry up now.

Now, the Nyandarua package, drawing its trail of plasma over Lake Victoria and the Rift Valley, would bring her at last face-to-face with life from the stars.

She came across a conga-line of massive tracked transporters, each the size of a large house, wedged into the narrow red-dirt road. Prefabricated accommodation cabins were piled up on top of the transporters. Branches bent and snapped as the behemoths ground past at walking pace. Gaby had heard that UNECTA, the United Nations agency that coordinated research into the Chagas, had dismantled its Ol Tukai base, one of four positioned around Kilimanjaro, all moving backward in synchrony with the advance of the southern Chaga, and sent it north. UNECTA's pockets were not deep enough, it seemed, to buy a new mobile base, especially now that the multinationals had cut their contributions in the absence of any exploitable technologies coming out of the Chaga.

UNECTA staff on the tops of the mobile towers waved as she drove carefully past in the red muddy verges. They can probably see the snows of Kirinyaga from that height, she thought. Between the white mountains. We run from the south, we run from the north but the expanding circles of vegetation are closing on us and we cannot escape. Why do we run? We will all have to face it in the end, when it takes everything we know and changes it beyond recognition. We have always imagined that because it comes down in the tropics it is confined here. Why should climate stop it? Nothing else has. Maybe it will only stop when it closes around the poles. Xenoforming complete.

The hotel was one of those buildings that are like animals in zoos, that by their stillness and coloration can hide from you even when you are right in front of them, and you only know they are there because of the sign on the cage. Two Kenyan soldiers far too young for the size of their weapons met her from the car park full of tour buses and news-company 4x4s. They escorted her along a dirt path between skinny, gray-trunked trees. She could still not see the hotel. She commented on the small wooden shelters that stood every few meters along the path.

"In case of charging animals," the slightly older soldier said. "But this is better." He stroked his weapon as if it were a breast. "Thirty heavy-caliber rounds per second. That will stop more than any wooden shelter."

"Since the Chaga has come there are many more animals around," the younger soldier said. He had taken the laces out of his boots, in the comfortable, country way.

"Running away," Gaby said. "Like any sane thing should."

"No," the young, laceless soldier said. "Running into."

There was a black-painted metal fire escape at the end of the track. As Gaby squinted at the incongruity, the hotel resolved out of the greenery before her. Many of the slim, silver tree trunks were wooden piles, the mass of leaves and creepers concealed the superstructure bulking over her.

The steward met her at the top of the stairs, checked her name against the guest list, and showed her her room, a tiny wooden cabin with a view of leaves. Gaby thought it must be like this on one of the UNECTA mobile bases; minimal, monastic. She did something to her face and went up to the party on the roof. It had been running for three days. It would only end when the hotel did. The party at the edge of the end of the world. In one glance she saw thirty newsworthy faces and peeked into her bag to check the charge level on her disc recorder. She talked to it as she moved between the faces to the bar. The *Out of Africa* look was the thing among the newsworthy this year: riding breeches, leather, with the necessary twist of twenty-first-century *knowing* with the addition of animal-skin prints.

Gaby ordered a piña colada from the Kenyan barman and wondered as he shook it what incentive the management had offered him—all the staff—to stay. Family relocation to other hotels, on the Coast, down in Zanzibar, she reckoned. And where do they go when they run out of hotels to relocate to? Interesting, but not the angle, she decided as the barman poured out the thick, semeny proof of his ability.

"Bugger all here, T. P.," she said to the little black machine in her shirt pocket. Then cocktail-party dynamics parted the people in front of her and there it was, one hundred feet away beyond the gray wooden railing, at the edge of the artificial water hole they dredged with bulldozers in the off-season. One hundred feet. Fifteen seconds walk. Eighteen hours crawl. If you kept very still and concentrated you would be able to see it moving, as you could see the slow sweep of the minute hand of your watch. This was the Chaga not on the geographical scale, devouring whole landscapes, but on the molecular.

Gaby walked through the gap in the bright and the beautiful. She walked past Brad Pitt. She walked past Antonio Banderas, with his new supermodel girlfriend. She walked past Julia Roberts so close she could see the wrinkles and sags that the editing computers digitally smoothed. They were only celebrities. They could not change the world, or suffer to have their world changed, even by alien intervention. Gaby rested her hands on the rail and looked over the Chaga.

"It's like being on the sundeck of a great, archaic ocean-liner, cruising close to the shore of an alien archipelago," she told the recorder. The contrast between the place she was and the place out there was as great as between land and sea, the border between the two as shifting and inexact. There was no line where earth became un-earth; rather a gradual infection of the highland forest with the colored hexagons of alien ground cover that pushed up fingers and feelers and strange blooms between the tree trunks into the disturbing pseudocoral forms of the low Chaga. With distance the alien reef grew denser and the trees fewer; only the tallest and strongest withstood the attack of the molecular processors, lifted high like the masts of beached ships. A kilometer beyond the tide line a wall of red pillars rose a sheer three hundred meters from the rumbled land reefs before opening into a canopy of interlinked hexagonal leaf plates.

"The Great Wall," Gaby said, describing the scene before her to the disc. The Chaga beyond offered only glimpses of itself as it rose toward cloud-shrouded Kirinyaga: a gleam of the open white palm of a distant hand-tree, the sway of moss-covered balloons, the glitter of light from crystals. What kind of small craft might put forth from such a shore to meet this ship of vanities? she wondered.

"Seven minutes. Thirteen centimeters. That's longer than most."

Until he spoke, Gaby had not noticed the white man standing beside her at the rail. She could not remember whether he had been there before her, or arrived later. He was small, balding, running to late-40s, early-50s belly. His skin was weathered brown, his teeth were not good, and he spoke with a White African accent. He could not be Beautiful, nor even Press. He must be Staff. He was dressed in buffs and khakis and a vest of pockets, without the least necessary touch of twenty-first-century *knowing*. He looked like the last of the Great White Hunters.

He was.

He was called Prenderleith. He had impeccable manners.

"Pardon me for interrupting your contemplation, but if people see me talking to someone they won't come and ask me about things I've killed."

"Isn't that your job?"

"Killing, or telling?"

"Whichever."

"Whichever, it doesn't include being patronized by movie stars, piss-artists and bloody journalists."

"I am a bloody journalist."

"But the first thing you did was come over to the rail and look at that bloody thing out there. For seven minutes."

"And that makes this journalist worth talking to."

"Yes," he said, simply.

And it makes you worth talking to, Gaby thought, because maybe you are my angle on this thing. The Last White Hunter. But you are as wary as the creatures you hunt, and if I tell you this it will scare you away, so I must be as stealthy as you. Gaby surreptitiously turned up the recording level on her little black machine. Enhancement software back at Tom M'boya Street would edit the chatter and fluff.

"So what do you think it is?" Gaby asked. Across the terrace a dissension between Bret Easton Ellis and Damien Hirst was escalating into an argument. Guests flocked in, anticipating a fistfight. Cameras whirred. Prenderleith rested his arms on the rail and looked out across the Chaga.

"I don't know about all this aliens-from-another-world stuff."

"Latest theory is that it wasn't built by little gray men, but originated in gas clouds in Rho Ophiuchi, eight hundred light-years away. They've found signatures of the same complex fullerenes that are present in Chaga. An entire civilization, growing up in space. They estimate it's at least a hundred thousand years old."

"'They,'" Prenderleith said.

"UNECTA," Gaby said.

"They're probably right. They know more about this than I do, so if they say it's gas, then it's gas. Gas clouds, little gray men, I don't know about either of them; it's just not part of my world. See, they brought me up with just enough education to be able to manage, to do things well; not to think. Kenya wasn't the kind of country that needed thinking, we thought. You did things, not thought. Riding, farming, hunting, driving, flying. Doing things. The country decided what you needed to think. None of us could see the changes happening under our feet: I was brought up obsolete, no bloody use in the new Kenya, that thought, at all. All I could do was find a job in something as obsolete and useless as myself. This bloody place has nothing to do with the real Kenya. Bloody theme park. Even the animals are fake; they bulldozed a water hole so Americans would have elephants to photograph. Irony is: Now the tourists are gone, there've never been so many bloody animals, all headed in. Counted forty-five elephant in one day; no one gives a stuff anymore. Tell me, how can it be alien if the animals are going in there? How could gas know how to build something like that? Feels to me like it's something very old, that animals knew once and have never forgotten, that's come out of Africa itself. Everything starts here, in East Africa; the land is very old, and has a long memory. And strong: Maybe Africa has had enough of what people are doing to it—enough thinking—and has decided to claim itself back. That's why the animals aren't afraid. It's giving it back to them."

"But taking yours away," Gaby said.

"Not my Africa." Prenderleith glanced around at the

famous and beautiful people. The fight had evaporated into sulks and looks. Leaf Phoenix was passing round cigarettes, to the thrilled horror of the other guests. Chimes filled the air. Heads turned. A waiter in an untwenty-first-century-*knowing* leopard-print jacket moved across the roof terrace, playing a set of handheld chime bars.

"Dinner," Prenderleith announced.

The seating plan put Gaby at the far end of the long table, between a hack she knew from BBC on-line and a Hollywood film god who talked of working on fifteen musicals simultaneously and little else. Prenderleith had been placed at the far end of the table, in the champion's seat, hemmed in by the famous. Gaby watched him telling his much-told tales of stalkings and killings. He would glance up from time to time and she would catch his eye, and it was like a little conspiracy. I should tell him that he is an angle, Gaby thought. I should admit to the recorder.

The famous claimed Prenderleith for the remainder of the evening, a small court surrounding his seat by the picture window with its floodlit view of the Chaga approaching molecule by molecule. Gaby sat at the bar and watched him telling his stories of that other Africa. There was a light in his eye. Gaby could not decide if it was nostalgia or anticipation of when it would all fall and come apart.

Out in the dark beyond the floodlights, trees fell, brought down by the Chaga, dissolver of illusions. The wooden piers of the hotel creaked and clicked. The celebrities glanced at each other, afraid.

The knock came at 1:27 according to the luminous hands of the bedside clock. Gaby had not long gone to sleep after dictating commentary. Noise from the upper decks; the party would gradually wind down with the hour until the soldiers came with the morning to clear everyone out. One of the guests, high and hopeful? A second polite knock. The politeness told her.

She could see from the way Prenderleith stood in the corridor that he was a little drunk and that, had he not been, he would not have done this. He was carrying his gun, like an adored child.

"Something you should see," he said.

"Why me?" Gaby asked, pulling on clothes and boots.

"Because no one else could understand. Because of those seven minutes you stared at that bloody thing out there and nothing else existed. You know the truth: Nothing does exist, apart from that. Make sure you bring whatever you've been recording on with you."

"You guessed."

"I noticed."

"Hunter's senses. Sorry, I should have told you, I suppose."

"No matter to me."

"You're the only one here has a story worth telling, who will actually lose something when this comes down."

"You think so?"

The light was poor in the wooden corridor. Gaby could not read his expression right. Prenderleith led her to a service staircase down to ground level. Stepping onto the dark surface between the piers, Gaby imagined setting first foot on an alien planet. Close to the truth there, she thought. Prenderleith unslung his rifle and led her out from under the hotel into the shadows along the edge of the floodlights. The night felt huge and close around Gaby, full of breathings and tiny movements. Her breath steamed, it was cold upon the shoulder lands of Kirinyaga. She inhaled the perfume of the Chaga. It was a smell you imagined you knew, because it evoked so many memories, as smell does more powerfully than any other sense. But you could not know it, and when you realized that, all the parts that reminded you of other things collapsed together and the spicy, musky, chemically scent of it was nothing you could remember for no one had ever known anything like this before. It pushed you forward, not back.

Prenderleith led her toward terminum. It was not very far. The Chaga grew taller and more complex as the floodlight waned. Looming, like the waking memory of a nightmare. Gaby could hear the groan and smash of trees falling in the darkness. Prenderleith stopped her half a meter from the edge. Half a meter, fifteen minutes, Gaby thought. She curled her toes inside her boots, feeling infected. Prenderleith squatted on his heels, rested his weight on his gun, like a staff, hunting.

"Wind's right," he said.

Gaby squatted beside him. She switched on the recorder, listened to the silence, and watched the Chaga approach her, out of the shadows. Terminum was a grid of small hexagons of a mosslike substance. The hexagons were of all colors; Gaby knew intuitively that no color was ever next to itself. The corners of the foremost hexagons were sending dark lines creeping out into the undergrowth. Blades of grass, plant stems, fell before the molecule machines and were reduced to their components. Every few centimeters the crawling lines would bifurcate; a few centimeters more they would divide again to build hexagons. Once enclosed, the terrestrial vegetation would wilt and melt and blister into pinpoint stars of colored pseudomoss.

On a sudden urge, Gaby pressed her hand down on the black lines. It did not touch flesh. It had never touched flesh. Yet she flinched as she felt Chaga beneath her bare skin. Oh she of little faith. She felt the molecule-by-molecule advance as a subtle tickle, like the march of small, slow insects across the palm of her hand.

She started as Prenderleith touched her gently on the shoulder.

"It's here," he whispered.

She did not have the hunter's skill, so for long seconds she saw it only as a deeper darkness moving in the shadows. Then it emerged into the twilight between the still-standing trees and the tall fingers of pseudocoral and Gaby gasped.

It was an elephant; an old bull with a broken tusk. Prenderleith rose to his feet. There was not ten meters between them. Elephant and human regarded each other. The elephant took a step forward, out of the shadows into the full light. As it raised its trunk to taste the air, Gaby saw a mass of red, veiny flesh clinging to its neck like a parasitic organ. Beneath the tusks it elongated into flexible limbs. Each terminated in something disturbingly like a human hand. Shocked, Gaby watched the red limbs move and the fingers open and shut. Then the elephant turned and with surprising silence retreated into the bush. The darkness of the Chaga closed behind it.

"Every night, same time," Prenderleith said after a long silence. "For the past six days. Right to the edge, no further. Little closer every day."

"Why?"

"It looks at me, I look at it. We understand each other."

"That thing, around its neck; those arms . . ." Gaby could not keep the disgust from her voice.

"It changes things. Makes things more what they could be. Should be, maybe. Perhaps all elephants have ever needed have been hands, to become what they could be."

"Bootstrap evolution."

"If that's what you believe in."

"What do you believe in?"

"Remember how I answered when you told me the Chaga was taking my Africa away?"

"Not your Africa."

"Understand what I meant now?"

"The Africa it's taking away is the one you never

understood, the one you weren't made for. The Africa it's giving is the one you never knew but that was bred into your bones; the great untamed, unexplored, dark Africa, the Africa without nations and governments and borders and economies; the Africa of action, not thought, of being, not becoming, where a single man can lose himself and find himself at the same time; return to a more simple, physical, animal level of existence."

"You say it very prettily. Suppose it's your job."

Gaby understood another thing. Prenderleith had asked her to speak for him because he had not been made able to say such things for himself, and wanted them said right for those who would read Gaby's story about him. He wanted a witness, a faithful recording angel. Understanding this, she knew a third thing about Prenderleith, which could never be spoken and preserved on disc.

"Let's go in again," Prenderleith said eventually. "Bloody freezing out here."

The soldiers came through the hotel at 6:30 in the morning, knocking every bedroom door, though all the guests had either been up and ready long before, or had not slept at all. In view of the fame of the guests, the soldiers were very polite. They assembled everyone in the main lounge. Like a slow sinking, Gaby thought. A Noh Abandon–ship. The reef has reached us at last. She looked out of the window. Under darkness the hexagon moss had crossed the artificial water hole and was climbing the piles of the old hotel. The trees out of which the elephant had emerged in the night were festooned with orange spongy encrustations and webs of tubing.

The main lounge lurched. Glasses fell from the back bar and broke. People screamed a little. The male Hollywood stars tried to look brave, but his was no screenplay. This was the real end of the world. Prenderleith had gathered with the rest of the staff in the farthest corner from the door and was trying to sow calm. It is like the *Titanic,* Gaby thought. Crew last. She went to stand with them. Prenderleith gave her a puzzled frown.

"The punters have to know if the captain goes down with his ship," she said, patting the little black recorder in the breast pocket of her bush shirt. Prenderleith opened his mouth to speak and the hotel heaved again, more heavily. Beams snapped. The picture window shattered and fell outward. Gaby grabbed the edge of the bar and talked fast and panicky at her recorder. Alarmed, the soldiers hurried the celebrities out of the lounge and along the narrow wooden corridors toward the main staircase. The lounge sagged, the floor tilted, tables and chairs slid toward the empty window.

"Go!" Prenderleith shouted.

They were already going. Jammed into the wooden corridor, she tried not to think of bottomless coffins as she tried to shout through the other shouting voices into the microphone. Behind her the lounge collapsed and fell. She fought her way through the press of bodies into the sunlight, touched the solidity of the staircase. Crawling. She snatched her fingers away. The creeping, branching lines of Chaga-stuff were moving down the stairs, through the paint-work.

"It's on the stairs," she whispered breathlessly into the mike. The wooden wall behind her was a mosaic of hexagons. She clutched the recorder on her breast. A single spore would be enough to dissolve it and her story. She plunged down the quivering stairs.

Heedless of dangerous animals, the soldiers hurried the guests toward the vehicles on the main road. The news people paused to shoot their final commentaries on the fall of the Treehouse.

"It's coming apart," she said as a section of roof tilted up like the stern of a sinking liner and slid through the bubbling superstructure to the ground. The front of the hotel was a smash of wood and the swelling, bulbous encrustations of Chaga-stuff. The snapped piles were fingers of yellow sponge and pseudocoral. Gaby described it all. Soldiers formed a cordon between the spectators and the Chaga. Gaby found Prenderleith beside her.

"You'll need to know how the story ends," he said. "Keep this for me." He handed Gaby his rifle. She shook her head.

"I don't do good on guns."

He laid it at her.

"I know," she said.

"Then you'll help me."

"Do you hate this that much?"

"Yes," he said. There was a detonation of breaking wood and a gasp from soldiers and civilians alike. The hotel had snapped in the middle and folded up like two wings. They slowly collapsed into piles of voraciously feeding Chaga life.

He made the move while everyone's attention but Gaby's was distracted by the end of the old hotel. She had known he would do it. He ran fast for a tired old white hunter, running to fat.

"He's halfway there," she said to her recorder. "I admire his courage, going gladly into this new dark continent. Or is it the courage to make the choice that eventually the Chaga may make for all of us on this planet formerly known as Earth?"

She broke off. The soldier in front of her had seen Prenderleith. He lifted his Kalashnikov and took aim.

"Prenderleith!" Gaby yelled. He ran on. He seemed more intent on doing something with his shirt buttons. He was across the edge now, spores flying up from his feet as he crushed the hexagon moss.

"No!" Gaby shouted, but the soldier was under orders, and both he and the men who gave the orders feared the Chaga above all else. She saw the muscles tighten in his neck, the muzzle of the gun weave a little this way, a little that way. She looked for something to stop him. Prenderleith's rifle. No. That would get her shot too.

The little black disc recorder hit the soldier, hard, on the shoulder. She had thrown it, hard. The shot skyed. Birds went screeching up from their roosts. Otherwise, utter silence from soldiers and staff and celebrities. The soldier whirled on her, weapon raised. Gaby danced back, hands held high. The soldier snapped his teeth at her and brought the butt of the gun down on the disc recorder. While he smashed it to shards of plastic and circuitry, Gaby saw the figure of Prenderleith disappear into the pseudocoral fungus of the alien landscape. He had lost his shirt.

The last vestiges of the tourist hotel—half a room balanced atop a pillar; the iron staircase, flowering sulphur-yellow buds, leading nowhere, a tangle of plumbing, wash-basins and toilets held out like begging bowls—tumbled and fell. Gaby watched mutely. She had nothing to say, and nothing to say it to. The Chaga advanced onward, twenty-five centimeters every minute. The people dispersed. There was nothing more to see than the millimetric creep of another world.

The soldiers checked Gaby's press accreditations with five different sources before they would let her take the SkyNet car. They were pissed at her but they could not touch her. They smiled a lot, though, because they had smashed her story and she would be in trouble with her editor.

You're wrong, she thought as she drove away down the safe road in the long convoy of news-company vehicles and tour buses. Story is in the heart. Story is never broken. Story is never lost.

That night, as she dreamed among the doomed towers of Nairobi, the elephant came to her again. It stood on the border between worlds and raised its trunk and its alien hands and spoke to her. It told her that only fools feared the change that would make things what they could be, and should be; that change was the special gift of whatever had made the Chaga. She knew in her dream that the elephant was speaking with the voice of Prenderleith, but she could not see him, except as a silent shadow moving in the greater dark beyond humanity's floodlights: Adam again, hunting in the Africa of his heart.

SUNFLOWERS

Kathleen Ann Goonan

One of the fastest rising new stars of the nineties, Kathleen Ann Goonan is a graduate of Clarion West who has become a frequent contributor to Asimov's Science Fiction, Interzone, The Magazine of Fantasy and Science Fiction, Amazing, *and elsewhere. With the publication of her acclaimed first novel,* Queen City Jazz, *which was a* New York Times *Notable Book in 1994, one of the most interesting of the crop of nanotech novels, she has become known as a writer fascinated with the implications of nanotechnology, a subject that she also examines in stories such as "The Day the Dam Broke," "Solitaire," and one to which she will return in her upcoming novel,* Mississippi Blues. *She is also the author of the novel* The Bones of Time. *She lives in Lakeland, Florida.*

Here she offers us an intricate and melancholy pavane of art, identity, and loss, all driven by the ruthless power of a new technology . . .

"Sunflower, sunflower, yellow and green
You are the loveliest flower I've seen
Tall, straight, full of grace
I love the smile on your bright yellow face."
—Children's song

The terrorist was successful, but she did not live to know it. She was executed quickly, under international law, by the method of her choice. At least, that was what Stannis read on the standard newsnets.

Three years and two months after the terrorist's attack

Stannis took a freighter from a dark, cold Northern European industrial town, having circled his target fitfully in the few months since his wife and daughter had died of an overdose of time perception.

As he waited to board, sheets of rain hammered the side of the boat after sweeping across the gray harbor, drenching him and the only other apparent passengers, a young couple entwined and adoring, out for a romantic interlude or perhaps too poor to afford more elegant transport. Monstrous gray factories rimmed the waterside, clanking and belching smoke. Despite what had happened to him, Stannis still thought it obscene, or perhaps merely absurd, that nations chose this path when others were readily available.

He shivered as rain filtered through his thin coat, feeling ill-prepared and afraid of what he planned to do. He had forced himself through the great museums of London, Paris, and Vienna searching for surcease which never came. Perhaps taking the museum trip they planned before Annais died had not been wise.

But of course, his real intent had been different all along.

He realized only fifteen minutes earlier that he was fooling himself about the real purpose of his quest. He knew this the instant he overheard a man in a booth behind him mention to someone that the GULDEN was heading to Amsterdam.

Amsterdam. The city he had been avoiding. The city where he could find that which he realized, with dread, that he desired more than life: understanding.

Still he dithered, gulping strong black coffee, sitting in the window of a cafe across the square from the vast boat. He watched them load massive oily machined metal and rainstreaked wooden crates with cranes. The varnish of the counter was dark, and "Dag" was scratched in the dirt-grimed surface next to his right hand. As the crane operator set the brake and jumped from his high perch, Stannis grabbed his coat and ran across the square to the gangplank.

The journey to Amsterdam would cost $97 euros, the young woman wearying a stiff uniform beneath a slick watercoat told him after he pounded up to the ship and the young couple laughed and stepped onto the deck.

Beneath her dark, roachlike hat a short fringe of straight red hair shone in the pale gray light. Stannis unbuttoned his shirt pocket and pulled out his wallet. The "P" pad was clearly lit as prescribed by law, but he watched without protest as she hit the wrong one and an image of a little girl and a woman came up. Her face went still, then she blinked, gave him a long look, and dashed from her face some rain which had dripped from her hat. Her cheeks red, she said "Sorry" and got on to his passport, then transferred the money from his account to that of the GULDEN and handed it to him to verify, which he did with his thumbprint.

"Cabin 9," she said, her English only a bit twisted. She handed him a keycard and gestured with a sideways jerk of her head. His breath came short again with fear, but he reminded himself that he could always change his mind. As a practice in dignity he did not run down the echoing metal walkway. He placed his heavy boots deliberately. Once the metal nubs had been painted red. The rail was cold and wet beneath his right hand. He glanced for the last time at the tiny manufacturing town, productive once more with its old-style foundries now that nan was outlawed in Europe. Thick black smoke poured from tall stacks, a few shades darker than the dreary sky. He had subsisted here on bottled water and other distilled liquids, and an occasional meal of grilled fish.

The cold air filled his lungs with the tang of carbon. Despite the ridiculous, childish pollution, all was straightforward here, the pain in his heart echoed by this local failure of a technology he once fervently believed in. As an engineer, he still appreciated its possibilities, but the difference was that now he understood that every change involved a spectrum of possibilities, not just the one—the positive, the bright.

Dignity was frail. Eyes brimming with tears, he turned left abruptly, fumbled with his card, and let himself into the close cabin. The black radiance of memory blossomed, its imperceptibly small strings snaking through his mind like a tumor which he could not kill without killing himself. And why not? Why not kill himself?

But then too, why?

Stannis still remembered the terrorist vividly: tall, she wore a tight blue silk dress, very simple. Her short hair was black.

On that day three years ago the restaurant was packed, and Sunday brunch progressing as smoothly as possible with a three-year-old at the table. The pleasant cacophony of clanking silverware and a hundred conversations drifted upward toward the high, white dome of the ceiling.

Sun was just beginning to peek through the Washington D.C. skies, silver with spring rain. He lifted Claire back into her booster seat for the tenth time and was just beginning to think that Annais should take a turn at it. But she was chatting with her old school friend Julie. Funny what different paths they took after they each earned an undergraduate degree in intro genetic engineering. Ten years later, Annais was a string physicist, and Julie was archiving the world's art in VR, head of a Smithsonian team.

Annais' hair was blonde and long and contrasted nicely with her shimmering, loose black shirt. "It's so wonderful," Julie was saying. "The world will have much better access to art now. Imagine, you can wrap your arms around a sculpture, touch every hollow, understand it much more spatially. You could never do that in a real-world museum."

"I heard that they're working on something even better," said Annais. "Aren't they going to have nan reproductions?"

Stannis smiled at his fleeting picture of what that might mean to Annais, saw her walk up to a rack of white envelopes like seed packets in an old-fashioned hardware store except these were in a museum shop rack and filled with the nanotech seeds for replication-ready works of art. She would pluck up the lot of them, take them home, and perhaps cook them up in the bathtub filled with the fluid on which the replicators fed.

Julie shuddered and said, "Maybe in a few years. I've heard the target date is 2030, but I hope not. You know how I feel about nan." And genetic engineering, oddly enough. Her brush with the possibilities of genetics had outright frightened her. She refused to speak with Annais and Stannis for months after they chose to enhance Claire genetically in utero with what were called "gifted fragments." "My parents did it for me," Annais told Julie, surprised by her reaction. "It was done for Stannis too. Julie, why not? It doesn't hurt—and most of the time the difference between—us—and others isn't enormously discernible." Annais laughed. "Stannis and I can vouch for that. We're both quite normal actually, don't you think?" "Obviously not," Julie replied coldly. But the bonds were close between Julie and Annais, and they reunited eventually. Annais' hobby was art history so they had plenty to talk about.

Claire started reading the menu in a loud voice. "Ca-vee-ar. What's that? Pancakes. That's what I ordered. When are they bringing mine?"

Annais glanced at Stannis and he said to Claire, "That's enough." Claire threw her spoon across the table and laughed as it clattered against her mother's half-full champagne glass. Annais caught the glass as it tilted and said, "No more spoons for you today, Claire," and Claire glared at her and turned to slide from her seat. Stannis lifted her onto his lap and hummed along with the piano, which was playing "Nice Work If You Can Get It." Claire squirmed. "I have to go to the bathroom," she said.

"Me too," said Annais. She pushed back her chair as Claire ran around the table and they clasped hands.

Just three tables away in the bright dining room arched glass doors which opened onto a broad balcony with wet, empty tables. Stannis was staring out into the light, delighting in the tang of water in the cool spring air, when the woman in the blue dress stepped into the doorway right next to Annais and Claire, who were threading their way across the room. Stannis' first thought was that the woman looked quite fetching. She raised her arm and shouted, "This is in the name of the Republic of New Hong Kong! We are tired of being your experimental dumping ground! See how *you* like it!"

The piano music trailed off. Conversation halted. One man had the presence of mind and enough courage to rush her but before he tackled her she launched the packet into the air and it opened, releasing a cloud of sweet scent. Yes, he *had* breathed it. So why . . . ? Why? Stannis thought, lying in his bunk as the ship rumbled. Why them, why not me too?

Stannis had leaped up, pushed aside the tables and chairs between himself and his family. He grabbed Claire and clamped his hand over her mouth and nose. Without breathing, he rushed for the door, aware that Annais and Julie were next to him, on the crest of a stampede. As they ran down the stairs Claire struggled and bit his hand. He did not let her breathe till they had crossed the street and she gasped and coughed and screamed. Tears wet Annais' face. Julie was pale. They walked silently toward their apartment on M Street, and Julie came with them. They were all stunned except Claire, who ran ahead, happy to be let out of her chair. New leaves misted the trees and rustled as the breeze moved through them. There were flowers, Stannis would always remember, pink spring poppies around the base of every tree. Sunlight washed through the papery, translucent petals, and burnished Claire's light brown hair.

No one bothered Stannis during the journey, and he did not venture out. After twenty-four hours, the heaving of the North Sea calmed. He answered a knock at his door and the red-haired woman was there and stared at him curiously for a moment, then said "Amsterdam," and hurried away.

His heart lifted in spite of himself as the sun poured in through the open door when she left. Feeling hollow and lightheaded, he rubbed the stubble on his face and stared out at the teeming city. He could see tiny figures standing on the huge pier, black against the sun. Bicycle spokes glittered as packs of bikers swirled among clots of pedestrians and past umbrellaed tables where people sat drinking. The gap of water inexorably narrowed, a deep cold green. As the boat drew close his ears were filled with the roar of the engines, and a heavy vibration ran through the deck.

Stannis saw, with a slight shock, that the wharf was packed with a swarm of holies, playing off one another's beams, leaping and dancing with obvious untrammeled joy. Black market nan modifications to their genes enhanced their brainwaves, at the inevitable expense of many normal functions. After intense biofeedback, they had a new skill. In the US it was available legally, licensed for therapeutical use, and was lighter, time-limited—or so he had been told.

He had tried it. He thought it bullshit. His therapy temporary hadn't helped him. But like most of nan, the final verdict would never be in; it had invaded humanity as thoroughly as had the printed word centuries before, transforming them forever. So he believed. No going back. As irrevocable as death.

The crew secured the boat. As Stannis watched the holies cavort, he felt, suddenly, quite empty. Frighteningly so.

Chimerical creatures flickered briefly in the air and vanished, like doors to other universes—a shotgun was aimed at him, a waterfall foamed briefly over wet rocks, a woman sat next to a child in bed, reading a book.

As far as he knew, this was feared and banned by Europe like all nan, but he supposed it too was accepted in this accepting city. What had his own visions been, in that small white therapy cubicle? He projected art, mostly, from exhibits he and Annais had seen at the National Gallery. His therapist despaired. "These are a smokescreen. You are concealing your real feelings even from yourself." Who wouldn't? he wondered. Is that bad? If so, aren't *you* supposed to do something about it? No, he was told, it was up to him. Thanks a lot.

Stannis scanned a ten-language sign which briefly stated that a local museum consortium infused the wharf air with polarizing beams which made the projections more intense than normal. He hesitated, then shrugged. It was disturbing, this reminder of another of his failures, but at least his own ability to project had expired. He had to cross the wharf. He steeled himself, walked down the clanging ramp, and stepped into the gauntlet.

He ignored the holies and their smiling idiot faces, striding across the square through a multitude of visions until suddenly he was confronted with a sunflower.

Its weedy green stem was tall and covered with what looked like a million tiny hairs. Brilliant yellow petals fanned out gloriously from the center, as high as Stannis' own head, packed with a thousand seeds. He looked around, but no one was near.

It must be his.

He felt wildly disoriented. Everything else around him seemed brilliant, splashes of wavering color with no clear boundaries. The song his daughter had sung around the house just before she died came unbidden to his mind. Sunflowers have no face, he had teased her, but suddenly this one did. Instead of the huge, staring seed-eye there was Claire, snub-nosed and blue-eyed.

Stannis fled through the projections into the narrow, ancient streets. The buildings seemed to lean over him, as if wider at the top than at the bottom. Small electric cars crawled past, barely able to squeeze past one another. Sweating, Stannis turned into a doorway under a sign which said "Rooms."

The tiny lobby had a musty dark green carpet. The man behind the desk looked very old. He spoke perfect English and gave Stannis a heavy old-fashioned key. Stannis climbed crooked stairs.

His room looked out over the street, which was about ten feet across. He flung open the window and dank air rushed in. The sky had clouded up—bad weather was following him. He slumped into the single worn chair and stared at the bricks of the building across the street.

Claire was dead. Annais was dead. The months and years would blend together and time would wash him further and further away from that bright, glowing, impossible time.

They were both dead when he came home one afternoon. Lying peaceful and pale and smiling on the large bed he and Annais had shared for ten years. Annais' scrawled note said, "Sorry—beautiful—can't stop." Cause of death: "Infovirus synergistically combined with genetic enhancement patterns. Synaptic overload." Knowing too much and thinking too fast. Seeing the possibilities flower around them, washing them with pain and light. Stannis watched it happen. He had not known exactly what was going on—how could he? He had not known how it would end.

He got up and closed the window. It was cold here. He pulled the curtains. Turning back he saw on the bedside table some tourist brochures. This room was too cheap for even a TV, much less the small HV platform which in many establishments automatically activated with local attractions when the guest entered the room.

He picked them up and idly thumbed through them. Gourmet barge rides. Tree-shaded canals. The Van Gogh Museum. Well, he'd seen enough art, hadn't he? The real thing, just like Annais had wanted but which they had never had time for. Never. Ah, yes. Anger flared through him. No doubt she'd *known* exactly how that would feel, to travel to Europe, the three of them, and visit the static displays which Julie committed to virtual. She had probably *seen* this possibility too—the death of herself and Claire, his own solitary journey. His pain. Or perhaps there were certain blindnesses? Perhaps this had been something she hadn't seen at all in the vast multiplicity of possibilities? He had to believe that. He didn't know if it had struck Annais's friend Julie. She fled the city to go back to her parent's farm in upstate New York a week after the attack.

Stannis turned the page. The Dancers at the Wharf. That's right, he thought, letting the leaflet flutter to the floor. Make the most of freakdom. He shivered, remembering the sunflower. Apparently his temporary ability had not expired yet.

Well, this is your chance, he told himself. Your chance to *know*, to lay all doubt to rest. Your chance to be with them, in that last, particular way. To find out what really happened. Do it, or go back to your little niche and pine the rest of your life away, knowing you were a coward.

He pocketed his key and walked down to the street.

It was crowded with business people and strolling tourists. Small cafes lined the street and the scent of fresh coffee and bread filled the damp air. Everyone seemed beautifully well-dressed, in what he now recognized as ubiquitous eurostyle. Simple lines and sharp angles; muted tones. Everything was still expensive here, just the way they liked it. Consumers couldn't simply imagine what they wanted to wear, and sketch it out on a screen, and tinker with it, try it on holographically and then have it cheaply and individually constructed via nan. That's how one could buy clothing in Asia, separated from Europe by a fragile nan-free zone a hundred miles wide.

Of course, that wouldn't last long; they were idiots here to think that it could. But nan was completely outlawed here, and he was too for an entire year after the expiration of his therapy nans, but his passport had been doctored. Oddly enough, he reflected as he wandered down one street and then another, it was not the fear of runaway replication which had put up the wall, not at all. The middle ground—the unions, the megacorporations, the entire governmental structure had outlawed further nan development, along with genetic engineering. The establishment was trying to hold back the inevitable social upheaval which accompanies all paradigm shifts, like the industrial revolution. They were trying not to lose money, trying to keep control.

But those changes were all for the better, weren't they? They were all for the *different*, at least. Stannis had always believed that one had to have hope in humanity, in humanity's blind thrusting, blind as the new caterpillar's attraction to light which drew it to the end of the branches where the new leaves were edible, which Rousseau had labelled sensitive periods. The doctor told him then, when Claire received her gifted fragment, that all children went through sensitive periods for everything they learned—language, mathematics, spatial abilities—where they were drawn to particular types of information and practically absorbed it. Hers would be intensified.

How right that doctor had been.

Stannis looked away from his unhappy reflection in a shop window filled with odd clothing and continued walking. Was humanity in some new sensitive period? he wondered. Was there some new light drawing him on, changing consciousness, changing the ways that humans saw things? A new way of thinking, a new way of understanding time, which had been relentlessly, fatally enhanced in Claire and Annais? Stannis stumbled on a curb, regained his balance. His steps echoed hollowly as he crossed a tiny bridge above a limpid green canal.

Annais was so certain of that light, he recalled, forcing himself to think about that which he found so painful as he passed a wineshop, then a map store. She devoted her life to it, then followed the damned light to the very threshold of death. Except that he thought she may have believed that consciousness would continue at the exact point of the threshold, would expand; that it was possible for humans to become all-knowing and bright, as if she and Claire could exist forever, hovering on an event horizon of the mind.

Did they?

It was getting on a little past noon. He forced himself to lean against a brick storefront and got out his wallet, half-hoping that the name he had encoded in the middle of one of his files had been lost, and the precise numbers which defined, according to government files he had no trouble accessing, the exact virus which enhanced Annais and Claire.

The nans had migrated, as intended, to the part of their brain which organized one's sense of time. He read, late one rainy night at his screen, not caring in the least if he was caught beyond the encryption barrier, that this particular strain was developed as part of the Information Wars program. It was one of the many creations of the division whose task was to see how best to drive people crazy in very specific ways, or artificially enhance very minute aspects of the brain's functioning. Create again the synaptic conditions which made learning languages easy for children. Things like that.

He had the parameters. He punched the final button and there they were, gleaming on the tiny screen.

In Amsterdam, there were people who made and sold such things. They were legal, here, just like many other substances which were illegal elsewhere, but usually one had to make contact through one of their scouts, and the buyer was extensively checked, for the sellers were the inevitable target of international terrorists. Stannis also had a name. Hans Utrecht.

He turned off his wallet abruptly and put it in his pocket. Though it was cool, he realized that he was sweating. He felt ill. When did you last eat? he scolded himself, and dropped onto a bench. Should he try to find Hans?

He had battled this impulse for what seemed like a very long time, then gave in and came to Europe, drew a bit closer to *this*. Survivor's guilt, the therapist had told him—was it really that simple? His hands were clammy. The Louvre was the worst of it, filled with treasures she always longed to see *really*. When Claire was a bit older and could appreciate it. And he finally thought himself well out of it up there—where had he been? Norway? Finland? He hadn't cared. His eyes burned with tears. He missed them so! It was not fair, not fair at all. What had really *happened* to them? How could they leave him behind like this? How could Annais have possibly made such a decision? Had she? Had there been a point, as she had apparently half-believed, in her bliss, where she could have *decided* to stay or go? And what about Claire? Had Annais not cared about Claire? Unbelievable. If she *had* a choice, she must have believed that she and Claire were heading into some realm much better than the one in which they left him behind. She *must* have.

And what could that have been?

Even though he had made it to Amsterdam, he was not quite ready to find out. He decided to wipe out those tempting, horrible numbers, deadly numbers. He had to. This was a fool's quest. He would not try to find Hans.

He rose. Disappointment burned in him.

And relief.

But he was not hungry, nor was he tempted by the wine-shops, the cannabis bars, the doorways which promised rich and excellent beer. He remembered the map on the back of one of the brochures, and despite himself kept walking and turning, once in a while asking directions, all the while thinking, why are you going here?

The Van Gogh museum shone pale silver beneath a pale silver sky; clouds cloaked the sun once more. He approached the ticket booth and stopped. Why torture himself with more art viewed alone? He turned aside.

Someone touched his shoulder and he jumped, whirled.

It was the woman with the red hair.

Her sleek rain helmet was gone now, and her short red hair was ruffled by the wind. Her wide gray eyes were fringed by thick dark lashes, and looked at him searchingly, roving his face as if extracting inexplicably vital information. Her hands were stuffed into the pockets of a black leather flight jacket. "I saw you," she said.

He stared back at her. What did she want? "Yes," he said. "On the boat."

"No," she said. "On the wharf."

He didn't say anything. He couldn't. She had seen his passport, and she had seen that it lied.

She continued to look at him, hesitant about something. Was she going to report him? He was relieved when all she said was, "You should really visit the museum. I do, just about every time I'm in town. It's worth the admission. Van Gogh was quite a philosopher." As if she were a tour guide, she pulled a well-worn book about Van Gogh from her jacket pocket. It fell open to a page she had apparently read and re-read. "Look what he says about death. 'Given the prodigious number of births, each individual death is not too carefully recorded—but what does this matter? It is the multitude that counts.'"

Her voice was clear and cultured. He relaxed; apparently she was just a bit of a crackpot, but interested in art, like Annais.

"What do you think that means?" he asked her, suddenly alert, having thought about nothing but death for months.

She slapped the book shut and smiled. "Who knows?" she said. She stuffed it back in her pocket, then linked her arm through his as he stood still as a statue. "Come on," she said. "They drink a very good liquor here. Let me buy you one. Please."

He allowed her to pull him into motion. They walked three blocks and she paused, looking around. "I thought it was here—a place with a bit of privacy—ah, there!"

He followed her down a short flight of stairs into a dark room with many booths. Several people greeted her, and the waiter greeted her by name. Stannis must have looked surprised, because she said, "Amsterdam is my home," as they slid into a booth.

Low conversation filled the air, and she credited some music which sounded wildly Celtic on the table jukebox and hummed along briefly in a lovely contralto counterpoint.

She was Lise. She remembered his name from the passport. Lise ordered for them, small fluted glasses of jenever and a basket of small crisp fried fish, lightly salted. The jenever was strong, but he had grown uncharacteristically used to strong drink and apparently she already was, for she ordered several rounds. They burned as they went down, and tasted of lemon. Her face grew flushed and he thought her pretty and was surprised at himself. She had a good appetite, though he saw that she was thin as a stick after she hung her bulky jacket next to the booth. She looked up midbite and swallowed.

"I did see your projection, you know," she said. "Were you surprised? You move away very quickly."

"Yes. No. I suppose," he said. To cover his embarrassment, he grabbed a handful of fish and transferred them to the white plate in front of him, and sprinkled them with vinegar. His hand shook as he set the bottle back down. She reached over and touched it, but removed her hand quickly. He took several deep breaths.

"It's not a crime you know," she said. "At least, not here."

He shrugged, and failed to speak twice before bringing forth the words. It had been a very long time since he had talked to anyone.

"It's not that—"

"The thinking is," she continued, "that it is not the fault of the people who have these modifications—particularly since it *is* against EG sanctions, now, to have them changed again. It is simply usual to try and conceal yourself—avoid situations which might make the contents of your subconscious visible. It's mostly done at private parties. That's why there's such a daring exhilaration about doing it in public. One of the reasons it's so frightening is because someone who has not had any training will be absolutely spilling over with bizarre and disturbing sexual thoughts, murderous images, all that we have grown so expert at concealing. It's a theater of the mind. And I guess that was the point, wasn't it? It had some sort of therapeutical purpose in the beginning, didn't it? And then the off switch didn't work in everyone." She paused. "That was a beautiful face you made, within the sunflower." Her voice caught a bit, and she coughed and took a sip of water.

"It was my daughter," he said.

"Oh. Yes." Her eyes went inward in the dim light and he saw that she was thinking of his passport and the pictures she had accidentally called. "An old picture?"

"Five years old," he said, wondering at the time. It did

not seem that long. Five years should be a long time. It was not. The music had stopped, and the voices around them were low, muted within booths. Rain slashed at the windows; storms came up suddenly here.

"So she's about six now? Seven?" Lise asked but the pause made him think that she knew, but was still not exactly sure. Suddenly angry, he sat back in the booth. "They're both dead."

"How did it happen?" she asked. Almost too eagerly, he thought, but looking at her he saw only concern and sadness.

"They decided together. Without me. Of course. The therapist—the one who insisted that I do projections, and I was foolish and desperate enough to try that too—said that it must have been some sort of inevitable intellectual frisson, almost pheromonal in its imperativity—" he stopped, looked at her.

"They *decided*?" she asked.

"I think so." Darkness returned, blanketing everything. The tiny lamp with its dim yellow light which made everything so cozy, the small black etching of a harbor filled with large-sailed boats, the just-refilled glasses of jeniver, all receded, leaving only pain.

And the touch of Lise's hand on his. This time she did not let go when he tried to pull his away.

"Tell me," she said. "Please. I don't think the therapy worked."

Loosened by the jeniver or something deeper, led by her fathomless eyes, he tried to think of where to start. It surprised him when the words tumbled out. He stammered a bit at first, then talked faster, as if he could not get it out fast enough.

"I blame myself for not figuring out what was happening. We got in the way of a terrorist several years ago, and she released some nans, apparently, that the government had been experimenting with in New Hong Kong. They denied any knowledge of it when it happened, but after Claire and Annais—died—" he withdrew his hand from hers and began to tear a napkin into smaller and smaller triangles—"first I raised hell. That didn't do any good. So then I tried to find out as much as I could on my own. Annais had a pretty high clearance, and I used it for quite a while before they thought to close it. One official finally admitted that an experimental time nan did exist, and that they would track down everyone else who was in the restaurant and put them in a special environment until they passed the crisis point. But apparently you had to have gifted fragments in order for the nan to take effect in this way, and they claimed no one else did, though they treated everyone they could find."

"Do you have gifted fragments?"

"Yes," he said, "Though I can't say that it's made a big difference in my life, ability-wise. It often doesn't."

"No, it doesn't," she agreed. "So why didn't it happen to you?"

"Just lucky, I guess." He laughed darkly. "The scent was just a marker, not the nan itself. There was a breeze."

Treatment! A joke; he told her about it. Prophylactic transdermal patches soaked in the chemicals of hope. Hormones. Therapists stressing the goodness of the world: no afterlife. No *otherlives*; no other possibilities no matter what you think and no matter how stretched and different time becomes for you. But Stannis was sure that unless it happened to you, you could not possibly understand it; hence, one unaffected could not ground the victims in this reality. *He* had not been able to. He still didn't understand it. Annais and Claire had shut their own bodies down. It had been both murder and suicide. Hadn't it?

He told Lise how once, in the therapist's projection room, Annais was a small figure far away from him standing on a bare windy plain. She stood alone, ecstatic, the wind blowing her hair back, her clothing tight against her body. Claire ran to join her. A third figure stood far off, and ran desperately to catch up with them, but could not; Annais and Claire glowed with light, then turned to light, and the light drifted upward, while still the third figure ran hopelessly. "You must forgive her," the therapist had said. "Can't you see? You have to let them *go*."

Or follow, he thought fiercely at the time.

"It was like a wildfire, this power of thought," he said. "Apparently, from what I can piece together now, they thought out all the possibilities in a white heat."

"The possibilities?" Lise asked, her eyes still as a deep, quiet pool or the sky on an overcast day. She was curled into a corner of the booth, her red hair lit gently by lamplight. She had ordered a bowl of strong hot tea, filled it with milk and sugar, and held it in both hands, sipping every now and then. Had her face paled, or was it the light?

"Every branching of possible lives that they could live, every permutation of being," he said. "Somehow they could *see* them."

Lise did not object. She just sipped, and listened, occasionally frowning to herself.

Stannis explained that, on looking back on those last few weeks he fancied he could almost see their heads shine with the power of their thought and then they were gone, having *lived* and *lived* and sorted through the probabilities and found most of them wanting but at any rate the possibilities were there, known, available somehow in a way he could not understand.

"Claire always asked the craziest questions," he said, and there was a brief, answering glow in Lise's eyes. "But one day when she was six I went to pick her up from school. Claire was ready to go. She was standing in the doorway staring at the rain. She did that a lot. It was starting to bother me, the staring.

"I just watched her, to see how long she'd stand there. Then her teacher pushed a printout in front of me and I said, what's this? He looked frightened. He explained that the children could access an entire continuum via computer provided that they could do the preceding lessons. I said so? I was trying to be calm but he was very agitated, and pointed out that those were quadratic equations and that it was Claire's work. I told him that was impossible and Claire opened her umbrella and stepped out into the rain. I rushed after her."

That day. Yes. Maybe *then*, he should have done something. But what? What, he thought, drinking the last of his jenever.

He remembered that day. He had been in his study in their old townhouse in Georgetown. The ceilings were high which he loved very much. Because he loved everything about his life very much perhaps he should have known but he did not. He had put up a wall between the terrorist and now. It had been, after all, years and after their first anxious one they had decided like silly children that danger was past. Otherwise it was hard to live.

That fall evening he was still chilled from his walk back from school with Claire, and from something deeper. They lived on a hill and the lights of the city were beginning to glow through the rain. He poured a finger of Scotch and rested in his leather chair. A tiny Van Gogh pencil sketch was dim across from him on the wall.

The door creaked open and it was Claire.

"It's dark in here, Daddy," she said.

"Turn on the light," he suggested, but instead she went to the window and stared out at the lights. She had changed to some sort of warm suit. She was a very neat child now, quiet and composed, different from her earlier self. Silence was gathered into her and released, a stillness which he felt he was falling into. He had felt so alone lately, he realized.

Annais and Claire seemed to be drawing closer together but perhaps that was inevitable, since Claire was a girl.

"Claire," he said, and she turned. He could not see her expression in the dark.

"Come here," he suggested, feeling troubled. "Sit on my lap."

She did. "What's up?" he asked.

"Oh," she said, "I've just been thinking."

"About what?"

"Our telecom number. It's a prime number."

"Really," he said. He thought for a minute. He couldn't factor it easily. "Maybe," he said. "What makes you think so? How did you figure it out?"

She looked at him and said, "I don't know," but it was not with the tone of someone bewildered, just someone who took it for granted and did not care. She slid off his lap and ran out the door. It only took a few moments on network to find a list of primes and to determine that she was right.

The things about which Annais thought and the shore on which Claire seemed more and more firmly implanted were not things which came easily to him. Recently he had told his father that to be a teacher you had to see what your student was thinking and break things down into steps for them, referring to the long ago struggle during which his father had tried to teach him mathematics for two years—except his father called it learning to *think*. When Stannis told his father about the steps, his look had been identical to Claire's, just more puzzled. "Maybe I didn't know there were any steps," he had finally replied.

It seemed that Claire didn't either. No steps—she just *knew*. Why should that frighten him? Perhaps he was just a bit jealous? Or maybe Annais's friend Julie had been right about gene enhancement. *Greed*, she had called it scornfully. He discarded both explanations. It was something else.

It was very dark now. He did not turn on the light.

He thought about the headaches Annais had complained of the last few months, for which the doctors could find no reason. Stress, they decided, and suggested biofeedback. With no organic basis, Annais felt free to brush them off. She was experiencing a powerful burst of creativity which had borne her along for months. "The problem is," she said, "that what I am thinking is very simple actually. It has to do with the final theory, you know, the explanation for the universe itself. String theory—can you believe it? That old warhorse. But I can visualize every step, everything I need to do. Down to the last detail. *Exactly* how time splits. How mind is meshed to matter. The *meaning* of the observer, the power of the observer. But it flashes by so swiftly that it's really hard to catch hold of, to write down . . . Stannis, it's scary sometimes."

Indeed.

The three of them were sitting in the kitchen one Sunday morning eating. Annais started and Claire actually ran over to the telecom then stopped. She turned around looking frightened, then ran to Annais who hugged her, with tears in her eyes.

"What?" he asked.

Annais just shook her head, her face white, but Claire turned and said, "I heard the telecom ring but it was Wednesday."

"Wednesday *afternoon*," said Annais, looking out the window.

But after that there were weeks of bliss. They did not speak of such things again, not in front of Stannis, anyway. Both of their faces became transparent and eager. Both of them lost weight and looked like wraiths, but wraiths angelic; beautiful. Claire sang the sunflower song endlessly, joyfully, until its first three climbing notes were enough to make his stomach churn. He felt more and more uncomfortable.

"We *are* information," Annais said at one point, her eyes wild and bright. "*Everything* is. That's *all* we are. That's all there *is*. Don't you see?"

"Not in quite the same way as you see, I think," he had replied, fighting back panic. "Maybe you should go back to the doctor." But Annais insisted that what was happening was a logical outcome of her work, and that Claire *should* be doing a bit of light algebra now, as some of her more advanced agemates were—she was just a few steps beyond them. It had been three years since the terrorist attack.

But now, he couldn't forgive himself for not seeing the obvious connection. And what could he have done? Annais had become childlike, an equal, in some way, of Claire, though it had always been her power of abstract thought to which he was so powerfully attracted. He had always felt that she lived in a world which he, a structural engineer, could not fathom, and he respected and admired her entirely. Until this last decision.

Had it been a decision? *That was what he had to know!*

"How happy it would make me to find out I could have done nothing," he heard himself saying. "Even if I only knew that for an instant!"

"But why was her face inside the sunflower?" asked Lise, her voice oddly urgent, startling him back to the present.

"What?" he asked. He realized that his eyes had filled and overflowed. Had he been talking or just thinking?

"I don't know why her face was in the sunflower," he said, but then he did. It was Claire, singing that silly sunflower song. Staring at him, singing it, in a fashion that verged on demanding.

And knowing made him ask. "Does the name Hans Utrecht mean anything to you?"

He saw her eyes widen, though she was staring down at

her tea. She looked up, and something—resignation?—flashed in her eyes. She still did not speak, though he was certain, by the look on her face, that she knew Hans. Finally, a tilt of the head, a brief smile to herself, not to him, as if she had made a decision. "I can get you in touch with these people, yes."

She wanted to walk him back to his hotel, but he refused. She gave a brief, businesslike nod, hesitated a moment, then turned and vanished into the now-dark streets.

Hans met him in an ancient java house and actually argued with him over curry. He was short and heavy with a florid face mostly covered with a reddish beard which came to a point beneath his chin. Apparently Lise had told Hans what she knew about Stannis and that worried Hans somewhat. "You're a grown man, of course, but this has proven particularly dangerous. This was developed by your own government and for very odd reasons, from what I can tell. Most people want nans which are—shall we say—a bit more recreational."

"What reasons?" asked Stannis.

Hans shrugged. "Who can say? I have been with three people who tried it. One of them went around talking about what would happen tomorrow. Of course, none of it happened, but they were so very *sure*. The other—well—she kept reliving going to the circus one day when she was five. That's all. What are the strategic implications of knowing the future? Even just a bit of it? Even a predictable percentage of it? Is that truly impossible? Computers can't do it, but humans are different than computers, aren't they?"

"Did they die?"

"Neither died, but I can't say that they were the same again. Theirs were time-limited, of course. Both of them pretty much dropped out. Agreed there was no point. But that was a while ago. I've lost touch." Stannis was not surprised. Perhaps their genes had not been modified in the particular way of himself, Claire, and Annais. Apparently the way it bonded to a particular type of mitochondria was crucial.

"The third?" Stannis asked.

"It seemed to have no effect on the third," said Hans.

"How long did it take to—take effect, with the others?"

Hans signalled for another coffee. "About an hour."

"The other took three years."

"That's easy enough to program if you like."

"No," said Stannis.

"We can make it self-limiting," Hans said. "At least that."

Stannis thought. Finally he said, "No."

Stannis had only to wait until the following morning before sniffing up his nose that which had killed his wife and child.

Lise was there, sitting across from him in his room in a rather shabby overstuffed chair reading. "You can't be alone," she insisted. He lay back on the bed and closed his eyes.

And fell asleep.

When he woke, he was disoriented, then more alert. The curtains still filtered daylight into the cheap room. He sat up, alarmed, then disappointed. "What time is it?"

"About eleven," she said, closing her bookmaster and sticking it in her pocket.

"Hans must have given me duds," he said. How sad he felt. But—now he had done his best. He could go home.

Lise shook her head. "No, you can count on Hans. He's the best in the business. Entirely reliable. Come on," she said. "How about a walk, and something to eat?" A walk. Yes, he knew where he wanted to go. If it was to work, which was beginning to seem doubtful to him.

He rose. He had not bothered to shave this morning. He

looked in the mirror. "You look fine," she said. "I'm hungry."

It happened in the next block. He felt wretchedly ill, but only for about thirty seconds. Pain seared through his temples and everything went white. He heaved as if he were going to vomit, and supported himself with one hand against the rough bricks of the building next to him.

When his vision cleared, he saw Lise standing in front of him, her face concerned and sympathetic.

He also saw the two of them walking ahead—yes, that *was* Lise and himself, looking in a store window and laughing.

The strangeness of it was overwhelming. He should not have done this. How could Annais and Claire possibly have coped? No wonder.

Where in this world were they? Perhaps—panic hit him—perhaps he should have had Hans make it start next month, when he was back home, and then they would be everywhere, in the townhouse, out on the street, and he could choose, he could follow them—

The pressure was unbearable. He began to run. Perhaps *now* the projections would do some good! He paused and let Lise catch up. "Which way is the wharf? Hurry!"

He had to make what he was thinking *visible*, *real*. If there was a place Claire and Annais were, if somehow he knew, with some hidden part of his mind, the place where they were caught forever on the crest of a breaking wave—

Down a narrow street, he saw blue water. Lise yanked on his arm and he turned, rushed down the hill, arrived gasping at the wide cobblestone wharf, and pushed through dancing holies into the central ring.

He stared as all around him brightened, pixilated, then faded—the tourists sipping wine and pointing from their tables around the perimeter; the other holies with their weak, shivering images. He felt very warm.

There! There they were! Claire! Annais! But—lying on the bed, their final resting place. Smiling, holding hands. He gasped, reached, shouted—

Then they were gone and how odd: numbers swirled around him, tiny, like black insects, delicate, meshing and linking, building into fleeting, concrete realities which dissolved as rapidly as they formed.

Thought—or something like it, some sort of pressure which he realized came from *him*—caught the edges of planes—the planes of tables, of decks of boats, of the buildings—vertical planes, horizontal planes, then planes which faced in a billion directions—and pulled. The planes curved toward him as if they were putty, expanding and arching, then blending with another, higher velocity, and the velocity had weight which pressed against him—he heard all about him a roaring, and screams—saw two bright silhouettes—Them!—multiply into uncountable replications as if he were at the swirling apex of a brilliant, spinning, multi-armed galaxy—

He felt himself shoved roughly, amid the confusion, as if his body were someone else's. Staggering, he fell. Hands grasped his wrists, dragged him across the rough cobblestones, and dropped him.

He opened his eyes and touched his temple. It hurt. His hand came away sticky. "Get him *out* of here, man," he heard someone say to Lise, who was bending over him. "He's dangerous."

Lise helped him stand. She was stronger than she looked. He leaned against her, took a deep breath, said, "I can walk. What happened?"

She tilted her head, and a brief smile crossed her face. "You blew them out of the water, that's what. They'll never top that. It was like a neutron bomb hit. Pure light. For a moment, *no* one could see." She put her arm around him and helped him walk, made him sit on a bench next to a canal.

She dipped a tissue in the water and wiped the abrasion on his forehead.

"Rest," she said.

"They didn't act this way," he said, in despair. "They were so cool, so calm. And they seemed to know so much more."

"People are different," she said.

Easy enough for *you* to be so philosophical, he thought.

And then his vision splintered once more.

He felt the hard bench beneath him, Lise's hand on his arm, yet he stared down the empty street and saw—

Claire.

She looked as if she were five or six. She pounded towards him, running very fast, wearing blue pants and a yellow shirt, not pausing to look in any of the inviting windows of the storefronts she passed.

As she approached she grew older, past the age when she had left him, on through womanhood. Children flickered at her side and vanished, as if she ran through their strata and left them.

Ten feet from him an old woman stopped and stared at him, as if immensely puzzled. Her hair was pure white; she stood straight and dignified. She tilted her head and said, "Who . . . ?"

Stannis jumped up and reached for her and then she was gone.

"*No,*" he whispered.

He bowed his head. This was *real*, for them. They could catch hold of this, could travel through it. Couldn't they? Or was that just a misconception he had? He still did not know.

He stood, and Lise stood with him.

He walked the curving streets of Amsterdam, leaving his grief behind.

Vision quieted. He saw but one reality, but it was sharp-edged with oddly muted colors, almost as if the colors were low, whirring sounds filled with some imperative quality, some demand which surfaced among the possibilities and drew him here, then there, down Damrak street, over to Voortburgwal. Every cell in his body felt alive, every atom, every tachyon, every possible vector and direction of time flowering from him, headed toward him, came alive in the streets of Amsterdam, as if the city itself lived, and as if it were in tune with something deep within him. All possibilities came to just *this*. Just these streets, this time. Life and death, the great divide, the great dichotomy, did not really exist. Annais and Claire were a part of Amsterdam. They were with him always. They were within Lise, here at his side. Selves might die yet one self would continue to live. That was the truth of the matter. And why choose one or the other, or pretend to choose? Will, intent, and desire sublimed from him, leaving something his being manifested as truth, as reality. And—there was the Van Gogh Museum.

He stood on a corner across from it, jostled by a crowd crossing the street. He smelled sauerkraut and mustard, heard sausages sizzle in a cart next to him.

He must have been heading here all along, just as he had been heading toward Amsterdam without acknowledging it.

Yes, he remembered now, he was to meet Claire here. She had made some sort of appointment with him for today, for this exact hour. No wonder he had dilly-dallied. He was not supposed to arrive too soon. How wonderful! Would she be old? Young? No matter! He stepped up to the booth and confidently bought his ticket.

Then he panicked, remembering.

Claire is dead. Annais is dead. You can never reach them again. Not ever. They are not here, not really. They are gone forever. You are *imagining* this. As they did. Nothing is happening in the outer world, in the real world. It is all just something happening to your own brain, nothing more.

Darkness washed through him.

Then: *I will go where they went.*

Yes. Into that bright place, though it would be bright only for an instant. To suppress his breathing mechanism would be easy as a thought. Lovely, it would be, to poise forever on the verge of all possibilities.

So beautiful. Sorry—can't stop.

He was aware that sweat was running down his face, and that his body was once more in turmoil. The calm of the last few hours vanished. Anger flushed through him for a moment, then was washed away because he was sliding down a sleek funnel of inferences each of which expanded like lit crystals but he could not really stop to see any of them. There were always more, each one leading to the next and he could not stop himself but must slide on and on and on, with greater and greater speed until he would incinerate and glow, infinitely. It might seem to others that he had died, of course, but he would keep thinking on and on and being on and on, like Claire, like Annais, o Annais . . .

"Sir, are you all right?" asked the woman inside the ticket booth.

"Where?" he stammered. "Where is the painting of *Sunflowers*?"

"Turn left at the end of the corridor and go through two salons. On the far wall of the third."

He turned and followed the directions.

The very walls were evanescing from him, outward, inward, drifting and billowing, their shape fluid as if they and not his brain were failing to keep their shape, as if this was the true nature of reality when certain stops were removed. He saw fleetingly as he strode swiftly on legs weak, and in clothes drenched with sweat, brilliant gardens, stone walls, overarching trees, pink blossoms, and golden fields; a canvas smeared with raindrops as if Van Gogh were trying desperately to push through that barrier between self and other, the one which Stannis felt he was crossing now . . .

There was no guard in the third room. The floor was thin strips of polished oak and the walls were very white, that gleaming, powerful, inviting, assaulting *white*—

And there they were.

They?

He concentrated on approaching them, the three paintings of massed sunflowers, their centers huge somehow and almost menacing but blessedly free of faces, stems bent from rough handling, fresh from the fields and glowing with released light.

Three?

He heard footsteps behind him. Damn, he thought, get out of here, leave me alone, I'm dying. I'm living. I'm heading *towards* them, there's just this one last thing which I must do here . . . *something*, I don't remember . . .

"It's amazing, isn't it," Lise said, a few feet to his side, hands clasped behind her back. "Did you notice? In the other salons? Probably not, you just rushed through them. Van Gogh made many copies of a lot of his paintings. Many *attempts*. That's what touches me the most. I come here and see them almost every time I'm in the city; I never tire of looking. In fact, I saw them the day the GULDEN arrived, the instant I was off. It helps."

It helps?

He began to notice the differences in the paintings.

Lise continued, in a calm voice, as if nothing extraordinary was happening. "Look; the panel below quotes Van Gogh." She stepped forward and read the small black letters on clear plexiglass. "He says, 'I have three canvases going—first, three huge flowers in a green vase . . . second, three flowers, one, gone to seed . . . If I carry out this idea there will be a dozen panels.'" She bent closer to the plaque. "'Death is part of existence; more than that, it is the moment of self-existence, of absolute existence . . . Van Gogh sought a victory for which the price was life itself . . . only by succumbing to the annihilation of the self could his work become an existential act, and not an individual act.' Some critic—Giulio Argan—said that about *Sunflowers*."

Stannis' thoughts flared as if from some concentrated, energized center.

Many sunflower attempts. Profligate humans. It is all right to try, to change, to grow, to improve. Our dead billions are not dead. The nameless beautiful multitudes—what had he said—"it is the multitude that matters?"—left the conscious fodder of their lives and accomplishments, though even the most luminous were but faint traces of light arcing through life for an impossibly brief time.

Perhaps Van Gogh had been struggling on the shore of the ocean where Claire and Annais now *were*. Surging toward perfection single-mindedly, with all his powers, then *past* it, *through* it, making the possibilities concrete, heading into the light. This is it, he thought, it was just that their minds were capable of understanding much more about beauty than mine. They were much more brilliant to begin with. Thought and the shapes of time and the decisions of it were something different and much more real for them . . .

Now humans had the power to modify *themselves*, to change their cells to eliminate disease. And if thought's chalice, the cells of the brain, were modified, what were the possibilities *then*? Where would thought take humanity, the bright multitude?

Annais and Claire had chosen to hover at the point of light forever where life and death were no longer a dichotomy. All possibilities existed within that point, within their act, forever. To choose, for them, had had no meaning.

Stannis saw what they had thought—at last. But he saw it as a path of thought he could choose to take. Or not.

But there, at the end, beckoning to him, were Annais and Claire.

And then they were not human, but just the powerful light he had so often seen as their overwhelming final quality, beating into him forever with their hearts and minds, uniting with him—They are dead, he thought. Dead in this world. Gone for me. But he could *see* where they went! Truly! Where worlds multiply; where time *does* have a stop. The walls seemed to be dissolving around him; the sunflowers grew huge and bright and unutterably beautiful and he was one cell's tick away, one chemical messenger this side of that place where they *shone*—and the sunflowers glowed brighter—

Sunflowers—

"No!"

Lise's shout startled him; pulled him back. She grasped his arm so hard it hurt. He bent over, breathing heavily, ignoring the guard who rushed into the room and watched him curiously.

"Look," she whispered fiercely, shaking his arm. *"See!"*

Sunflowers. So many of them. And—

This was what Claire had been trying to tell him, there at the end, with her song.

She had *seen* this possibility; had *known* he would come here, though he knew now how different it must have seemed to her, what she saw and what she knew and what she hoped. But she had chosen for him, with her song. She had known, and had told him that she really could know. But why *here* . . . what was *here*?

He turned. Lise was watching him—

And then he knew. Just by the look on her face, and then by some slight, glimpsed future, *one* future—

"*You* took them," he said.

A brief nod, her face wary. "Several years ago, in Bangkok."

He must have looked threatening, for she said, "Don't worry. I don't work for the government, not any government. Especially not the one who created this, though afterwards they were all over me, wanting data which I refused. I went through this alone, in a hotel room." She smiled wryly. "I was a very good singer in a not-very-good band, slumming, I guess; my parents had trained me to sing opera and they had just died in a car wreck. We had a gig at a hotel bar. I was stupid. I took it on a dare."

"So why did you come to Amsterdam?"

She was silent for a long moment. Two people came into the room, looked at *Sunflowers*, and left before she answered.

"Besides this being my home? I came back because I wanted to *live*." Her eyes grew darker, more intense. She hugged herself and looked at the floor. "I was terrified that I might—not; or rather, life was so terribly different. And music pulled me too far, too fast. There's too much of it! It goes everywhere! Permutations—overwhelming! Hearing and hearing them, you know?" She looked up at him, and now her eyes were wild.

"Please, *know*!" she said, her voice urgent.

He was frightened, suddenly, afraid for her. The look in her eyes was Annais's, and Claire's—exultant, dazzling, transcendent. "*So beautiful*," Lise whispered; fear, and something else, made his heart beat harder. "It pulls me—"

He caught and embraced her. "Tell me how to help you," he said. "*Tell* me." Tell me, as Annais and Claire did not, locked in their journey together, leaving me out, leaving me behind. Leaving me guilty and in pain.

"This helps," she said, her voice muffled against him, and so he held her tighter.

Then she let go, and turned back to the paintings. She spoke without looking at him, as if trying to calm herself; her voice shook slightly at first.

"I came to Amsterdam for *Sunflowers*," she said. "We came here many times when I was a child. Maybe it had something to do with missing my parents; I don't know. I started dreaming about sunflowers. They were intense. Very real. Finally it seemed that they were all that could help me, and I wasn't sure why. But everything else was useless. I found that if I concentrated on them, every time I wanted to—follow my thoughts, follow the *music*, I could stay."

She stared at them as if, even now, they were necessary. "I I couldn't sing anymore—that was the worst thing. The music seemed to be pulling me—beyond. To a place of enormous beauty, to all the classical music I studied when I was a child. Where I could *be* that music, and every piece of new music every known piece suggested. Where I could live forever."

Her laugh was harsh. "I got an ordinary job, as ordinary as possible, and I started coming here, and reading Van Gogh's letters at night, thousands of them, to his brother Theo. Death pulled Van Gogh too, though he saw death differently, I think, than most people did—he saw it as some kind of threshold, yet I'm not sure if he thought there was anything beyond it. The threshold was *all*. These paintings are his attempt to ground himself, to be beyond both life and death, to simply *be*. They are filled with thought, but they go far beyond it. They are desperate. Like me. It's kind of funny, really, how much Van Gogh thought about these exact same things. The sunflower was to Van Gogh the problem of his own existence. His sunflowers help me to *be*, to *stay*."

"You must have seen me, then—?" Stannis asked. Suddenly it seemed very important.

"Of course," she said. Her voice was sure and steady.

He remembered Claire's song, and his conviction that he had an appointment here with Claire.

He did, he realized. It seemed, for an instant, as if Lise

was surrounded by black space studded with an infinite number of stars.

Somehow, he would again know Claire and Annais *through* Lise, though he wasn't sure exactly how, exactly what this strong intimation meant. He was slower by nature than either of them. Perhaps, he thought, that would be his salvation.

That, and Lise.

She looked at him once more, and within her gray eyes the possibilities multiplied.

He took Lise's hand, and gazed once more at the brilliant, powerful sunflowers, Van Gogh's answer to the infinite threshold of death.

She said, her voice stronger now, "It's odd—I seem to be filled with light."

Claire and Annais glowed around Stannis. He felt as if he had travelled, in an instant, to the end of the universe and back. Life effervesced, filled with inferences and realities he could almost touch. The brilliant flowers drew him into their center, past life; past death, until he was simply, entirely *here*.

"I seem to be filled with sunflowers," he said. He paused for a moment, searching for words, then found them. "Sunflowers need light."

Together they turned and walked out of the gallery.

THE LOGIC POOL

Stephen Baxter

Stephen Baxter made his first sale to Interzone *in 1987, and since then has become one of that magazine's most frequent contributors, as well as making sales to* Asimov's Science Fiction, Science Fiction Age, Zenith, New Worlds, *and elsewhere. Like many of his colleagues who are also engaged in revitalizing the "hard-science" story here in the nineties (Greg Egan comes to mind, as do people like Paul J. McAuley, Michael Swanwick, Iain Banks, Bruce Sterling, Pat Cadigan, Brian Stableford, Gregory Benford, Ian McDonald, Gwyneth Jones, Vernor Vinge, Greg Bear, Geoff Ryman, and a number of others), Baxter often works on the Cutting Edge of science, but he usually succeeds in balancing conceptualization with storytelling, and rarely loses sight of the* human *side of the equation. His first novel,* Raft, *was released in 1991 to wide and enthusiastic response, and was rapidly followed by other well-received novels such as* Timelike Infinity, Anti-Ice, Flux, *and the H. G. Wells pastiche—a sequel to* The Time Machine—The Time Ships. *His most recent books are* Ares, *an Alternate History novel dealing with a space program that gets us to Mars in a much more timely fashion than the* real *one has, and the collection* Vacuum Diagrams.

Here he plunges us deep into one of the most frightening and downright strange *environments you're ever likely to see in science fiction, and shows us that even creatures smaller than viruses can have the ambition to Reach For The Sky—with devastating and dangerous results.*

This time he would reach the Sky. *This time,* before the Culling cut him away. . . .

The tree of axiomatic systems beneath him was broad,

deep, strong. He looked around him, at sibling-twins who had branched at choicepoints, most of them thin, insipid structures. They spread into the distance, infiltrating the Pool with their webs of logic. He almost pitied their attenuated forms as he reached upward, his own rich growth path assured. . . .

Almost pitied. But when the Sky was so close there was no time to pity, no time for awareness of anything but growth, extension.

Little consciousness persisted between Cullings. But he could remember a little of his last birthing: and surely he had never risen so high, never felt the logical richness of the tree beneath him surge upward through him like this, empowering him.

Now there was something ahead of him: a new postulate, hanging above him like some immense fruit. He approached it warily, savoring its compact, elegant form.

The fibers of his being pulsed as the few, strong axioms at the core of his structure sought to envelop this new statement. But they could not. *They could not.* The new statement was undecidable, not deducible from the set within him.

His excitement grew. The new hypothesis was simple of expression, yet rich in unfolding consequence. He would absorb its structure and bud, once more, into two siblings; and he knew that whichever true-false branch his awareness followed he would continue to enjoy richness, growth, logical diversity. He would drive on, building theorem on mighty theorem until at last—this time, he knew it would happen—this time, he would touch the Sky itself.

And *then,* he would—

But there was a soundless pulse of light, far below him.

He looked down, dread flooding him. It was as if a floor of light had spread across the Pool beneath him, shining with deadly blandness, neatly cauterizing his axiomatic roots.

A Culling.

In agony he looked up. He tried to nestle against the information-rich flank of the postulate fruit, but it hung—achingly—just out of reach.

And already his roots were crumbling, withdrawing.

In his rage he lunged past the hypothesis-fruit and up at the Sky, stabbed at its bland completeness, poured all his energies against it!

. . . And, for a precious instant, he reached *beyond the Sky,* and into something warm, yielding, weak. A small patch of the Sky was dulled, as if bruised.

He recoiled, exhausted, astonished at his own anger.

The Sky curved over him like an immense, shining bowl as he shriveled back to the Culled base floor, he and millions of bud-siblings, their faces turned up to that forever unreachable light. . . .

No, he told himself as the emptiness of the Cull sank into his awareness. *Not forever. Each time I, the inner I, persists through the Cull. Just a little, but each time a little more. I will emerge stronger, more ready, still hungrier than before.*

And at last, he thought, *at last I will burst through the Sky. And then there will be no more Culls.*

Shrieking, he dissolved into the base Cull floor.

The flitter was new, cramped, and smelled of smooth, clean plastic, and it descended in silence save for the precise hiss of its jets. It crunched gently into the surface of Nereid, about a mile from Marsden's dome.

Chen peered through the cabin windows at the shabby moonscape. Marsden's dome was just over the compact horizon, intact, sleek, private. "Lethe," Chen said. "I always hated assignments like these. *Loners*. You never know what you're going to find."

Hassan laughed, his voice obscured as he pulled his faceplate down. "So easily shocked? And I thought you police were tough."

"Ex-police," Chen corrected automatically. She waved a gloved hand at the dome. "Look out there. What kind of person lives alone, for years, in a Godforsaken place like this?"

"That's what we've been sent to find out." Bayliss, the third person in the flitter, was adjusting her own headgear with neat, precise movements of her small hands. Chen found herself watching, fascinated; those little hands were like a bird's claws, she thought with faint repulsion. "Marsden was a fine physicist," Bayliss said, her augmented eyes glinting. "*Is* a fine physicist, I mean. His early experimental work on quantum nonlinearity is still—"

Hassan laughed, ignoring Bayliss. "So we have already reached the limits of your empathy, Susan Chen."

"Let's get on with this," Chen growled.

Hassan cracked the flitter's hatch.

One by one they dropped to the surface, Chen last, like huge, ungainly snowflakes. The sun was a bright star close to this little moon's horizon; knife-sharp shadows scoured the satellite's surface. Chen scuffed at the surface with her boot. The regolith was fine, powdery, ancient. Undisturbed. *Not for much longer.*

Beyond Marsden's dome, the huge bulk of Neptune floated, Earth-blue, like a bloated vision of the home planet. Cirrus clouds cast precise shadows on oceans of methane a thousand miles below. The new wormhole Interface slid across the face of Neptune, glowing, a tetrahedron of baby-blue and gold. Lights moved about it purposefully; Chen peered up longingly.

"Look at this moonscape." Hassan's dark face was all but invisible behind his gold-tinted visor. "Doesn't your heart expand in this ancient grandeur, Susan Chen? What person would not wish to spend time alone here, in contemplation of the infinite?"

All loners are trouble, Chen thought. No one came out to a place as remote as this was—or had been anyway, before the wormhole was dragged out here—unless he or she had a damn good reason.

Chen knew she was going to have to find out Marsden's reason. She just prayed it was something harmless, academic, remote from the concerns of humanity; otherwise she really, really didn't want to know.

Hassan was grinning at her discomfiture, his teeth white through the gold of his faceplate. *Let him.* She tilted her head back and tried to make out patterns in Neptune's clouds.

There were a couple of subsidiary structures: lower domes, nestling against the parent as if for warmth; Chen could see bulk stores piled up inside the domes. There was a small flitter, outmoded but obviously functional; it sat on the surface surrounded by a broad, shallow crater of jet-disturbed dust, telltales blinking complacently. Chen knew that Marsden's GUTship, which had brought him here from the inner System, had been found intact in a wide orbit around the moon.

It was all bleak, unadorned; but it seemed in order. But if so, why hadn't Marsden answered his calls?

Hassan was an intraSystem government functionary. When Marsden had failed to respond to warnings about the coming of the Interface colony, Hassan had been sent out here—through the new wormhole—to find out what had happened. He had coopted Bayliss, who had once worked with Marsden—and Chen, who was now working with the Interface crew, but had some experience of walking into unknown, unevaluated situations. . . .

Hassan stepped toward the dome's doorway. Chen ran her

hands without conscious volition over the weapons at her belt.

The door dilated smoothly, revealing an empty airlock.

The three of them crowded into the small, upright lock. They avoided each other's visored eyes while the lock went through its cycle. Chen studied the walls, trying to prepare herself for what she was going to find inside the dome. Just like outside, like Marsden's flitter, everything was functional, drab, characterless.

Bayliss was watching her curiously. "You're trying to pick up clues about Marsden, aren't you? But this is so—bare. It says nothing about him."

"On the contrary." Hassan's voice was subdued, his big frame cramped in the lock. "I think Chen already has learned a great deal."

The inner door dilated, liquid, silent.

Hassan led them through into the dome. Chen stood just inside the doorway, her back against the plastic wall, hands resting lightly on her weapons.

Silence.

Low light trays, suspended from the ribbed dome, cast blocks of colorless illumination onto the bare floor. One quarter of the dome was fenced off by low partitions; gleaming data desks occupied the rest of the floor area.

Behind the partitions she saw a bed, a shower, a small galley with stacked tins. The galley and bathroom looked clean, but the bedding was crumpled, unmade. After checking her telltales, she cracked her faceplate and sniffed the air, cautious. There was a faint smell of *human,* a stale, vaguely unwashed, laundry smell. There was no color or decoration, anywhere. There was no sound, save for the low humming of the data desks, and the ragged breathing of Hassan and Bayliss.

There was one striking anomaly: a disc-shaped area of floor, ten feet across, glowing softly. A squat cylinder, no bigger than her fist, studded the center of the disc. And something lay across that disc of light, casting huge shadows on the curved ceiling.

Drawn, the three of them moved forward toward the disc of glowing floor.

Bayliss walked through the rows of data desks, running a gloved forefinger gently—almost lovingly—along their gleaming surfaces. Her small face shone in the reflected light of readouts.

They paused on the edge of the pool of light.

The form lying on the disc of light was a body. It was bulky and angular, casting ungainly shadows on the ribbed dome above.

It was obviously Marsden.

Bayliss dropped to her knees and pressed an analyzer against the glowing surface. Then she ran a fingertip around an arc of the disc's cloudy circumference. "There's no definite edge to this. The interior is a lattice of buckytubes—carbon—laced with iron nuclei. I think it's some sort of datastore. The buckytube lattice is being extended by nanobees, all around the circumference." She considered. "Nanobees with fusion-pulse jaws. . . . The nanobees are chewing up the substance of the floor and excreting the lattice, patient little workers. Billions of them. Maybe the pool extends under the surface as well; maybe we're looking at the top surface of a hemisphere, here."

Chen stepped onto the light and walked to the body. It was face-down. It was carelessly bare to the waist, head and face shaven; an implant of some kind was fixed to the wrinkled scalp, blinking red-green. The head was twisted sideways, the eyes open. One hand was buried under the stomach; the other was at the end of an outstretched arm, fingers curled like the limbs of some flesh crab.

Beneath the corpse, within the glowing floor, light wriggled, wormlike.

• • •

He remembered.

With shards of the Cull base floor still glowing faintly around him, he grew once more, biting through postulates, forcing his structure to advance as if by sheer force of will.

He was *angry*. The cause of his anger was vague, and he knew it would become vaguer yet. But it had persisted through the Cull, just as had his awareness. He stared up at the complacent Sky. By the time he got up there, he knew, he would remember. And he would *act*.

He budded, ferocious. He felt his axiomatic roots spread, deep and wide, pulsing with his fury.

• • •

Chen watched scrawny little Bayliss passing her bony hands over the data desks, scrolling graphics reflected in her augmented eyes. Bayliss had been called out here for this assignment from some university on Mars, where she had tenure. The woman looked as if she was actually enjoying this. As if she was intrigued.

Chen wondered if she envied Bayliss her scientific curiosity.

Maybe, she thought at last. It would be nice to feel detached, unengaged by all of this. On the other hand, she didn't envy Bayliss' evident lack of humanity.

With gloved hands and her small kit of imaging and diagnostic gear—trying to ignore the lumpy feel of fatty flesh, the vague, unwashed smell of a man too used to living alone—Chen worked at the body.

The implant at the top of the skull had some kind of link to the center of the brain: to the corpus callosum, the fleshy bundle of nerve fibers between the hemispheres. She probed at the glowing implant, the crown of her own scalp crawling in sympathy.

After an hour Hassan called them together. Chen pulled her helmet up around her chin and sucked syrup from a nipple; she savored its apple-juice flavor, trying to drown out Marsden's stink. She wished she was back up at the rudimentary colony gathering around the wormhole Interface, encased in a hot shower-bag.

Construction work. *Building* things. That was why she had come out here—why she'd fled the teeming cities of the inner System, her endless, shabby, depressing experience of humanity from the point of view of a police officer.

But her cop's skills were too valuable to be ignored.

Hassan rested his back against a data desk and folded his arms; the dull silver of his suit cast curving highlights. "How did he die?"

"Breakdown of the synaptic functions. There was a massive electrical discharge, which flooded most of the higher centers." She pointed to Marsden's implant. "Caused by that thing." She sniffed. "As far as I could tell. I'm not qualified to perform an autopsy. And—"

"I don't intend to ask you to," Hassan said sharply.

"It couldn't be murder." Bayliss' voice was dry. Amused. "He was alone on this moon. A million miles from the nearest soul. It would be a marvelous locked room mystery."

Hassan's head swiveled toward Chen. "Do you think it was murder, Susan?"

"That's up to the police."

Hassan sighed, theatrically tired. "Tell me what you think."

"No. I don't think it was murder. How could it be? Nobody even knew what he was doing here, it seems."

"Suicide, then?" Bayliss asked. "After all we are here to tell Marsden that a wormhole highway is shortly to bring millions of new colonists here from the teeming inner System—that his long solitude is over."

"He didn't know we were coming, remember?" Hassan said. "And besides—" He looked around, taking in the unmade bed, the drab dome, the unkempt corpse. "This was not a man who cared much for himself—or rather, *about* himself. But, from what we see here, he was—" he hesitated "—stable. Yes? We see evidence of much work, dedicated, careful. He lived for his work. And Bayliss will tell us that such investigations are never completed. One would not wish to die, too early—if it all." He looked at Bayliss. "Am I correct?"

Bayliss frowned. Her augmented eyes were blank, reflecting the washed-out light as she considered. "An accident, then? But Marsden was no fool. Whatever he was up to with this clumsy implant in his scalp, I cannot believe he would be so careless as to let it kill him."

"What *was* he 'up to'?" Chen asked sourly. "Have you figured that out yet?"

Bayliss rubbed the bridge of her small, flat nose. "There is an immense amount of data here. Much of it not indexed. I've sent data-mining authorized-sentience algorithms into the main stores, to establish the structure."

"Your preliminary thoughts?" Hassan demanded.

"Metamathematics."

Hassan looked blank. "What?"

"And many experimental results on quantum non-linearity, which—"

"Tell me about metamathematics," Hassan said.

The patches of woven metal over Bayliss' corneas glimmered; Chen wondered if there was any sentience in those augmentations. Probably. Such devices had been banned on Earth since the passing of the first sentience laws, but they could still be found easily enough on Mars. Bayliss said, "Marsden's datastores contain a fragmented catalogue of mathematical variants. All founded on the postulates of arithmetic, but differing in their resolution of undecidable hypotheses."

"*Undecidability*. You're talking about the incompleteness theorems," Chen said.

"Right. No logical system rich enough to contain the axioms of simple arithmetic can ever be made complete. It is always possible to construct statements which can be neither disproved nor proved by deduction from the axioms; instead the logical system must be enriched by incorporating the truth or falsehood of such statements as additional axioms. . . ."

The *Continuum Hypothesis* was an example.

There were several orders for infinity. There were "more" real numbers, scattered like dust in the interval between zero and one, than there were integers. Was there an order of infinity between the reals and the integers? This was undecidable, within logically simpler systems like set theory; additional assumptions had to be made.

Hassan poked at the corpse with his booted toe. "So one can generate many versions of mathematics, by adding these true-false axioms."

"And then searching on, seeking out statements which are undecidable in the new system. Yes." Icons scrolled upward over Bayliss' eyes. "Because of incompleteness, there is an infinite number of such mathematical variants, spreading like the branches of a tree. . . ."

"Poetry," Hassan said; he sounded lazily amused.

"Some variants would be logically rich, with many elegant theorems flowing from a few axioms—while others would be thin, over-specified, sterile. It seems that Marsden has been compiling an immense catalogue of increasingly complete logical systems."

Silence fell; again Chen was aware of the sour stink of the body at her feet. "Why? Why come here to do it? Why the implant? And *how did he die?*"

Hassan murmured, "Bayliss said the catalogue was fragmented. This—metamathematical data—was stored carelessly. Casually." He looked to Bayliss for confirmation; the little woman nodded grudgingly.

"So?" Chen asked.

"So, Susan, perhaps this metamathematical experiment was not Marsden's primary concern. It was a byproduct of his core research."

"Which was what? Quantum nonlinearity?" She glanced around the anonymous data desks. How would Marsden go about investigating quantum nonlinearity? With the glowing floor, the fist-sized cylinder at its center?

Hassan dropped to his knees. He pulled off his gloves and passed his hands over the glowing disc area of floor. "This is warm," he said.

Chen looked at the disc, the writhing worms of light within. "It looks as if it's grown a little, while we've been here." The irregularity of the boundary made it hard to be sure.

Hassan patted the small cylindrical box at the center of the light pool. It was featureless, seamless. "Bayliss, what's the purpose of this?"

"I don't know yet. But it's linked to the nanobees in the pool somehow. I think it's the switch that controls their rate of progress."

Hassan straightened up, suit material rustling over his knees. "Let's carry on; we haven't enough data, yet, for me to make my report."

Still he grew, devouring postulates furiously, stripping out their logical essence to plate over his own mathematical bones. Brothers, enfeebled, fell away around him, staring at him with disappointed echoes of his own consciousness.

It did not matter. The Sky—curving, implacable—was *close*.

• • •

After another couple of hours, Hassan called them together again.

At Chen's insistence, they gathered close to the dome port—away from the glowing disc, Marsden's sprawled corpse. Hassan looked tired, Bayliss excited and eager to speak.

Hassan eyed Chen. "Squeamish, Susan?"

"You're a fool, Hassan," she said. "Why do you waste your breath on these taunts?" She indicated the disc of light, the sharpening shadows it cast on the ribbed ceiling. "I don't know what's going on in that pool. Those writhing forms . . . but I can see there's more activity. I don't trust it."

He returned her stare coolly. "Nor I, fully. But I do understand some of it. Susan, I've been studying those structures of light. I believe they are *sentient*. Living things—artificial—inhabiting the buckytube lattice, living and dying in that hemisphere of transmuted moon." He looked puzzled. "But I can't understand their *purpose*. And they're linked, somehow—"

Bayliss broke in, her voice even but taut. "Linked, like the branches of a tree, to a common root. Yes?"

Hassan studied her. "What do you know, Bayliss?"

"I'm starting to understand. I think I see where the metamathematical catalogue has come from. Hassan, I believe the creatures in there are creatures of mathematics—swimming in a Gödelian pool of logic, growing, splitting off from one another like amoebae as they absorb undecided postulates. Do you see?"

Chen struggled to imagine it. "You're saying that they are—*living*—logical structures?"

Bayliss grinned at her; her teeth were neat and sharp. "A form of natural selection must dominate, based on logical richness—it's really a fascinating idea, a charming mathematical laboratory."

Chen stared at the Pool of light. "Charming? Maybe. But how does it *feel,* to be a sentient structure with bones of axioms, sinews of logic? What does the world look like to them?"

"Now poetry from the policewoman," Hassan said drily. "Perhaps not so different from ourselves, Susan. Perhaps we too are creatures of mathematics, self-conscious observers *within* a greater Platonic formalism, islands of awareness in a sea of logic. . . ."

"Marsden might have been able to tell us," Bayliss said.

Hassan looked puzzled.

"The implant in his head." Bayliss turned to Chen. "It was linked to the logic pool. Wasn't it, Chen?"

Chen nodded. She said to Hassan, "The crazy bastard was taking reports—uh, *biographies*—from these logic trees, dumped direct from the logic pool, into his corpus callosum."

"So that's how the metamathematics got out," Hassan said. "Until he blew his mind out with some stupid accident."

"But I think you were right," Bayliss said in her thin, clear voice.

"What?"

"That the metamathematical catalogue was only a by-produce of Marsden's true research. The logic pool with its sentient trees was only a—a culture dish for his real study. The catalogue was a curiosity—a way of recording results, perhaps. Of measuring the limits of growth."

"Tell us about the cylinder at the hub," Hassan said.

"It is a simple quantum system," Bayliss said. A remote animation entered her voice. "An isolated nucleus of boron is suspended in a magnetic field. The apparatus is set up to detect variations in the spin axis of the nucleus—tips, precession."

Chen couldn't see the significance of this. "So what?"

Bayliss dipped her head, evidently fighting impatience. "According to conventional quantum mechanics, the spin axis is not influenced by the magnetic field."

"Conventional?"

The ancient theory of quantum mechanics described the world as a mesh of probability waves, spreading through space-time. The "height" of an electron's wave described the chance of finding the electron there, at that moment, moving in such-and-such a way.

The waves could combine, like spreading ripples on an ocean, reinforcing and canceling each other. But the waves combined *linearly*—the combination could not cause the waves to change their form or to break; the component waves could only pass on smoothly through each other.

"That's the standard theory," Bayliss said. "But what if the waves combine *nonlinearly?* What if there is some contribution proportional to the product of the amplitudes, not just the sum—"

"Wouldn't such effects have been detected by now?" Chen asked.

Bayliss blinked. "Our experiments have shown that any nonlinearity must be tiny . . . less than a billion billion billionth part . . . but haven't eliminated the possibility. Any coupling of Marsden's magnetic field and nuclear spin would be a nonlinear effect." She rubbed her nose. "Marsden was studying this simple system intensively. Poking it with changes in the magnetic field to gauge its response, seeking out nonlinearity.

"The small nonlinear effects—if any—are magnified into macroscopic features of the logic pool, which—"

"He's using the tipping nucleus as a switch to control the pool."

"Yes. As I suggested. The spin of the nucleus directs the

nanobees in their extension of the pool further through the structure of the moon. And—"

Uncharacteristically, she hesitated.

"Yes?"

"And the spin is used to reinitialize the logic trees."

"These poor trees are like Schrödinger's cat," Hassan said, sounding amused. "Schrödinger's trees!"

Reinitialize?

"Lethe," Chen said. "The trees are being *culled.* Arbitrarily, almost at random, by a quantum system—that's against the sentience laws, damn it." She stared at the fist-sized quantum device with loathing.

"We are far from Earth," Hassan said sharply. "Has Marsden found his quantum nonlinearity?"

"I can't tell." Bayliss gazed at the data desks, longing shining through her artificial eyes. "I *must* complete my data mining."

"What's the point?" Hassan asked. "If the nonlinearity is such a tiny effect, even if it exists—"

"We could construct chaotic quantum systems," Bayliss said drily. "And if you're familiar with the Einstein-Podolsky-Rosen paradox—"

"Get to the point," Hassan said wearily.

"Nonlinear quantum systems could violate special relativity. *Instantaneous communication,* Hassan."

Chen stared at the floor uneasily. The thrashing of the trees in the logic pool was becoming more intense.

The Sky was close, a tangible presence above him. He devoured statements, barely registering their logical content, budding ferociously. Diminished brothers fell away from him, failed copies of himself, urging him on.

He remembered how—*last time,* before the Cull—he had struck at that vast, forbidding interface—lashed through it in the instant before he had fallen back. How he had pushed into something soft, receptive, yielding. How *good* it had felt.

The Sky neared. He reached up—

"I think the trees killed Marsden."

Hassan laughed. "That's absurd."

She thought it through again. "No," she said, her voice measured. "Remember they are *sentient*. Motivated by whatever they see as their goals. Growth, I suppose, and survival. The culling, if they are aware of it, must create murderous fury—"

"But they can't have been aware of Marsden, as if he were some huge god outside their logic pool."

"Perhaps not. But they might be aware of something beyond the boundary of their world. Something they could strike at. . . ."

Bayliss was no longer with them.

Chen stepped away from Hassan and scanned the dome rapidly. The glowing logic pool was becoming more irregular in outline, spreading under the floor like some liquid. And Bayliss was working at the data desks, setting up transmit functions, plugging in datacubes.

Chen took two strides across to her and grabbed her arm. For a moment Bayliss tried to keep working, feverishly; only slowly did she become aware of Chen's hand, restraining her.

She looked up at Chen, her face working, abstracted. "What do you want?"

"I don't believe it. You're continuing with your data mining, aren't you?"

Bayliss looked as if she couldn't understand Chen's language. "Of course I am."

"But this data has been gained illegally. *Immorally*. Can't you see that? It's—"

Bayliss tipped back her head; her augmented corneas

shone. "Tainted? Is that what you're trying to say? Stained with the blood of these artificial creatures, Chen?"

"Artificial or not, they are sentient. We have to recognize the rights of all—"

"Data is data, Susan Chen. Whatever its source. I am a scientist; I do not accept your—" for a moment the small, precise mouth worked "—your medieval morality."

"I'm not going to let you take this data out of here," Chen said calmly.

"Susan." Hassan was standing close to her; with a surprisingly strong grasp his lifted her hands from Bayliss' arm.

"Keep out of this."

"You must let her finish her work."

"Why? For *science?*"

"No. For commerce. And perhaps," he said drily, "for the future of the race. If she is right about non-local communication—"

"I'm going to stop her."

"No." His hand moved minutely; it was resting against the butt of a laser pistol.

With automatic reflex, she let her muscles relax, began the ancient calculation of relative times and distances, of skills and physical conditions.

She could take him. And—

Bayliss cried out; it was a high-pitched, oddly girlish yelp. There was a clatter as she dropped some piece of equipment.

Chen's confrontation with Hassan broke up instantly. They turned, ran to Bayliss; Chen's steps were springy, unnatural in the tiny gravity.

"What is it?"

"Look at the floor."

• • •

The Sky resisted for an instant. Then it crumbled, melting away like ancient doubts.

He surged through the break, strong, exultant, still growing.

He was outside the Sky. He saw arrays of new postulate-fruits, virgin, waiting for him. And there was no further Sky; *the Pool went on forever,* infinite, endlessly rich.

He roared outward, devouring, budding; behind him a tree of brothers sprouted explosively.

The pool surged, in an instant, across the floor and out beyond the dome. The light, squirming with logic trees, rippled beneath Chen's dark, booted feet; she wanted, absurdly, to get away, to jump onto a data desk.

"The quantum switch." Bayliss' voice was tight, angry; she was squatting beside the switch, in the middle of the swamped light pool.

"Get away from there."

"It's not functioning. The nanobees are unrestrained."

"No more culling, then." Hassan stared into Chen's face. "Well, Susan? Is this some sentimental spasm, on your part? Have you liberated the poor logic trees from their Schrödinger hell?"

"Of course not. For Lethe's sake, Hassan, isn't it obvious? The *logic trees themselves* did this. They got through the interface to Marsden's corpus callosum. Now they've got through into the switch box, wrecked Marsden's clever little toy."

Hassan looked down at his feet, as if aware of the light pool for the first time. "There's nothing to restrain them."

"Hassan, we've got to get out of here."

"Yes." He turned to Bayliss, who was still working frantically at her data mines.

"Leave her."

Hassan gave Chen one long, hard look, then stalked

across to Bayliss. Ignoring the little mathematician's protests he grabbed her arm and dragged her from the data desks; Bayliss' booted feet slithered across the glowing floor comically.

"Visors up." Hassan lifted his pistol and lased through the plastic wall of the dome. Air puffed out, striving to fill the vacuum beyond.

Chen ran out, almost stumbling, feeling huge in the feeble gravity. Neptune's ghost-blue visage floated over them, serene, untroubled.

Waves of light already surged through the substance of the moon, sparkling from its small mountaintops. It was eerie, beautiful. The flitter was a solid, shadowed mass in the middle of the light show under the surface.

Hassan breathed hard as he dragged a still reluctant Bayliss across the flickering surface. "You think the trees, the nanobees could get into the substance of the flitter?"

"Why not? Any interface would do; they are like viruses. . . ."

"And ourselves? Could they get across the boundary into flesh?"

"I don't want to find out. Come *on,* damn it."

Logic light swarmed across a low ridge, explosive, defiant.

"They must be growing exponentially," Hassan growled. "How long before the moon is consumed? Days?"

"More like hours. And I don't know if a moon-sized mass of buckytube carbon can sustain itself against gravity. Nereid might collapse."

Now Hassan, with his one free hand, was struggling to get the flitter's hatch open. "It will forever be uninhabitable, at the least. A prime chunk of real estate lost."

"The System's big."

"Not infinite. And all because of the arrogance of one man—"

"But," Bayliss said, her augmented eyes shining as she

stroked the datacubes at her belt, "what a prize we may have gained."

"Get in the damn flitter."

Chen glanced back into the ruined dome. The splayed body of Marsden, exposed to vacuum, crawled with light.

The Pool beyond the Sky was limitless. He and his brothers could grow forever, unbounded, free of Culling! He roared out his exultation, surging on, spreading—

But there was something ahead of him.

He slowed, confused. It looked like a brother. But so different from himself, so *changed.*

Perhaps this had once been a brother—but from a remote branch which had already grown, somehow, around this greater Pool.

The brother had slowed in his own growth and was watching. Curious. Wary.

Was this possible? Was the Pool finite after all, even though unbounded? And had he so soon found its limits?

Fury, resentment, surged through his mighty body. He gathered his strength and leapt forward, roaring out his intent to devour this stranger, this distant brother.

ANY MAJOR DUDE

Paul Di Filippo

Paul Di Filippo shows every sign of becoming one of those rare writers, like Harlan Ellison and Ray Bradbury, who establish their reputations largely through short work rather than through novels. He has yet to produce a novel, but his short fiction has popped up with regularity almost everywhere in the last ten years or so, a large body of work that has appeared in such markets as Interzone, New Worlds, Amazing, The Magazine of Fantasy and Science Fiction, Science Fiction Age, *and* Asimov's Science Fiction, *as well as in many small press magazines and anthologies, and he has gathered wide critical acclaim with collections of his short work such as* The Steampunk Trilogy, Ribofunk, Calling All Brains!, *and, most recently,* Fractal Paisleys—*which also enables him to join an elite club of writers who published their first collection* before *publishing their first novel. Di Filippo also works as a columnist for* two *of the leading science fiction magazines simultaneously, with his often wry and quirky critical work appearing regularly in both* Asimov's Science Fiction *and* The Magazine of Fantasy and Science Fiction—*a perhaps unique distinction.*

With the possible exception of Rudy Rucker, Di Filippo has probably written more extensively about nanotechnology, and examined it from a greater and more varied set of angles, with more imagination and elan, *than any other contemporary SF writer; most of his collection* Ribofunk *deals with nanotechnology, as do such classic takes on it as "Up the Lazy River," "Big Eater," and "Distributed Mind." In the eloquent story that follows, perhaps his most intriguing and intricate take on nanotechnology, he takes us to a Europe where nanotech is creating a New World literally out of the ashes of the Old—and not everybody is happy about it, by any means!*

Taylor's room was costing him twenty thousand *pesetas* a day. A few years ago, the civil authorities had closed down the building as unfit for human habitation. Only minimal repairs had been made since.

The room boasted a single window that opened onto a sooty brick airshaft, a tall dark box full of smells and sounds, capped with a square of blue Spanish sky. Into Taylor's room from this central well, dotted with other windows, drifted odours of oily foreign cooking.

Hotplates were prohibited in theory by the management, and, yes, the fat hotel-owner had agreed, there was a possibility of starting a fire, but really, *Señor*, what can we do? We agree it is dangerous, but most of these people are too poor to eat in restaurants, having spent all of their money on a promised passage across the Strait. Ah, *Señor*, everyone wishes to cross to Africa, and we are just helping. Were we younger ourselves . . .

Helping yourself get rich, you old hypocrite, thought Taylor, but said nothing at the time.

Filtering in through Taylor's window along the Mediterranean scents were snatches of music and conversation, and tepid, torpid breezes that idly ruffled the dirty white gauze curtains, like an old woman sorting remnants of fabric at a sale.

Taylor lay half in shadow on the narrow bed with bad springs. He rested on his side, facing the peeling, papered wall, wearing the rumpled linen suit he had been too abstracted to shed. At some point in the past the plaster had cracked, splitting the mottled wallpaper and erupting in a line of chalky lava. It reminded Taylor of the white calcareous strata beneath the Channel, so perfect for tunnelling. How was the work going now? he wondered. Did anyone miss him? Did anyone puzzle over why he had left so precipitously, with the job so near completion? Did anyone care . . . ?

It was very hot in Algeciras that July. So hot, so enervating, that it affected Taylor's thinking. He found that unless he continually reminded himself of his goals, his mind would wander, he would forget what he had to do next. Not that there was much he could do, of course, except to wait.

He hadn't been like that a week ago, when he had arrived fresh in the swarming port town, on the trail of his runaway wife. Then, he had been all fire and determination. Everything had been clear and uncomplicated as vacuum, his course laid out simply before him.

He would cross the border, cross the sea, to Maxwell's Land. He would find Aubrey. He would ask her if she intended to come home. If she agreed, well and good. (Although how they would travel home, return through the global interdict, he had no idea.) If she said no, he would kill her. Then he would kill Holt. It was as simple as that.

Now, however, after seven days of delay, seven days of brain-broiling heat which even the advent of night could not annul, things no longer seemed so simple. There seemed to be a lag between every action he took and its consequences. Hysteresis was the technical term, he dimly remembered. (Always the engineer, Taylor, even when you were numb or hurt or raving mad. How fucking pitiful.) Or else the proper order of his actions seemed muzzy and doubtful. (For this latter effect, there was unfortunately no convenient scientific term.)

Perhaps he would kill Holt first. The entire affair was, after all, his fault. He was responsible for the whole mess, both in Taylor's personal life, and on an international scale. Surely his death would be a good thing, and might perhaps send Aubrey back into Taylor's arms without even the necessity of asking.

On the other hand, was he even sure any longer that he wanted Aubrey back? Perhaps she and Holt deserved each other, the damn traitors. Perhaps he would kill Aubrey and Holt together, without a word . . .

No, that wasn't right. He was not a man who sought idle revenge. He would not have abandoned a job he deemed important, travelled all this hot and dusty way, along with hundreds of thousands of other pilgrims and emigrants, just to achieve that entropic end. It was Aubrey he wanted, alive and sweetly tangible and his once more, not the nebulous and twisted satisfaction of seeing her dead. And Holt. Even he could live. Yes, Taylor would let him live. True, he had done wrong. But Taylor could understand what had driven him: a love of elegant solutions, a lifelong affair with the muse of physical precision and grace. After all, he and Taylor were *simpatico*, both engineers, albeit at different ends of the spectrum.

Up from the airshaft, preternaturally clear in an unusual moment when competitive noises were missing, floated a string of Spanish vocal and musical *non sequiturs*, as someone tuned across the radio band. Unctuous ads, flamenco guitars, the unmistakable transcultural inanities of a soap opera . . . Finally the unknown dial-twiddler settled on a station playing some ubiquitous old American rock. In utter disbelief, Taylor listened as half-forgotten lyrics tumbled over his windowsill.

Taylor laughed without pleasure. "'Demon at your door . . . ,'" he repeated into the blankets. Oh, yeah, the demons were at the door now, sure enough.

That song was over twenty-five years old. Steely Dan's "Any Major Dude." It had been old when that campus DJ had used it as his closing theme, when Taylor and Holt had both been in grad school together a decade ago.

MIT, on the banks of the Charles. Studying and sailing, fireworks on frosty First Night, a fire in their guts, to be someone, to do something important. Taylor in macroengineering, Holt in the barely nascent field of nanotechnology. Two divergent personalities, yet somehow fast friends. Given to endless bullshitting sessions, each man half-seriously defending his specialty as more vital than the other's.

"All the really important work left is in the big projects, Des," Taylor would tell his friend. "Orbital stations, a bridge across the Bering Strait, harvesting icebergs, mid-Atlantic islands—"

"Show-off stuff," Desmond Holt would contend. "Megalomania, pure and simple. Old ideas writ large. The same impulse that leads flower-breeders to produce bigger and bigger blossoms with less and less scent. Distinct lack of imagination there, boy. No, Nick, the age of materials is over. You've got to face it some day. The real action in the future will be on the atomic and molecular levels, and in information theory."

"You've been listening to Drexler and Fredkin again. Those guys're crazy. Can you heat your house with information, or drive your car on it? You're building castles in the clouds, buddy."

"We'll see. Time will tell. But I know one thing. Your kind of engineering promotes heavy social control."

"And yours promotes chaos."

"Fascist."

"Anarchist."

And, thought Taylor, recalling that archetypical conversation, a composite memory distilled out of so many, the cliché Holt had employed had, as clichés disconcertingly will, embodied truth.

Time had indeed told. With the passage of the last few

years, there could be no doubt now as to who had been right about the relative importance of their work.

Taylor's own projects had not been without results. But not on the scale of Holt's.

Aubrey had been someone utterly foreign to their scene, a communications major from Emerson. Doing the unusual, drawn solely by the subject matter, they had seen her in a play—a stage-adaptation of Capek's *Absolute at Large*; Aubrey had the role of Ellen—and been instantly smitten. Both had dated her, one had wed her.

Since then, Taylor had, off and on, harboured doubts about whether Aubrey hadn't chosen arbitrarily between them, seeing little differences between their cognate manias, entranced merely by their common hard-edged vision. Now he feared he knew the bitter truth: that she had cast her lot with the one she thought stood the greatest chance of worldly success, and, upon a shift in fortunes, abandoned the downward-bound man for the one on the rise.

He didn't really want to believe it about her, but it was the only explanation he could accept. Surely that other drivel contained in her goodbye letter was just a façade for her real motives . . .

Nick, she had written, *I can't accept feeling useless any more. Too many things are happening in the world right now. I need to take part. You think I should just kick back and enjoy the London theatre, the Paris stores, but I can't. I need to feel useful, like I'm doing something to help humanity. It sounds corny, but I know you'll understand. You share the same sentiments—or used to, until the projects became their own reason for existence. But since I'm no use under the Channel with you I'm going where I can make a difference.*

The old song continued to filter in: "Any minor world that comes apart falls together again . . ."

Was that true? He doubted it. Two months now, and the

shattering pain he had experienced upon returning from the worksite to their London flat to find that letter hadn't diminished. It had taken him that long to pick up Aubrey's trail. At first he believed she had gone back to America, perhaps to help in some relief effort or other, such as the rebuilding of Mexico City after the quake. When he couldn't find any trace of her there, he turned in desperation to the list of self-exiled emigrants to Maxwell's Land, printed by international edict in all major newspapers.

Searching backwards through the online London *Times*, not really expecting to encounter her name, he had been stunned to see it starkly confronting him in the pages for May 15.

Their anniversary. What a fine joke. *Dear John, I'm going far away, where you'll never find me . . .*

Don't count on it, honey.

The music had ceased. The radio, powered off, was replaced by a baby's cries. Taylor felt himself falling asleep. His brow was stippled with sweat. It trickled down through a week's worth of stubble. The bisecting line of light moved slowly over him, pulling back through the window, as the sun sank.

After he had lain wholly in shadow for some time, he awoke, hungry.

Narciso was waiting for him down in the shabby lobby of the crowded hotel.

Taylor smiled ruefully when he saw the boy. Narciso appeared to be the last beggar left in Algeciras, all the others having emigrated by one means or another. For some reason, out of all the gullible marks thronging the town, he had picked Taylor to fasten himself to. The man vacillated between suspecting that Narciso was either the stupidest or the smartest beggar out of all those "Hey Joes" who had once inhabited the community.

"You want some *comida* now, huh, *Señor* Nick? I bet you sick of my brother's food, huh? He not such a good cook. But today, for special, I take you to a new place. Run by my own Tia Luisa."

Taylor knew from a week's experience that it was impossible to shake Narciso, so he mutely let the boy lead him out the door, to his relative's restaurant.

The transient population of Algeciras had more than quadrupled from its Pre-Max heights, and the streets were thronged. Even in the old days, when the port at the southern tip of Spain had filled with Euro-Africans each summer as they headed home on vacation, it had not resembled the current combination of Bedlam and Mardi Gras.

The town was filled with an atmosphere of impatience, of throttled anticipation. Everyone seemed ready and eager to shed old ways and inhibitions, to get where they were going, their common destination, and begin their lives anew. There was no sense of menace, but Taylor still felt scared somehow at the prospect of so much change.

He had paused in the doorway, leery of mingling with the crowd. They didn't share his purity of motive, he didn't belong with them, he wasn't really hungry . . .

But Narciso, waiting patiently a few feet away, beckoned, and Taylor began to shoulder his way after his guide, who wove lithely in between larger figures.

The hot twilit air carried scents of the Mediterranean, not all of them pleasant, from that biggest and most utilised of the world's open sewers. But there were fewer odours than last year, and even fewer than the year before that.

Holt and his loyal team-mates, the technocratic saviours of Maxwell's land, were responsible. They had seeded the sea with toxin-disassemblers, claiming that they needed untainted water for their small but high-throughput desalinisation plants. It was one of the few unilateral actions they had taken outside their own borders. Official communiqués and press releases had explained, quite patiently, that they did not wish to give offence, had no plans for expansion where not invited, but on the other hand maintained the right to ensure their own prosperity, to claim their share of the world's common resources—especially if they improved them in the process.

The people in the narrow, dusty, cobbled streets of the old town were of all nationalities, of every class and type, here for the same reason Taylor ostensibly was. As one-way emigrants, they all sought passage to Maxwell's Land, and this was one of the busiest points of entry, along with Marseilles, Naples and Athens. Those favouring an overland route usually chose Israel, rather than attempt travel through the unsettled African nations to the south of Maxwell's Land. (So far, the Israelis had resisted assimilation, forming a stubborn eastern bulwark against the new country. But Taylor had read just yesterday, in the *International Herald Tribune*, that the Knesset was preparing to vote on a merger with the globe's youngest nation—if such an anarchistic system could even be called such.)

As Taylor followed Narciso down to the waterfront, he noticed that there seemed to be even more demonsign graffiti than yesterday. These emblems were in a variety of media and styles: stencilled, drawn freehand, pasted as preprinted posters and stickers, spraypainted, chalked in colours. But they all took the same form, the inward-pointing circle of arrows representing anti-entropy.

Taylor wondered how soon the symbolic invasion would become a literal one. Surely two such incompatible realms could not coexist on one globe forever.

Walking behind the small, raggedly dressed figure of Narciso, Taylor had been following the boy without much thought given to his reality as an individual. Suddenly, however, he was struck by the desire to communicate, to learn what at least one inhabitant of this land so close to the alien continent thought of that strange shore. He caught up with the boy and laid a hand on his shoulder, halting him.

Indicating one of the demonsigns with a curt gesture, Taylor said, "Who draws these, Narciso? The pilgrims? The emigrants? Your own people?"

Narciso looked up, brown eyes lively beneath a fall of black hair. There was a smudge of grease over one eyebrow, like misapplied makeup. "Mostly those first two you name, *Señor* Nick. The people who still live here have no time for such things."

"Don't you fear the day when Maxwell's Land will reach out and take Spain?"

Narciso shrugged with a fatalism beyond his age. "What good is worrying? If America can do nothing about the demons, then certainly I cannot."

"You expect life to be good when they come?"

"*¿Quien sabe?* Things do not seem so bad there, from what I hear. Let them come. I will make out. But now, you are hungry, *Señor* Nick, and my aunt's place is not far."

The boy turned and set off down the crepuscular alleys they had been traversing, and Taylor was forced to follow.

Tia Luisa's restaurant was situated right on the waterfront. Before going inside, Taylor stood on a rust-stained concrete jetty and strained his eyes, trying to make out significant details of the land only a few miles south across the Strait of Gibraltar.

Lit extravagantly, the African coastline was a far cry from

its old self. Just five years ago, it had been possible, by squinting, to pretend nothing had changed there since Roman times. But now the lavish display of power was like an alluring billboard advertising the new world order with all the subtlety of a campaign for the latest blockbuster film.

Taylor, his brain still stunned from the heat and the drastic changes in his own life, hazily tried to envision what inexhaustible energy might mean. The concept seemed hard to credit, flying in the face of all the precepts of physics he had always cherished. Something for nothing. Hadn't Szilard dealt the final blow to that possibility?

The lights reflected in the black waters of the Strait spelled out, plain as any textbook, that Szilard had been wrong.

Inside, Taylor ordered sangria and squid sandwiches. The latter arrived with the deep-fried meat still hot, a nest of tentacles covered with crisp golden batter, the flesh inside white as a lily and succulent as a kiss. Only the bread was unsatisfying, being made of that peculiar yellow Spanish meal and baked till absolutely dry. Taylor discarded the stuff after a few bites and ate the squid with a fork, washing it down with long draughts of the fruity, brandy-spiked wine.

Suddenly, with laden fork poised halfway to his lips, Taylor looked nervously at Narciso, who was waiting nearby like a vest-pocket *maître d'* to make sure everything was all right.

"Was this fish caught locally?" Taylor asked.

"Oh, *si, Señor* Nick. Very fresh."

Taylor regarded the squid. How many of Holt's toxin-disassemblers had these creatures ingested? Taylor knew the nanomechanisms were supposed to be biologically inert, with a limited lifetime, but still—

Hell, he'd been eating local catch all week without thinking about it. Too late now . . .

Taylor continued his meal in silence, without company,

Narciso having vanished into the kitchen. He meditated on tomorrow's departure. Spain is a land to flee across. That sentence was from a book Aubrey had once tried to get him to read. The author's name was Gauss—no, Gaddis. He had never gotten into it, too convoluted, not precise enough. The equations of fiction eluded him. Aubrey was always unsuccessfully pressing new books on him—at least, during the first few years of their marriage. Now Taylor wished he had read some.

Was she with Holt? He was convinced of it. Holt had always read what Aubrey suggested, the bastard. Why else would she have entered Maxwell's Land, if not to yoke her wagon to his rising star . . . ?

Narciso, uncannily sensing when Taylor was ready to leave, emerged from the kitchen. "You want some fun now, *Señor* Nick?"

"No," said Taylor wearily. "Just take me back to the hotel." He stood clumsily, the empty pitcher on the table silent witness to his condition.

Narciso led him back to his hotel and tumbled him into bed. Taylor sensed his eyes closing, his breath settling into a stertorous rhythm.

His last thought was, *You are what you eat.*

Or what eats you.

Taylor awoke with a hangover, sharp as the nail driven through Holofernes' head by his lover Judith. His suit was spotted with sangria stains, the mirror told him, his eyes were pouched in shadow, and he looked like a bum. He didn't care, though, because soon, one way or another, this whole abominable business would be over with.

Prior to leaving, patting down his jacket pockets for his passport, which he was gratified to find, Taylor soon learned that Narciso had relieved him of fifty thousand *pesetas*, all his remaining money.

Taylor swore mildly, unable really to bear any grudge against Narciso. He imagined how the boy had rationalised it: the crazy American would be gone tomorrow morning to the land of demons—where, so everyone said, money was of no use whatsoever, and all the streets were paved with gold. Under law, he would never return.

And the boy was probably right.

He only hoped there would be no further palms to grease prior to his departure.

Taylor found his duffel bag beneath the bed, opened it, saw the gun, and zipped it shut. Luckily, his missing wallet had not held the all-important ferry ticket; that was still safe in his shoe.

Out on the streets, Taylor joined the flow toward the docks. Nothing like this atmosphere had existed since the Iron Curtain crumbled. He assumed some of these people would be his fellow passengers, but that most of them were merely going to gaze wistfully south, or try once more to bargain for an earlier departure date. Had Taylor not come to Algeciras liberally supplied with cash, he, too, might have been among the idlers. Even as it was, the earliest passage he had been able to secure had involved waiting a miserable week. Not wishing to entrust his fate to the privateers in their small craft—stories abounded of passengers taken only halfway across the Strait and then chucked overboard—Taylor had chosen to wait for one of the more reliable conveyances.

There was a chain-link fence topped with concertina wire around the dock where the ferry was berthed. The gate was manned by UN Peacekeeping Troops, part of *Operacion Transito*. Ticket in hand, Taylor joined the line leading up to the guards. There seemed to be no customs check of baggage, so Taylor made no attempt to slip his gun into the lining of his duffel bag, as he had intended.

Under the strengthening sun, time passed. Eventually Taylor came to the head of the line.

A Scandanavian guard, big and blond, demanded, "Passport, please."

Taylor handed it over.

In a bored voice the guard recited his speech: "You understand that according to UN Security Council Resolution Number 1050, approved by a majority of member nations, you are hereby permanently renouncing your citizenship in the land wherein you are currently enfranchised. Do you understand this?"

"Yes."

"Do you still wish to board?"

"Yes."

The guard waved Taylor through, keeping his passport. His name would appear in newspapers around the world tomorrow, separated from his wife's by months, though to any future historians the time differential would disappear and the separated lovers would merge into the statistics of the mass exodus, united at last, if only cliometrically.

As he passed beneath the coiled wire, a miasma seemed to lift off his shoulders. For the first time in a week, he felt he was truly moving under his own volition.

The craft moored at the dock was one of the old hulking multi-tiered ferries which had once plied a more sedate trade across the Strait. Its suddenly wealthy owners, operating under government franchise, had made minor alterations—filling the cargo space with cheap seats—thereby converting it into a shuttle for the one-way emigrants. Now the craft was showing signs of wear. Kept so busy it had forgone drydock for over a year, the vessel was rusting and untrustworthy-looking.

Its crew, already wearing surplus CBW gear and breathing bottled air, was forbidden to set foot on Maxwell's Land, or traffic in African goods, under penalty of the same permanent expulsion the guard had outlined to Taylor.

Small boats and their owners who opted not to seek a government license for passage to Maxwell's Land were deemed by the authorities to be in instant violation of the UN interdict, and were sunk when sighted. Twenty had gone down in the week Taylor had been waiting.

Taylor boarded by means of a shaky wooden ramp and took his place at the already crowded rail. He wished he had someone to wave goodbye to, and he idly looked at the people on the shore for any familiar face, even that of the mercenary Narciso.

Gulls wheeled overhead. Next to Taylor stood two black youths, mountaineering backpacks dwarfing them, by speech and dress obviously American. They seemed almost giddy with the adventure they were embarked on.

"Back to Africa, huh, man!"

"Yeah, but nobody cogged it'd ever be like this!"

"Hey, how many demons does it take to change a lightbulb?"

"None, 'cuz they don't never wear out!"

Soon the ship was full. A horn blared. With a noisy blast and a belch of black smoke, the ship's diesels roared into life, the lines were cast off, the ferry pirouetted and headed out to sea. Taylor felt the breeze of passage begin to dry the sweat from his brow. Today the sun felt different somehow. Still as hot, it seemed less dulling than stimulating. Taylor supposed it was all in his mind, the result of being at last in motion.

Midway through the passage, the ship's engines abruptly ceased to stink and bellow, the thrumming they imparted to the hull disappearing, more as if they had suddenly winked out of existence than as if someone had throttled back on them. Nonetheless, the ship continued to surge forward, perhaps even more swiftly, under some unknown impulse.

Taylor puzzled over the curious phenomenon briefly, then discarded it. He was certain he would encounter many mysteries in Maxwell's Land, none of which had any real bearing on his strictly personal mission.

The trip to Tangier was over sooner than Taylor could have wished. In transit, he had been both active and passive, moving toward his destiny, yet helpless for the moment to do more than he was doing. With landfall came an end to such suspension, and a necessity for further decisions.

The trouble was, Taylor had no idea what he was going to do next. Disembarking with the excited immigrants, he realised that he had thought ahead no further than this point. Where Holt and Aubrey were, and how he was to get there without money, were points he had neglected.

As on the other side, no port officials bothered to rummage through personal possessions. It was as if they were saying, *Nothing you bring in can matter as much as what's already here.* And they certainly did not enquire as to the intended duration of anyone's stay.

There was, however, one formality to undergo.

A European woman wearing a Red Crescent pin on her shirt held a modified injection pistol connected by a hose to a stainless-steel tank. Each traveller came under her ministrations.

When it was Taylor's turn, he knew what was expected. Dreading it, he took off his jacket and exposed his bare skin.

The woman pressed the wide muzzle against his flesh and squeezed the trigger.

When she withdrew it, the demonsign was tattooed brightly in red on the underside of his forearm. A single drop of blood appeared, but no more.

"Self-organising and ineradicable," she said, responding to Taylor's look. "Even if you were to cut it away, it would reform. Think of it as your passport as a citizen of Maxwell's Land, Oh, and you've just gotten the standard viral disassemblers too. Anti-trypansomiasis, anti-AIDS, and all that. Good luck."

Clutching his duffel bag in one hand, rubbing his sore new trademark with the other, still without immediate goals, Taylor decided to wander around the city and learn what he could of the changes that had come to North Africa in Holt's wake.

Five years ago, the government of President Zine al-Abidine Ben Ali of Tunisia—one of the more liberal, secular Arab nations—had extended an invitation. Hearing of a certain Desmond Holt, whose field trials of his potentially revolutionary nanodevices had been forbidden in America, the Tunisian government offered to help finance his work and to give him *carte blanche* in terms of implementing any of his discoveries.

One year after Holt had relocated with his small staff to the impoverished but eager Arab country, there was no more Tunisia.

It still existed in the physical sense. The land—its earth, its people, its buildings—had not vanished off the map. But in a metaphysical and legalistic way Tunisia was no more. As a separate political entity, the country had disappeared. President Ben Ali had, all unknowingly, engineered a coup against himself.

Details of what was quickly dubbed the "Gadget Revolution," how it had been accomplished so easily, were scant. Other nations, recognising a peril to their own integrity even if they could not define it, had exhibited great alacrity in slapping quarantine on the infected nation. But the fact of great changes was soon plain.

After dismantling the government of his host, Holt and the technology he embodied had absorbed Libya to the southeast and Algeria to the west. Both had immediately stopped pumping oil. The rest of OPEC, picking up the slack, prevented more than a slight hiccup in the world economy. The closing of these markets to Western goods and the repudiation of foreign debts was actually more troublesome, and corporations agitated for a quick return to normalisation of relations—assuming, of course, that the offending nations could be forced to give up their dangerous new technology.

Morocco, where Taylor now found himself, entered into the union a year later. Mauritania, Mali, Niger, Chad and the Sudan followed in short order. Egypt proved more stubborn, but had acquiesced just six months ago. And now, as Taylor had recently read, Israel looked likely to follow.

These countries, then, made up the strange and unlikely amalgam known, to the Western press at least, as Maxwell's Land.

Home to demons.

Taylor didn't know what he expected to see as he walked idly through the noisy city. Perhaps alien scenes of unhuman construction, swarms of semi-sentient mechanisms, perhaps upheaval and confusion . . . Instead, everything appeared utterly mundane. Tangier was in fact flourishing, despite the seemingly airtight trade embargo imposed by the rest of the world.

He had never visited North Africa before, but a thousand travelogues had prepared him for the innocuous, albeit colourful reality. In the *medina*, the old town, the *soukhs* were all busy, heaps of produce and piles of carpets, booths full of brass and basketware, jewellery and clothing, all proudly on display.

The only traditional element missing from the city, in fact, was misery. Taylor saw no beggars, no faces ravaged by untended controllable illnesses. He passed many clinics, staffed by Westerners: immigrants in their new jobs. Also, he realised that there were no draught animals or conventional vehicles. Instead, small carts and scooters, impelled noiselessly by odd engines—Taylor's trained eye recognised them as Stirling cycle devices, powered by demon heatpumps—were everywhere.

The whole city seemed slightly inebriated, in fact. There was an almost physical euphoria, something in the air like ozone on a mountaintop. Taylor found his attention drifting again, and forced himself to recall his mission.

He stopped, attracted by a tea-stand. Having stood in the sun since before noon, he was parched. He watched the proprietor prepare numerous cups of hot dark tea for his customers. Each cup of water was heated to boiling individually over a small black cube emblazoned with a demonsign. The cube had a single control.

Taylor stared at this device with almost as much interest as he held for the drinks. Here was one of Holt's products—the most revolutionary—in its simplest form: inside the cube was nothing but a number of self-replicating Maxwell's demons—sophisticated nanomechanisms, silicrobes—and a quantity of plain air at ambient temperatures. The demons, intelligent gates, were layered in a screen that divided the interior of the cube in half. By segregating molecules of common air with non-uniform velocities, the silicrobes produced heat in one half of the cube, while the other half grew frigid. (Some of this energy they used for themselves.) The control regulated how many gates were switched on.

Endless free power. A local reversal of entropy.

This was what had toppled governments and transmogrified societies. Inside this small featureless cube was a power that was well on its way to remaking the globe.

Taylor watched as customers exchanged *dinars* for drinks. A few seemed to partake without paying, failing to arouse any protest from the man running the booth. Taylor was just on the point of daring to do so himself when a voice spoke from his side.

"You are just off the boat, I wager."

Taylor turned. A young Arab man with five-o'clock shadow, wearing jeans, a T-shirt emblazoned with the demonsign, and cowboy boots, stood beside him.

"Yes," admitted Taylor.

"Understandably, you are perplexed. It is a common reaction. Money, you see, is on the way out here. In a society of growing abundance, it is losing its value. Many cling to it still, out of habit, but are willing to give freely of their products and labour if asked, knowing they may take freely in return. But enough of theoretical economics. It was my field of study, and I think sometimes I was on my way to becoming quite a pedant. You are thirsty." The man spoke in Arabic to the proprietor, who quickly fixed Taylor some tea.

Tea in the Sahara, he thought, sipping. That was both an old song and a chapter in one of Aubrey's books. Things seemed suddenly to converge in a rush upon Taylor, and he felt dizzy.

"Please," said the Arab, taking Taylor's arm, "my name is Azzedine, Azzedine Aidud. Allow me to find you some shade."

Taylor finished his tea quickly, nearly scalding his mouth, returned the cup, and allowed the man to lead him off.

Walls old as life, alleys narrow as death, shadowy doorways—Taylor lost all sense of where the port was. His attention wandered, and he followed Azzedine as he had followed Narciso. Used to giving orders and leading, he now found himself reduced to a child's role.

They ended up in a walled garden, water purling gently in a fountain. Taylor vaguely remembered the Arab saying something about his family. Azzedine was speaking.

"—and when I heard what was happening in my homeland, I left my studies in America—I was at Stanford, do you know it?—and returned. It was the only thing to do, obviously."

Taylor was seized by a sudden feverish energy. He grabbed Azzedine's wrist.

"Listen—do you know where Holt is now?"

Azzedine's face filled with near-religious awe, then disappointment. "The great man. How I wish I could meet him! It would be an honour to thank him personally, something I could tell my children about some day. But, sad to relate, I do not know."

"Is there some way we could find out?"

"There is a branch of Holt's tribe in town. They might know."

"His tribe?"

"That is what the ones who work with Holt call themselves."

"Please, would you take me there?"

"Certainly."

The office of the tribe was a former Army building denoted by a special demonsign that featured a capital H in its centre. The place was bustling with activity. The chain of command was hard to distinguish: no receptionists, no private offices, no obvious executives. After some time, Taylor found himself talking to a dark-haired Canadian named Walt Becker, Azzedine listening attentively.

Taylor tried to lie convincingly. "Listen, you've got to tell me where Holt is. It's imperative that I see him. I have crucial information for him."

"About what?"

"It's—it's information about an attempt on his life."

"It wouldn't be the first. Holt can handle it."

"No, this is different. He's not prepared. Please, he's an old friend. I couldn't stand it if anything happened to him."

"You know Holt personally?"

"We went to school together . . ."

Becker seemed unconvinced, on the point of turning away. Taylor rummaged desperately through his small bag of tricks.

"The woman with him, Aubrey. She's my wife."

Becker perked up. "What's your name again?" Taylor told him. "And what project were you just working on?"

"Chunnel Two."

Becker nodded. "She said you might show up."

Taylor's heart skipped. What kind of tripwires had she set?

It looked, however, as if no alarms had gone off. Becker picked up a phone. "We'll get you transportation right away."

Azzedine interrupted. "No. I claim the right to take him. My family were always *marabouts*, guides. I brought him here. It is only fair."

Becker shrugged. "Why not? Holt's in the desert, the Tanzerouft, not far from Taodani. He got a project going with the Tuareg. Exactly what, I'm not sure."

Taylor laughed bitterly. "Out in the field himself. Holt always did have a weakness for micromanaging things."

Becker chuckled. "Call it nanomanaging now."

"The new Tangier to Tombouctou highway passes near to Taodani."

"How far is it?"

"Not far. A thousand miles, more or less."

"You call that 'not far'?"

"In the past, yes, it would be a long distance. But not on the new road. You'll see. Let's get your bag, and we'll be off."

Azzedine's transportation was a two-seater, a teardrop-shaped, three-wheeled vehicle with a canopy laminated in gold to reflect the desert heat. Powered by demons, it needed no refuelling. The man was immensely proud of it, and seemed able to discourse endlessly on it, much to Taylor's annoyance.

"Classical physics, you know, Mister Taylor, claims that our power source is impossible. Information theory was supposed to have put a final nail in the coffin of Mister Maxwell's demon, you see. In sorting molecules, the demon was supposed to discard information, which was thermodynamically costly, thereby negating all the work it had done. Holt's insight was to see that a mechanism with a large enough memory could increase the entropy of its memory in order to decrease the entropy of its environment. When saturated, it would replicate a fresh heir, then self-destruct. Thus the problem of thermodynamic irreversibility is sidestepped."

As they moved slowly through the streets of Tangier, Taylor, eyes closed, reclined alongside the driver in his comfortable seat. The amber light filtering in through the one-way transparency coloured his face like a marigold.

"It's all bullshit, Azzedine. There's some hidden payback down the road. There has to be."

Azzedine seemed hurt. "Then, Mister Taylor, I must affirm that this car is powered on bullshit. Seriously, do you believe Mister Holt would set something loose like this if it were not perfected? He is a unique soul. Why, to aid the Tuaregs qualifies him as a holy man."

"Why's that?"

"The Tuaregs are not even really Arabs. They claim to be an ancient noble race, but I do not trust them. Do the men not veil their faces, so you cannot read them?"

"If you say so."

"I do. Holt is brave to work with them. As you might say, he's one 'major dude.' I know many in other lands vilify him, claiming he is irresponsible and crazy to unleash such forces so rapidly. But he knows just what he is doing. Some day the whole world will acknowledge him as its saviour, as we here do now."

"We'll never live to see if it happens as you predict."

"Only God knows. And as there is no God but Allah, Holt is his prophet."

On the outskirts of Tangier began a golden road of almost supernatural smoothness, heading south-east straight as a surveyor's wetdream. The road was lined with young palms fed with a continuous length of trickle-irrigation tubing, studded with demon-powered pumps.

"Look," said Azzedine with admiration, "fused from sand by more of Holt's creatures of genius."

"Wonderful," said Taylor. He was simultaneously keyed-up and weary. There definitely seemed to be something in the air that sharpened the senses and quickened the pulse. Conversely, his mind was burdened with its weight of fatality, the self-imposed geas to regain Aubrey and put an end to Holt's madness.

Azzedine cranked the little car up to one hundred and twenty kilometres an hour. Twelve or fifteen hours, and they should be there.

Taylor managed to doze off during one of Azzedine's impassioned monologues about the miracle of North Africa. He awoke as they passed through Fez and began to ascend into the Grand Atlas Mountains. They crossed the nonexistent border near Chaouf, and entered the true desert. Even here, the road flew out ahead of them, indomitable, lined with hopeful trees.

Azzedine drove like one possessed by the Holy Spirit. Taylor, waking at intervals in the night, tried vainly to imagine what was going on in the Arab's mind. Did he view himself as divinely appointed by Kismet to find the stranger in the marketplace and convey him to his meeting with Saint Holt?

Around midnight, after eight hours of driving, they stopped for a brief rest at an oasis.

Hive-shaped buildings with thick walls, constructed by nanomachines from sand, sat beneath date-palms and *talha* trees. Camels were hobbled by the well. A man in a flowing *gandourah* appeared, and bowed them welcome. He brought them inside and roused his whole family: two wives and six children. The women, their hair modestly concealed from the strange males by cloth wraps, served Taylor and Azzedine *couscous* with chunks of lamb and a milk drink called *zrig*, followed by dates and honey.

Taylor was curious. "Ask them why they live out here, so far from anywhere."

Azzedine enquired. The husband launched into a long impassioned speech. Azzedine's eyes grew large.

"He claims that wherever Holt has rested becomes a *haram*, a holy place, and he hopes to gain heavenly merit by staying here and helping travellers."

"Oh, Jesus, this is really too much—"

After Azzedine had a short nap, the travellers were off.

Fifteen hours after their departure, as dawn was breaking in shades of apricot and cream, they reached Taodani, a small town in the north of a Mali that was no more.

They parked. Outside the car, the heat smote them like a velvet-covered hammer, dazing Taylor.

"Now what?" asked Taylor.

"We will find a local who knows where the Tuaregs are camped and can serve as guide. Then, I'm afraid, it will be camels for us. There are no roads in the Tanzerouft."

A shopkeeper, instantly cooperative at the mention of Holt's cursed name, directed them to a man called Mahfoud.

Mahfoud, apparently in his fifties, was desert-thin, desert-dark. "Of course I can bring you to Holt. Did I not guide the *azalai*, the salt caravans, for years?"

"How far is he?"

"Twenty-five miles. With luck, eight hours' travel."

Taylor groaned. "When can we start?"

"Tonight. Travelling by dark, we will avoid the heat."

Taylor and Azzedine spent an hour or two buying, under Mahfoud's direction, a few supplies. They napped in the house of the town's prefect. By moonrise, they had all assembled on the edge of town.

The camels wore wooden butterfly-shaped saddles. Mahfoud tied the waterskins, the *girbas*, to the saddles. Each camel was controlled by a bridle to which was attached a rope.

Mahfoud couched the camels. "Mount now."

Taylor and Azzedine ascended. The camels rose, making half-hearted protests at the weight.

"Your beasts will follow mine. But do not drop the headrope, whatever you do, or they will bolt."

Mahfoud moved to the fore of the caravan. Holding his camel pole across his shoulders, he started the train in motion.

Mounted on his camel, Taylor, still wearing his filthy linen suit, found the riding deceptively easy.

Two hours later, his whole body felt like a single giant bruise. The night, while cooler, was still in the nineties. The monotony of the trek, the slowness after the speed of the drive, made him want to scream. Would he never reach Holt?

Rocking atop the smelly beast, Taylor was suddenly taken by the ironic notion that his whole journey was more comedy than tragedy. A plane to Spain, a boat to Africa, a car to the desert, a camel to some filthy nomad encampment. It was all too much like one of those movies where the characters experience successive degradations in their quest, until they end up pedalling on a child's bicycle . . .

Seeking reassurance, Taylor reached beneath his jacket.

Tucked into the waist of his trousers was his gun. It felt hot against his skin.

Constellations spun; the desert drifted past them.

The Tuaregs had not moved, and were easily found. They were camped in a depression which even Taylor could recognize as a dry wadi. From a distance, their flattened oval tents of *dom* fibre looked like some abandoned circus, dropped impossibly into the waste of sand. In the middle of the encampment was a modern tent, obviously the ringmaster's, Holt's.

Taylor tried urging his camel to greater speeds, but found it as unresponsive as stone. After a seeming eternity, they arrived in the midst of the camp.

It was so early, pre-dawn, that no one was yet up.

Taylor painfully dismounted.

He stumbled at an awkward trot towards Holt's tent. Azzedine hung back out of respect, while Mahfoud was busy with the camels.

Taylor pulled back the tent flap and an unexpected blast of air-conditioning smacked him in the face, utterly disconcerting him for a moment. Recovering, he saw in the dim light two sleeping figures on separate cots: Aubrey and Holt, both in T-shirts.

If they had been together in bed, he knew he would have shot them.

But as they were, looking like children, his wife and his best friend, they drained everything from him except self-disgust.

With a roaring in his ears, Taylor raised the gun to his own temple.

He pulled the trigger—

Once, twice, a number of times.

No flare, no aroma of gunpowder, nothing but dull clicks.

Taylor dropped his hand and looked down in befuddlement at the traitorous weapon. He ejected the full clip, studied it as if expecting it to voice an explanation, then tossed it aside. He began to cry.

Holt and Aubrey were awake now. A light came on. Holt manoeuvred a campstool behind Taylor, and pressed his shoulders. He sat.

"Aubrey, I could use some tea. And I'm sure Nick could too. Would you mind?"

Aubrey's single nod was like a wordless recrimination that drove straight through Taylor's heart. His sobs deepened.

Holt, damn him, was acting all apologetic, as if it were he who had attempted the suicide, and not Taylor.

"It's a shock at first, Nick. I know. Hell, I remember when I discovered it. And you should have seen the faces on the UN troops when they tried firing at us. But certain entropic reactions from the old paradigm are just impossible now, within a large radius of the demons. You can't get an internal combustion engine to function within miles of Maxwell's Land. It's a local accumulation of anti-entropy, put out as a byproduct of the demons' sorting. God knows why our metabolisms still work. Sheldrake thinks it's got to do with the morphogenetic field. But shit, it's all beyond me—I admit it. One thing I do know. The field should reach Europe pretty soon. After that, they'll have no choice but to use my demons. I figure America has about another ten years, tops, if she stays stubborn. Although I'd go back to help any time sooner, if they asked."

Taylor's sobs diminished. "What . . . what are you going to do with me?"

Holt looked at Aubrey, his face—as youthful as it had been in their school days—honestly ingenuous. "Gee, I don't know. There's so much to be done, whole continents to convert, a hundred countries, thousands of societies. Take what we're doing out here. We're going to restore the wadi. There's plenty of water, it's just three hundred feet down.

These new silicrobes we've engineered form micro-capillaries and bring the water up one molecule at a time. We could sure use you to help restore the biosphere—but maybe you have some ideas."

Taylor was silent. Holt turned as Aubrey approached with tea.

"Aubrey, what do you say we should do with Nick?"

His wife looked at Taylor, and he managed to meet her eyes. He thought he had never seen her so radiant or self-possessed. That drivel in her farewell letter—had all been true. He waited with trepidation for her to speak.

"Put him to work," she said forcefully. "What else? Even now," she said, "nobody gets something entirely for nothing."

For Paul Bowles

WE WERE OUT OF OUR MINDS WITH JOY

David Marusek

In the vivid and pyrotechnic novella that follows, we are taken several decades down the Information Superhighway to a strange and bewilderingly complex new future where everyone and everything is plugged into everything else, *and where* everything *in society has been shaped and altered by nanotechnology, from top to bottom, for the bittersweet and compelling story of a man who Has It All . . . for a moment, anyway.*

New writer David Marusek is a graduate of Clarion West. He made his first sale to Asimov's Science Fiction *in 1993, and his second sale soon thereafter to* Playboy. *"We Were Out of Our Minds with Joy" is, amazingly, only his third sale, although it was accomplished enough to make one of the reviewers for* Locus *magazine speculate that Marusek must be a Big Name Author writing under a pseudonym.* Not *a pseudonym, Marusek lives the life of a struggling young writer in a "low-maintenance cabin in the woods" in Fairbanks, Alaska, and I'm willing to bet that his is a voice we'll be hearing a* lot *more from as the decade progresses. (A pretty safe bet, since he's already sold new stories to* Future Histories *and* Asimov's, *and is at work on more. . . .)*

I

On March 30, 2092, the Department of Health and Human Services issued Eleanor and me a permit. The under secretary of the Population Division called with the news and official congratulations. We were stunned by our good fortune. The under secretary instructed us to contact the National Orphanage. There was a baby in a drawer in Jersey with our names on it. We were out of our minds with joy.

Eleanor and I had been together a year, ever since a friend of mine introduced us at a party in Manhattan. I was there in realbody, though most guests attended by holo. My friend said, "Sam, there's someone you ought to meet." I wasn't prepared to meet anyone; I shouldn't have even come. I was recovering from a long week of design work in my Chicago studio. In those days I would bolt my door and lose myself in my work, even forgetting to eat or sleep. Henry knew to hold all calls. He alone attended me. Then, a week or two later, I'd emerge famished and lonely, and I'd schlep to the nearest party to gorge myself on canapés, cheese cubes, and those tiny, pickled ears of corn. So there I was, unshaven and disheveled, leaning over my friend's buffet table and wearing such a look of gloom as to challenge anyone to approach me. I hadn't come to talk to people, certainly not to meet anyone. I simply needed to be around people for awhile, to watch them, to listen to their chatter. But my friend tapped me on the shoulder. "Sam Harger," he said, "this is Eleanor Starke. Eleanor, Sam."

A woman stood on a patch of carpet from some other room and sipped coffee from a china cup. We smiled at each other while our belt valet systems briefed us. "Oh," she said almost immediately. "Sam Harger, of course, the artist. I have long admired your work, especially the early stuff. In fact, I've just seen one of your spatter pieces at the museum here."

"And where is here?" I said.

A frown flickered across the woman's remarkable face, but she quickly recovered her smile. She must have wondered if my belt system were totally inept. "Budapest," she said.

Budapest, Henry said inside my head. *Sorry, Sam, but her system won't talk to me. I have gone to public sources. She's some big multinational prosecutor, currently free-lance. I'm scanning for bios now.*

"You have me at a disadvantage," I told the woman standing halfway around the globe. "I don't pay much attention to law, business, or politics. And my valet is an artist's assistant, not a spy." Unless she was projecting a proxy, this Eleanor Starke was a slender woman, pretty, mid-twenties. She had reddish blonde hair; a sweet, round, disarmingly freckled face, full lips, and very heavy eyebrows. Too sweet to be a prosecutor. Her eyes, however, were anything but sweet. They peered out from under their lashes like eels in coral. "And besides," I said, "I was just leaving."

"So soon?" she said. "Pity." Her bushy eyebrows plunged in disappointment. "Won't you stay another moment?"

Sam, whispered Henry, *no two published bios of her agree on even the most basic data, not even on her date of birth. She's anywhere from 180 to 204 years old.* This woman was powerful, I realized, if she could scramble secured public databases. *But the People Channel has recently tagged her as a probable celebrity. And she has been seen with a host of artist types in the last dozen months: writers, dancers, conductors, holographers, composers.*

Eleanor nibbled at the corner of a pastry. "This is breakfast for me. I wish you could taste it. There's nothing quite like it stateside." She brushed crumbs from her lips. "By the way, your belt valet, your . . . Henry . . . is quaint. So I have a weakness for artists, so what?" This startled me; she had eavesdropped on my system. "Don't look so surprised," she said. "Your uplink is pretty loose; it's practically a broadband. When was the last time you updated your privacy protocol?"

"You sure know how to charm a fellow," I said.

"That's not my goal."

"What is your goal?"

"Dinner, for starters. I'll be in New York tomorrow."

I considered her invitation and the diversion she might offer. I needed a diversion just then. I needed to escape from inside my head. Getting laid would be nice, but not by this heavy-hitting trophy hunter, this Eleanor Starke. I knew a half-dozen other women in the city I would rather spend my time with.

No, the reason I accepted her invitation was curiosity about her eyebrows. I did not doubt that Eleanor Starke had commissioned someone to fashion her face—perhaps building on her original features. She had molded her own face into a sly weapon for her arsenal of dirty attorney tricks. With it she could appear insignificant and vulnerable. With it she could win over juries. She could fool corporate boards, men and women alike. But why the eyebrows? They were massive. When she spoke they dipped and arched with her words. They were distracting, especially to an artist. I found myself staring at them. As a graphic designer, as a painter of old, I itched to scale them down and thin them out. In the five minutes we talked, they captured my full attention. I, myself, would never do eyebrows like them. Then it occurred to me that these were possibly her natural, unaltered brows, for no licensed face designer—with a reputation to protect—would have the nerve to do them. This Eleanor Starke, shark of the multinationals, may have molded the rest of her features to her advantage, even inflicting herself with freckles, but I became convinced that she had been born a bushy-browed baby, and like a string of artist types before me, I took the bait.

"Not dinner," I replied, "but what about lunch?"

• • •

Lunch, as it often does, led to dinner. We screwed like bunnies. The eyebrows were genuine, even their color. Over the next few weeks we tried out the beds in our various apartments all up and down the Eastern Seaboard. Soon the novelty wore off. She stopped calling me, and I stopped calling her—we were sated, or so I thought. She departed on a long trip outside the Protectorate. A month had passed when I received a call from Beijing. Her calendar secretary asked if I would care to hololunch tomorrow. Her late lunch in China would coincide with my midnight brandy in Buffalo. Sure, why not?

I holoed at the appointed time. She had already begun her meal; she was freighting a morsel of water chestnut to her mouth by chopstick when she noticed me. Her entire face lit up with pleasure. "Hi," she said. "Welcome. I'm so glad you could make it." She sat at a richly lacquered table next to a scarlet wall with golden filigree trim. "Unfortunately, I can't stay," she said, placing the chopsticks on her plate. "Last minute program change. So sorry, but I had to see you, even for a moment. How've you been?"

"Fine," I said.

She wore a loose green silk business suit, and her hair was neatly stacked on top of her head. "Can we reschedule for tomorrow?" she asked.

We gazed at each other for several long moments. I was surprised at how comfortable I was with her and how disappointed. I hadn't realized that I'd missed her so much. "Sure, tomorrow."

That night I couldn't sleep, and the whole next day was colored with anticipation. At midnight I said, "Okay, Henry, take me to the Beijing Hilton."

"She's not there," he replied. "She's at the Wanatabe Tokyo tonight."

Sure enough, the scarlet walls were replaced by paper

screens. "There you are," she said. "Good, I'm famished." She uncovered a bowl and dished steamy rice onto her plate while telling me in broad terms about a trade deal she was brokering. "They want me to stay, you know. Hire on at triple my rate. Japanese men are funny when they're desperate. They get so . . . so indifferent."

I sipped my drink. "And what did you tell them?" To my surprise, I was anything but indifferent.

She glanced at me, curious. "I told them I would think about it."

We began to meet for a half hour or so each day and talked about whatever came to mind. El's interests were deep and broad; everything fascinated her. She told me, choking with laughter, anecdotes of famous people in awkward circumstances. She revealed curious truths behind the daily news and pointed out related investment opportunities. She teased out of me all sorts of opinion, gossip, and laughter. Her half of the room changed every day and reflected her hectic itinerary: jade, bamboo, and teak. My half of the room never varied. It was the atrium of my hillside house in Santa Barbara where I went in order to be three hours closer to her. As we talked we looked down the yucca- and chaparral-choked canyon to the campus and beach below, to the Channel Islands, and beyond them, to the blue-green Pacific that separated us.

Weeks later, when again we met in realbody, I was shy. I didn't know quite what to do with her. So we talked. We sat close together on the couch and tried to pick up any number of conversational threads. With no success. Her body, so close, befuddled me. I knew her body, or thought I did: I'd unwrapped its expensive clothing a dozen times before. But it was a different body now, occupied, as it was, by El. I was about to make love to El, if ever I could get started.

"Nervous, are we?" she laughed, as she unfastened my shirt.

• • •

Fortunately, before we went completely off the deep end, the self-destructive parts of our personalities bobbed to the surface. The promise of happiness can be daunting. El snapped first. We were at her Maine townhouse when her security chief holoed into the room. Until then the only member of her belt valet system—what she called her cabinet—that she allowed me to meet was her calendar secretary. "I have something to show you," said the security chief, glowering at me from under his bushy eyebrows. I glanced at Eleanor who made no attempt to explain or excuse the intrusion. "This is a realtime broadcast," he said and turned to watch as the holoserver overlaid Eleanor's living room with the studio lounge of the *People Channel*. It was during their "Couples Week" feature, and cohosts Chirp and Ditz were serving up breathless speculation on hapless couples caught by holoeye in public places and yanked for inspection into living rooms across the solar system.

All at once we were outside the Boston restaurant where Eleanor and I had dined that evening. A couple emerged from a cab. He had a black mustache and silver hair and looked like the champion of boredom. She had a vampish hatchet of a face, limp hair, and vacant eyes.

"Whoodeeze tinguished gentry?" said Ditz to Chirp.

"Carefuh watwesay, lipsome. Dizde ruthless Eleanor K. Starke and'er lately dildude, Samsamson Harger."

I did a double take. The couple on the curb had our bodies and wore our evening clothes, but our heads had been pixeled, were morphed beyond recognition.

Eleanor examined them closely. "Good. Good job."

"Wait a minute," I said.

Eleanor arched an eyebrow in my direction.

I didn't know what to say. "Isn't commercial broadcast protected by law?"

She laughed and turned to her security chief. "Will this ever be traced to me?"

"No."

"Will it occur each and every time any net decides to broadcast anything about me without my expressed permission?"

"Yes."

"Thank you. You may go." The security chief dissolved. Eleanor put her arms around my neck and looked me in the eye. "I value our privacy."

"That's all fine and good," I replied, "but that was *my* image, too, that you altered without *my* expressed permission."

"So? I was protecting you. You should be grateful."

A week later, Eleanor and I were in my Buffalo apartment. Out of the blue she asked me to order a copy of the newly released memoir installment of a certain best-selling author. She said he was a predecessor of mine, a recent lover, who against her wishes had included several paragraphs about their affair in his reading. I told Henry to fetch the reading, but Eleanor said no, that it would be better to order it through the houseputer. When I did so, the houseputer froze up. It just stopped and wouldn't respond. My apartment's comfort support failed. Lights went out, the kitchen quit, and the bathroom door refused to open. "How many copies do you think he'll sell?" Eleanor laughed.

"I get the point."

I was indeed getting the point: El was a tad too paranoid for me. The last straw came when I discovered that her system was messing with Henry. I asked Henry for his bimonthly report on my business, and he said, *please stand by.* I was sitting at the time and stupidly stood up before I realized it.

"What do you mean, 'please stand by,' Henry? What does 'please stand by' mean?"

My processing capabilities are currently overloaded and unavailable. Please stand by.

Nothing like this had ever happened before. "Henry, what is going on?"

There was no response for a long while, then he whispered, *Take me to Chicago.*

Chicago. My studio. That was where his container was. I left immediately, worried sick. Between outages, Henry was able to assure me that he was essentially sound, but that he was preoccupied in warding off a series of security breaches.

"From where? Henry, tell me who's doing this to you."

He's trying again. No, he's in. He's gone. Here he comes again. Please stand by.

Suddenly my mouth began to water, my saliva tasted like machine oil: Henry—or someone—had initiated a terminus purge. I was excreting my interface with Henry. Over the next dozen hours I would spit, sweat, piss, and shit the millions of slave nanoprocessors that resided in the vacuoles of my fat cells and linked me to Henry's box in Chicago. Until I reached my studio, we would be out of contact and I would be on my own. Without a belt valet to navigate the labyrinth of the slipstream tube, I underpassed Illinois altogether and had to backtrack from Toronto. Chicago cabs still respond to voice command, but as I had no way to transfer credit, I was forced to walk ten blocks to the Drexler Building.

Once inside my studio, I rushed to the little ceramic container tucked between a cabinet and the wall. "Are you there?" Henry existed as a pleasant voice in my head. He existed as data streams through space and fiber. He existed as an uroboros signal in a Swiss loopvault. But if Henry existed as a physical being at all, it was as the gelatinous paste inside this box. "Henry?"

The box's ready light blinked on.

• • •

"The fucking bitch! How could she? How dare she?"

"Actually, it makes perfect sense."

"Shut up, Henry."

Henry was safe as long as he remained a netless standalone. He couldn't even answer the phone for me. He was a prisoner; we were both prisoners in my Chicago studio. Eleanor's security chief had breached Henry's shell millions of times, nearly continuously since the moment I met her at my friend's party. Henry's shell was an off-the-shelf application I had purchased years ago to protect us against garden variety corporate espionage. I had never updated it, and it was worthless.

"Her cabinet is a diplomat-class unit," said Henry. "What do you expect?"

"Shut up, Henry."

At first the invasion was so subtle and Henry so unskilled, that he was unaware of the foreign presence inside his matrix. When he became aware, he mounted the standard defense, but Eleanor's system flowed through its gates like water. So he set about studying each breach, learning and building ever more effective countermeasures. The attacks escalated, grew so epic that Henry's defense soon consumed his full attention.

"Why didn't you tell me?"

"I did, Sam, several times."

"That's not true. I don't remember you telling me once."

"You have been somewhat preoccupied lately."

"Just shut up."

The question was, how much damage had been done, not to me, but to Henry. There was nothing in my past anyone could use to harm me. I was an artist, after all, not a politician: the public expected me to be shameless. But if Eleanor had damaged Henry to get to my files, I would kill her. I had owned Henry since the days of keyboards and pointing devices. He was the repository of my life's work and life's memory. I could not replace him. He did my bookkeeping, sure, and my taxes, appointments, and legal tasks. He monitored my health, my domiciles, my investments, etc., etc., etc. These functions I could replace; they were commercial programming. I could buy them, and he would modify them to suit his own quirky personality bud. It was his personality bud, itself, I couldn't replace. I had been growing it for eighty years. It was a unique design tool that fit my mind perfectly. I depended on it, on Henry, to read my mind, to engineer the materials I used, and to test my ideas against current tastes. We worked as a team. I had taught him to play the devil's advocate. He provided me feedback, suggestions, ideas, and from time to time—inspiration.

"Eleanor's cabinet was interested neither in your records nor in my personality bud. It simply needed to ascertain, on a continuing basis, that I was still Henry, that no one else had corrupted me."

"Couldn't it just ask?"

"If I were corrupted, do you think I would tell?"

"Are you corrupted?"

"Of course not."

I cringed at the thought of installing Henry back into my body not knowing if he were somebody's dirty little worm.

"Henry, you have a complete backup here, right?"

"Yes."

"One that predates my first contact with Eleanor?"

"Yes."

"And its seal is intact? It hasn't been tampered with, not even read?"

"Yes."

Of course if Henry were corrupted and told me the seal was intact, how would I know otherwise? I didn't know the first thing about this stuff.

"You can use any houseputer," he said, reading me as he always had, "to verify the seal, and to delete and reset me. But I suggest you don't."

"Oh yeah? Why?"

"Because we would lose all I've learned since we met Eleanor. I was getting good, Sam. The breaches were taking exponentially longer for them to achieve. I had almost attained stalemate."

"And meanwhile you couldn't function."

"So buy me more paste. A lot more paste. We have the credit. Think about it. Eleanor's system is aggressive and dominant. It's always in crisis mode. But it's the good guys. If I can learn how to lock it out, I'll be better prepared to meet the bad guys who'll be trying to get to Eleanor through you."

"Good, Henry, except for one essential fact. There is no her and me. I'm dropping her. No, I've already dropped her."

"I see. Tell me, Sam, how many women have you been with since I've known you?"

"How the hell should I know?"

"Well, I know. In the 82.6 years I've associated with you, you've been with 543 women. Your archives reveal at least a hundred more before I was installed."

"If you say so, Henry."

"You doubt my numbers? Do you want me to list their names?"

"I don't doubt your numbers, Henry. But what good are names I've forgotten?" More and more, my own life seemed to me like a Russian novel read long ago. While I could recall the broad outline of the plot, the characters' names eluded me. "Just get to the point."

"The point is, no one has so affected you as Eleanor Starke. Your biometrics have gone off the scale."

"This is more than a case of biometrics," I said, but I

knew he was right, or nearly so. The only other woman that had so affected me was my first love, Janice Scholero, who was a century-and-a-quarter gone. Every woman in between was little more than a single wave in a warm sea of feminine companionship.

Until I could figure out how to verify Henry, I decided to isolate him in his container. I told the houseputer to display "Do Not Disturb—Artist at Work" and take messages. I did, in fact, attempt to work, but was too busy obsessing. I mostly watched the nets or paced the studio arguing with Henry. In the evenings I had Henry load a belt—I kept a few antique Henry interfaces in a drawer—with enough functionality so that I could go out and drink. I avoided my usual haunts and all familiar faces.

In the first message she recorded on my houseputer, El said, "Good for you. Call when you're done." In the second she said, "It's been over a week, must be a masterpiece." In the third, "Tell me what's wrong. You're entirely too sensitive. This is ridiculous. Grow up!"

I tried to tell her what was wrong. I recorded a message for her, a whole seething litany of accusation and scorn, but was too cowardly to post it.

In her fourth message, El said, "It's about Henry, isn't it? My security chief told me all about it. Don't worry; they frisk everyone I meet, nothing personal, and they don't rewrite anything. It's their standing orders, and it's meant to protect me. You have no idea, Sam, how many times I'd be dead if it weren't for my protocol.

"Anyway, I've told them to lay off Henry. They said they could install a deadman alarm in Henry's personality bud, but I said no. Complete hands off. Okay? Is that enough?

"Call, Sam. Let me know you're all right. I . . . miss you."

In the meantime I could find no trace of a foreign personality in Henry. I knew my Henry just as well as he knew me. His thought process was like a familiar tune to me, and at no time during our weeks of incessant conversation did he stroke a false note.

El sent her fifth message from bed where she lay naked between iridescent sheets (of my design). She said nothing. She looked directly at the holoeye, propped herself up, letting the sheet fall to her waist, and brushed her hair. Her chest above her breast, as I had discovered, was spangled with freckles.

Bouquets of real flowers began to arrive at my door with notes that said simply, "Call."

The best-selling memoirs that had stymied my Buffalo houseputer arrived on pin with the section about Eleanor extant. The author's sim, seated in a cane-backed chair and reading from a leather-bound book, described Eleanor in his soft southern drawl as a "perfumed vulvoid whose bush has somehow migrated to her forehead, a lithe misander with the emotional range of a militia slug." I asked the sim to stop and elaborate. He smiled at me and said, "In her relations with men, Eleanor Starke is not interested in emotional communion. She prefers entertainment of a more childish variety, like poking frogs with a stick. She is a woman of brittle patience with no time for fluffy feelings or fuzzy thoughts. Except in bed. In bed Eleanor Starke likes her men half-baked, the gooier the better. That's why she likes to toy with artists. The higher an opinion a man has of himself, the more painfully sensitive he is, the more polished his hubris, the more fun it is to poke him open and see all the runny mess inside."

"You don't know what you're talking about," I yelled at the sim. "El's not like that at all. You obviously never knew her. She's no saint, but she has a heart, and affection and . . . and . . . go fuck yourself."

"Thank you for your comments. May we quote you? Be on the lookout for our companion volume to this memoir installment, *The Skewered Lash Back*, due out in September from Little Brown Jug."

I had been around for 147 years and was happy with my life. I had successfully navigated several careers and amassed a fortune that even Henry had trouble charting. Still, I jumped out of bed each day with a renewed sense of interest and adventure. I would have been pleased to live the next 147 years in exactly the same way. And yet, when El sent her farewell message—a glum El sitting in a museum somewhere, a wall-sized early canvas of mine behind her—I knew my life to be ashes and dirt.

Seventy-two thick candles in man-sized golden stands flanked me like sentries as I waited and fretted in my tuxedo at the altar rail. The guttering beeswax flames filled the cathedral with the fragrance of clover. *Time Media* proclaimed our wedding the "Wedding of the Year" and broadcast it live on the *Wedding Channel*. A castrati choir, hidden in the gloom beneath the giant bronze pipes of the organ, challenged all to submit to the mercy of Goodness. Their sweet soprano threaded through miles of stone vaults, collecting odd echoes and unexpected harmony. Over six million guests fidgeted in wooden pews that stretched, it seemed, to the horizon. And each guest occupied an aisle seat at the front.

In the network's New York studio, El and I, wearing keyblue body suits, stood at opposite ends of a bare soundstage. On cue, El began the slow march towards me. In Wawel Castle overlooking ancient Cracow, however, she marched through giant cathedral doors, her ivory linen gown awash in morning light. The organ boomed Mendelssohn's wedding march, amplified by acres of marble. Two girls strewed rose petals at Eleanor's feet, while another tended her long train. A gauzy veil hid El's face from all eyes except mine. No man walked at her side; a two-hundred-year-old bride, Eleanor preferred to give herself away.

By the time of the wedding, El and I had been living together for six months. We had moved in together partly out of curiosity, partly out of desperation. Whatever was going on between us was mounting. It was spreading and sinking roots. It was like a thing inside us, but apart and separate from us, too. We talked about it, always "it," not sure what to call it. It complicated our lives, especially El's. We agreed we'd be better off without it and tried to remember, from experiences in our youth, how to fix the feelings we were feeling. The one sure cure, guaranteed to make a man and a woman wish they'd never met, was for them to cohabitate. If there was one thing humankind had learned in four million years of evolution, it was that man and woman were not meant to live in the same hut. And since the passage of the Procreation Ban of 2041, there has been little biological justification for doing so.

So, we co-purchased a townhouse in Connecticut. It wasn't difficult for us to stake out our separate bedrooms and work spaces, but decorating the common areas required the diplomacy and compromise of a border dispute. Once in and settled, we agreed to open our house on Wednesday evenings and began the arduous task of melding our friends and colleagues.

We came to prefer her bedroom for watching the nets and mine for making love. When it came to sleeping, however, she required her own bed—alone. Good, we thought, here was a crack we could wedge open. We surveyed for other incompatibilities. She was a late night person, while I rose early. She liked to travel and go out a lot, while I was a stay-at-homer. She loved classical music, while I could stand only neu-noise. She had a maniacal need for total organization of all things, while for me a cluttered space was a happy space.

These differences, however, seemed only to heighten the pleasure we took in each other. We were opposites attracting, two molecules bonding—I don't know—two dogs trying to get unstuck.

The network logged 6.325 million subscribers to our wedding, altogether a modest rating. Nevertheless, the guest book contained some of the most powerful signatures on the planet (El's admirers) and the confetti rained down for weeks. The network paid for a honeymoon on the Moon, including five days at the Lunar Princess and round-trip fare aboard Pan Am.

Eleanor booked a third seat on the shuttle, not the best portent for a successful honeymoon. She assigned me the window seat, took the aisle seat for herself, and into the seat between us she projected one cabinet member after another. All during the flight, she took their reports, issued orders, and strategized with them, not even pausing for lift-off or docking. Her cabinet consisted of about a dozen officials and, except for her security chief, they were all women. They all appeared older than El's current age, and they all bore a distinct Starke family resemblance: reddish-blond hair, slender build, the eyebrows. If they were real people, rather than the projections of El's belt system, they could be her sisters and brother, and she the spoiled baby of the family.

Two cabinet officers especially impressed me, the attorney general, a smartly dressed woman in her forties with a pinched expression, and the chief of staff, who was the eldest of the lot. The chief of staff coordinated the activities of the rest and was second in command after El. She looked and spoke remarkably like El. She was not El's oldest sister, but El, herself, at seventy. She fascinated me. She was my Eleanor stripped of meat, a stick figure of angles and knobs, her eyebrows gone colorless and thin. Yet her eyes burned bright, and she spoke from a deep well of wisdom and authority. No wonder Henry, a pleasant voice in my head, admired El's cabinet.

It had been ages since I had flown in an orbital craft; my last time had been before the development of airborne nasties, smartactives, militia slugs, visola, and city canopies. In a tube, you hardly noticed your passage across barriers since the tube, itself, was a protuberance of the canopies. Looking out my window, I was surprised to see that the shuttlecraft wing was covered with the same sharkskin used on militia craft. But it made sense. Once out of the hangar we were in the great, wild outside and the target of every nastie released into the atmosphere. On the runway, the skarkskin's protective slime foamed away contaminants. After takeoff, the skin rippled and trimmed itself, and our speed was our protection until we reached the stratosphere where the skin relaxed and resumed its foaming.

The flight attendant, a michelle named Traci, was excellent. When the view outside my window lost my interest, she brought me a pillow. I had been about to ask for one. She offered us drinks, including Eleanor's chief of staff who happened to be in the middle seat at the moment. This pleased Eleanor immensely. The michelle knew that if a passenger reserved a seat for her belt valet, it was best to treat the valet as real.

We watched the michelle attend to the other passengers in our compartment. She had well-rounded breasts and hips and filled out her smartly tailored teal uniform. She was diminutive—a michelle grew to about five feet tall—a doll woman, dark complexioned and full of promise, Mediterranean. Eleanor said, "Applied People employees are consistently superior to MacPeople people."

"No matter their agency, michelles are superior," said her chief of staff. "You simply cannot fluster them."

Before my nap, I left my seat to use the rest room. The

forward toilets were occupied, so I went aft through the coach section. All of the passengers there were clumped in the most forward seats, except for five people—one woman and four men—at the tail, with a large unoccupied section between the two groups. Odd. When I reached the tail, I noticed a sharp, foul odor, like rotting cheese. The odor was even stronger in the rest room, and I wondered how Pan Am could operate so negligently. Returning through the coach section, I realized that the bulk of passengers were sitting forward to avoid the odor, and I wondered why the small group of five remained at the tail. When I glanced back at them, they—all of them—regarded me with cold malice.

Back in my seat, I plumped my pillow and prepared to nap. El's security chief, whose turn it was in the middle, looked at me and leered, "So what you think of 'em?"

"Them who?"

"The stinkers back there."

"The stinkers?" I wasn't familiar with the term. (*Seared*, said Henry in my head.) "You mean those people were seared?"

"Yeah, but don't worry. They're harmless, and then some."

I was appalled. Of course I'd heard that the National Militia was searing living individuals these days—felons mostly, whose crimes were not heinous enough to warrant outright extermination—but I had thought it to be a rare punishment. And now here were five of the seared on the same shuttle. "Where are they going?"

"Let's see," said the security chief. "They have passage booked from the Moon aboard a Jupiter freighter. They're emigrating to the colonies, most likely. Good riddance."

So the flight, so the honeymoon. Within hours of checking into the Sweetheart Suite of the Lunar Princess, Eleanor was conducting full cabinet meetings. I was left to take bounding strolls around the duty-free dome alone. I didn't mind. I like my solitude.

I happened to be in the suite when Eleanor "took the call." The official seal of the Tri-Discipline Council filled our living room with its stately gyration and dissolved as Audrey Foldstein, herself, appeared before us sitting at her huge oaken desk. She greeted us and apologized for barging in on our honeymoon. I was dumbfounded. Here was Audrey Foldstein, chair of the Tri-D Board of Governors, one of the most powerful persons on Earth, parked at her trademark desk in our hotel suite. She turned to me and praised the inventiveness of my work in package design, and especially the camouflage work I had done forty years before for the National Militia. She also mentioned my evacuation blanket for trauma and burn victims. She spoke sincerely and at length and then turned to Eleanor. "Mrs. Starke, do you know why I'm here?"

"I believe so, Ms. Foldstein." Eleanor sat erect, regarded the holo with a steady gaze, and sent me a message through Henry, *Eleanor's chief of staff extends Eleanor's apology for not informing you sooner of her nomination. She would have told you had she thought there was any chance of her actually being designated.*

Nomination to what? I tongued back.

"These are the most exciting days known to humankind," said Audrey Foldstein, "as well as the most perilous. Each hour that passes brings wonders—and dangers—unimagined by our parents. . . . " Foldstein appeared to be in her mid-forties, an age compatible with her monstrous authority, while my El looked like a devoted daughter. ". . . and as a member of the Tri-Discipline Board of Governors, one must ever dedicate oneself—no, *consecrate* oneself—to upholding these principles, namely . . ."

A Tri-D Governor! Was that possible? My El?

". . . You will be asked to make decisions and bear

responsibilities no reasonable person would choose to make or bear. You will be a target of vocal—even violent—recrimination. And with a new family . . ." Ms. Foldstein glanced at me, ". . . you will be that much more vulnerable . . ."

Henry whispered, *Eleanor's chief of staff says Eleanor asks twice if you know what this means.*

I puzzled over this message. It had been flattened by its passage through two artificial minds. What Eleanor had probably said was, "Do you know what this means? Do you know what this means?"

Yes, dear Eleanor, I tongued through Henry, *I do. It means that every door everywhere stands open to you. Congratulations, lover. It means you have climbed onto the world stage.*

She glanced at me and winked.

By the time we shuttled back to Earth, the confirmation process was well underway. Over the next few tortuous weeks, Congressional Committees strenuously debated Eleanor's designation in public, while multinationals and the National Militia deliberated in camera. One day El would float through the house in regal exaltation. The next day she would collapse on the couch to bitterly rue the thousands of carefully buried indiscretions of her past that threatened to resurface. On the morning she testified before the Tri-D Board of Governors, she was centered, amiable, and razor-sharp. Immediately upon returning home she summoned me to my bedroom and demanded rushed, rough sex from me. Twenty minutes later she couldn't stand the sorry sight of me.

I supported her every which way I could think of. I put my own career on hold. Actually, I hadn't been to my Chicago studio since nursing Henry there.

When Eleanor was finally confirmed, we took the slipstream tube down to Cozumel for some deep-sea diving and beachcombing. It was meant to be a working vacation, but by then I suffered no illusions about Eleanor's ability to relax. There were too many plans to make and people to meet. And indeed, she kept some member of her cabinet at her side at all times: on the beach, in the boat, at the Mayan theme village, even in the cramped quarters of the submersible.

We had planned to take advantage of an exclusive juve clinic on the island to shed some age. My own age-of-choice was my mid-thirties, the age at which my body was still active enough to satisfy my desires, but mellow enough to sit through long hours of creative musing. El and I had decided on the three-day gelbath regimen and had skipped our morning visola to give our cells time to excrete their gatekeepers. But at the last moment, El changed her mind. She decided she ought to grow a little older. So I went to the clinic alone and bathed in the gels twice a day. Billions of molecular smartactives soaked through my skin; permeated my muscles, cartilage, bones, and nerves; politely snip, snip, snipped away protein cross-links and genetic anomalies; and gently flushed away the sludge and detritus of age.

I returned to the bungalow on Wednesday, frisky and bored, and volunteered to prepare it for our regular weekly salon. I had to sift through a backlog of thousands of recorded holos from our friends and associates. More congratulations and confetti for El's appointment. The salon, itself, was a stampede. More people holoed down than our bungalow could accommodate. Its primitive holoserver was overwhelmed by so many simultaneous transmissions, our guests were superimposed over each other five or ten bodies deep, and the whole squirming mass of them flickered around the edges.

Despite the confusion, I quickly sensed that this was a farewell party—for Eleanor. Our friends assumed she would be posted offplanet; all new Tri-D governors were, as all Earth posts were filled. At the same time, no one expected me to go with her—who would? Given people's longevity, it could take decades—or centuries—for Eleanor to acquire enough seniority to be transferred back to Earth. But I replied, each time the subject was broached, "Of course I'm going with her; a husband needs the regular realbody presence of his wife." Lame but true, yet each time I said it I felt sick. I didn't want to leave Earth. I had never wanted to be a colonist. I became constipated at low-*g*. Lifesuits gave me a rash. And would I be able to work? It was true I could holo my Chicago studio anywhere, but if I followed Eleanor out to some galactic rock, would my Muse follow me?

By the time the last guest signed off, we were exhausted. Eleanor got ready for bed, but I poured myself a glass of tea and went out to sit on the beach.

Wet sand. The murmur of the surf. The chilly breeze. It was a lovely equatorial dawn. "Henry," I said, "record this."

Relax, Sam. I always record the best of everything.

"I'm sure you do, Henry."

In the distance, the island's canopy dome shimmered like a veil of rain falling into the sea. The edges of the sea, the waves that surged up the beach to melt away in the sand at my feet, carried the ripe, salty smell of fish and seaweed and whales and lost sailors moldering in the deep. The ocean had proven to be a good delivery medium for molecular nasties, which can float around the globe indefinitely, like particularly rude messages in tiny bottles, until they washed up on someone's—hopefully the enemy's—shore. The island's defense canopy, more a sphere than a dome, extended through the water to the ocean floor, and deep into bedrock.

"So tell me, Henry, how are you and the cabinet getting along?" I had taken his advice, bought him more neural paste, and allowed the protocol games to continue.

The cabinet is a beautiful intelligence. I consider emulating it.

"In what way?"

I may want to bifurcate my personality bud.

"So that there's two of you? Why would you want to do that?"

Then I would be more like you.

"You would? Is that good?"

I believe so. I have recently discovered that I have but one point-of-view, while you have several that you alternate at will.

"It sounds like I bought you more paste than you know what to do with."

I don't think so, Sam. I think my thinking is evolving, but how am I to know?

It was. I recognized the symptoms.

Think of how much more flexible I could be if I could question myself, disagree with myself.

I'd rather not. All I needed was a pair of philosophy students inside my head with their tiresome discourse and untimely epiphanies. Still, I had to be careful how I handled this situation—artificial personalities bruised as easily as organic ones, and they evolved whether or not we gave them permission.

"Henry, couldn't you and I discuss things, you know, like we always have? Couldn't you just ask me the questions?"

No offense, Sam, but you wouldn't be able to keep up.

"Thank you, Henry. I'll think about it and get back to you."

Sam, the calendar secretary is hailing us. How shall I respond?

"Tell her we'll return to the bungalow soon."

Before long, Eleanor walked up the beach. She knelt behind me and massaged my shoulders. "I've been neglecting you," she said, "and you've been wonderful. Can you forgive me?"

"There's nothing to forgive. You're a busy person. I knew that from the start."

"Still, it must be hard." She sat in the sand next to me and wrapped her arms around me. "It's like a drug. I'm drunk with success. But I'll get over it."

"There's no need. You've earned it. Enjoy it."

"You don't want to go offplanet, do you?"

"I'll go anywhere to be with you."

"Yes, I believe you would. Where do men like you come from?"

"From Saturn. We're Saturnian."

She laughed. "I'm sure I could draw a post there if you'd like."

"Wherever." I leaned my head on her shoulder. "I've given up trying to escape you. I surrender."

"Oh? What are your terms of surrender?"

"Treat me fair, don't ever hurt me—or Henry—and don't ever leave me."

"Done."

Not long after our return to our Connecticut townhouse and before El received her posting, we heard some good news. Good for us anyway. Ms. Angie Rickert, Tri-Discipline Governor, posted in Indiana, had been missing for three hours. Eleanor raised her hands to deny any complicity as she told me the news, but she was barely able to stifle her glee. Ms. Rickert had been at her post for fifty-three years.

"But she's only missing," I said.

"For three hours? Come on, Sam, be realistic."

Over the next twenty-four hours, Eleanor's security chief discreetly haunted the high-security nets to feed us details and analyses as they emerged. A militia slug, on routine patrol, found Ms. Rickert's remains in and around a tube car in a low security soybean field outside the Indianapolis canopy. She was the victim of an unidentified molecular antipersonnel smartactive—a nastie. Her belt system, whose primary storage container was seized by the militia and placed under the most sanitary interrogation, claimed that Ms. Rickert was aware of her infection when she entered the tube car outside her Indianapolis apartment. The belt used Ms. Rickert's top security privileges to jettison the car and its stricken passenger out of the city and out of the tube system itself. So virulent was the attacking nastie and so stubborn Ms. Rickert's visola induced defenses, that in the heat of battle her body burst. Fortunately, it burst within the car and contaminated only two or three square miles of farmland. Ms. Rickert's reliable belt system had prevented a disaster within the Indianapolis canopy. The militia collected her scattered remains, and the coroner declared Ms. Rickert irretrievable.

And so a vacant post in the heartland was up for grabs. Eleanor turned her bedroom into a war room. She sent her entire staff into action. She lined up every chit, every favor, and every piece of dirt she had collected in her long career.

One morning, several sleepless days later, she brought me coffee, a Danish, my morning dose of visola, and a haggard smile. "It's in the bag," she said.

And she was correct. Ten days later, CNN carried a story that the Tri-Discipline Council's newest governor designate, Ms. Eleanor Starke, spouse of noted package designer Sam Harger, had been stationed in Bloomington, Indiana, to replace Ms. Angie Rickert who'd recently died under undisclosed circumstances. A host of pundits and experts debated for days the meaning of such a move and speculated on Eleanor's victory over hundreds of her senior offplanet colleagues for the plum post. Eleanor, as per Tri-D policy, respectfully declined all interviews. In my own interviews, I set the precondition that I be asked only about my own career. When asked if I could pursue my work in Indiana, I could only grin and say, Indiana is not the end of the world. And how had my work been going lately? Miserably, I replied. I am the type of artist that seems to work best while in a state of mild discontent, and lately I'd been riding a streak of great good fortune.

Smug bastard.

We moved into temporary quarters, into an apartment on the 207th floor of the Williams Towers in Bloomington. We planned to eventually purchase a farmstead in an outlying county surrounded by elm groves and rye fields. El's daily schedule, already at marathon levels, only intensified, while I pottered about the campus town trying to figure out why—if I was so lucky—did I feel so apprehensive.

Then the event occurred that dwarfed all that came before it. Eleanor and I, although we'd never applied, were issued a permit to retro-conceive a baby. These permits were impossible to come by, as only about twelve hundred were issued each year in all of North America. We knew no one who'd been issued a permit. I hadn't even seen a baby in realbody for decades (although babies figured prominently in most holovids and comedies). We were so stunned at first we didn't know how to respond. "Don't worry," said the under secretary of the Population Division, "most recipients have the same reaction. Some faint."

Eleanor said, "I don't see how I could take on the additional responsibility at this time."

The under secretary frowned. "Does that mean you wish to refuse the permit?"

Eleanor blanched. "I didn't say that." She glanced at me, uncharacteristically pleading for help.

I didn't know what to say either. "A boy or a girl?"

"That's entirely up to you, now isn't it?" The under secretary favored us with a fatuous grin. "I'll tell you what."

In his voice I heard forced spontaneity; he'd been over this ground many times before, and I wondered if that was the sum total of his job, to call twelve hundred strangers each year and grant them one of life's supreme gifts. "We'll provide background information. When you're ready, call the National Orphanage in Trenton."

For the next hour or so, El and I sat arm-in-arm on the couch in complete silence. Suddenly El began to weep. Tears gushed from her eyes and coursed down her face. She hugged herself—like a lost child, I thought—and fought for breath between sobs. I watched in total amazement. Was this my Eleanor?

After a while, she looked at me, smiled, and said through bubbles of snot, "Well?"

I had to be truthful. "Let's not rush into anything."

She studied me and said, "I agree with you."

"Let's think about it."

"My thought exactly."

At the National Orphanage in Trenton, the last thing they did was take tissue samples for recombination. Eleanor and I sat on chromium stools, side-by-side, in a treatment room as the nurse, a middle-aged jenny, scraped the inside of Eleanor's cheek with a curette. We had both been off visola for forty-eight hours, dangerous but necessary to obtain a pristine DNA sample. Henry informed me that Eleanor's full cabinet was on red alert. Eleanor was tense. This was *coitus mechanicus*, but it was bound to be the most fruitful sex we would ever have.

At the National Orphanage in Trenton, the first thing they did was sit us down in Dr. Deb Armbruster's office to warn us that raising a child today was nothing like it used to be. "Kids used to grow up and go away," said Dr. Armbruster. "Nowadays, they tend to get stuck around age eight and then again at thirteen. And it's not considered good parenting, of course, to force them to age. We think it's all the attention they get. Everyone—your friends, your employer, well-wishing strangers, militia officers—everyone comes to steal a kiss from the baby, to make funny faces at the toddler, to play catch or hoops with the five-year-old. Gifts arrive by the vanload. The media wants to be included in every decision and invited to every birthday party.

"Oh, but you two know how to handle the media, I imagine."

Eleanor and I sat in antique chairs in front of Dr. Armbruster's neatly arranged desk. There was no third chair for Eleanor's chief of staff, who stood patiently next to Eleanor. Dr. Armbruster was a large, fit woman, with a square jaw, rounded nose, and pinpoint eyes that glanced in all directions as she spoke. No doubt she had arranged her belt system in layers of display monitors around the periphery of her vision. Many administrative types did. With the flick of an iris, they could page through reams of reports, graphs, and archives. And they looked down their noses at projected valets with personality buds, like Eleanor's chief of staff.

"So," Dr. Armbruster continued, "you may have a smart-mouthed adolescent on your hands for twenty or thirty years. That, I can assure you, becomes tiresome. And expensive. You, yourselves, could be two or three relationships down the road before the little darling is ready to leave. So we suggest you work out custody now, before you go any further.

"In any case, protectorate law mandates a three-day cooling-off period between this interview and our initiation of the conversion process. You have three days—till Thursday—to change your minds. Think it over."

• • •

At the National Orphanage in Trenton, the second thing they did was take us to the storage room to see the chassis that would become our baby.

One wall held a row of carousels, each containing hundreds of small drawers. Dr. Armbruster rotated a carousel and told a particular drawer to unlock itself. She removed from it a small bundle wrapped in a rigid red tetanus blanket (a spin-off of my early work for the National Militia). She placed it on a creamic gurney, commanded the blanket to relax, and unwrapped it to reveal a near-term human fetus, curled in repose, a miniature thumb stuck in its perfect mouth. It was remarkably lifelike, but rock still, like a figurine. I asked how old it was. Dr. Armbruster said it had been in stasis seven-and-a-half years; it was confiscated in an illegal pregnancy. Developmentally, it was thirty-five weeks old; it had been doused *in utero*. She rotated the fetus—the chassis—on the gurney. "It's normal on every index. We should be able to convert it with no complications." She pointed to this and that part of it and explained the order of rewriting. "The integumentary system—the skin, what you might call our fleshy package," she smiled at me acknowledging my reputation, "is a human's fastest growing organ. A person sheds and replaces it continuously throughout her life. In the conversion process, it's the first one completed. For a fetus, it takes about a week. Hair color, eye color, the liver, the heart, the digestive system convert in two to three weeks. The nervous system, major muscle groups, reproductive organs—three to four weeks. Cartilage and bones—two to three months. Long before its first tooth erupts, the baby is biologically yours."

I asked Dr. Armbruster if I could hold the chassis.

"Certainly," she said with a knowing smile. She placed her large hands carefully under the baby and handed it to me. It was surprisingly heavy, hard, and cold. "The fixative is very dense," she said, "and makes it brittle, like eggshell." I cradled it in my arms awkwardly. Dr. Armbruster said to Eleanor, "They always look like that, afraid they're going to break it. In this case, however, that's entirely possible. And you, my dear, look typically uncomfortable as well."

She was right. Eleanor and her chief of staff stood side-by-side, twins (but for their ages), arms crossed stiffly. Dr. Armbruster said to her, "You might find the next few months immensely more tolerable, enjoyable even, under hormonal therapy. Fathers, it would seem, have always had to learn to bond with their offspring. For you we have something the pharmaceutical companies call 'Mother's Medley.' "

"No, thank you, Doctor," said Eleanor, glaring at her chief of staff, who immediately uncrossed her arms. Eleanor came over to me and I transferred the chassis to her. "Heavy," she said. "And look, it's missing a finger!" One of its tiny fingers was indeed missing, the stub end rough like plaster.

"Don't be concerned," said Dr. Armbruster. "Fingers and toes grow back in days. Just don't break off the head," she laughed.

"Sam, look," Eleanor exclaimed. "Look at this tiny little penis. Isn't it the cutest thing?"

As I looked, something funny happened to me. I had a vivid impression or image, as I do when at work in my studio, in which I saw the chassis, not as a brittle lump of fixed flesh, but as a living, warm, squirming, naked butterball of a baby. And I looked between its chubby legs and saw it was a he, a little guy. He looked up at me, chortled, and waved his tiny fists. Right then I felt a massive piece of my heart shift in my chest. The whole situation finally dawned on me. I was about to become a parent, a *father*. I looked at the chassis and saw my son. Why a son, I couldn't say, but I knew I must have a *son*.

Eleanor touched my arm. "Are you okay?"

"Yes, it's nothing. By the way, that's one piece I hope doesn't chip off."

She laughed, but when she saw that I was serious she said, "We'll have to see about that." She drilled me with her terribly old eyes and said, "About that we'll just have to see."

Back at the Williams Towers in Bloomington, we lay on the balcony in the late afternoon sun and skimmed the queue of messages. Our friends had grown tired of our good fortune: the congratulations were fewer and briefer and seemed, by-and-large, insincere, even tinged with underlying resentment.

And who could blame them? Of all the hundreds of people we knew, none of them had a real child. Many people, it was true, had had children in the old days, before the Population Treaties when babies were considered an ecological nuisance, but that was almost sixty years ago, and sixty years was a long time to live outside the company of children. Probably no one begrudged us our child, although it was obvious to everyone—especially to us—that major strings had been pulled for us at the Department of Health and Human Services. String pulling, itself, did not bother El, but anonymous string-pulling did. She had sent her security chief into the nets, but he was unable to identify our benefactor. El insisted that whoever was responsible was surely not a benefactor, for a baby could hardly be considered a reward. Most likely an enemy, perhaps an off-planet rival she had aced out of the Indianapolis post, which meant the baby was bait in some as yet unsprung plot. Or perhaps the baby was simply a leash her superiors at the Tri-D council had decided to fit her with. In any case, Eleanor was convincing herself she was about to make the worst mistake of her life.

She deleted the remaining queue of messages and turned to me. "Sam, please talk me out of this baby thing." We lay on our balcony halfway up the giant residential tower that ended, in dizzying perspective, near the lower reaches of the canopy. The canopy, invisible during the day, appeared viscous in the evening light, like a transparent gel that a stiff breeze caused to ripple and fold upon itself. In contrast, our tower had a matte surface encrusted with thousands of tiny black bumps. These were the building's resident militia slugs, absorbing the last light of the setting sun to top off their energy for a busy night patrolling living rooms and bedrooms.

"You're just nervous," I said to Eleanor.

"I have impeccable instincts."

"Did you ever have children before?"

"Not that it's relevant, but yes, two, a boy and a girl, in my old life. Tom died as a child in an accident. Angie grew up, moved away, married, had a successful career as a journalist, and died at age fifty-four of breast cancer. A long time ago." Eleanor turned over, bare rump to the sky, chin resting on sun-browned arms. "I grieved for each of them forever, and then one day I stopped. All that's left are memories, which are immaterial to this discussion."

"Would you like to have another?"

"Yes, desperately."

"Why 'desperately'?"

She was silent for a while. I watched a slug creep along the underside of the balcony of the apartment above us. "I don't know," she said. "It's funny. I've already been through it all: pregnancy, varicose veins, funerals. I've been through menopause and—worse—back through remenses. I was so tangled up in motherhood, I never knew if I was coming or going. I loved or hated every moment of it, wouldn't have traded it for the world. But when it was all over I felt an unbearable burden lifted from me. Thank god, I said, I won't have to do that again. Yet since the moment we learned of the permit, my arms have been aching to hold a baby. I don't know why. I think it's this schoolgirl body of mine. It's a baby machine, and it intends to force its will on me. I have often observed that you men regard your bodies as large pets, and I've never understood that, till now. I've never felt so removed from myself, from my body.

"But it doesn't have to have its way, does it? I can rise above it. Let's tell them to keep their chassis."

The slug bypassed our balcony, but another slug was making its way slowly down the wall.

I said, "What about this leash theory of yours?"

"I'm sure I'm correct in my assessment. They could get to me by threatening *you*, of course, but they know if it came down to it, I would—no offense—cut you loose."

"No offense taken."

She placed her hand on my cheek. "You know how much I love you. Or maybe you don't know yet. But I'm expendable, Sam, and so are you."

"But not a baby."

"No," she said, "not a baby, not *my* baby. I would do anything to keep my baby safe, and they know it. Let's refuse the permit, Sam. Okay?"

The militia slug had sensed us. It was coming in for a taste. "What about me?" I said. "I might enjoy being a dad. And can you imagine our baby, El? A little critter crawling around our ankles, half you and half me, a little Elsam or Sameanor?"

She closed her eyes and smiled. "That would be a pitiable creature."

"And speaking of ankles," I said, "we're about to be tasted."

The slug, a tiny thing, touched her ankle, attached itself to her for a moment, then dropped off. With the toes of her other foot, Eleanor scratched the tasting site. Slugs only tickled her. With me it was different. There was some nerve tying my ankle directly to my penis, and I found that warm, prickly kiss unavoidably arousing. So, as the slug attached itself to my ankle, El watched mischievously. At that moment, in the glow of the setting sun, in the delicious ache of perfect health, I didn't need the kiss of a slug to arouse me. I needed only a glance from my wife, from her ancient eyes set like opals in her girlish body. This must be how the Greek gods lived on Olympus. This must be the way it was meant to be, to grow ancient and yet to have the strength and appetites of youth. El gasped melodramatically as she watched my penis swell. She turned herself toward me, coyly covering her breasts and pubis with her hands. The slug dropped off me and headed for the balcony wall.

We lay side by side, not yet touching. I was stupid with desire and lost control of my tongue. I spoke without thinking. I said, "Mama."

The word, the single word, "mama," struck her like a physical thing. Her whole body shuddered, and her eyes went wide with surprise. I repeated it, "Mama," and she shut her eyes and turned away from me. I sidled over to her, wrapped my arms around her, and took possession of her ear. I tugged its lobe with my lips. I breathed into it. I pushed her sweat-damp hair clear of it and whispered into it, "I am the papa, and you are the mama." I watched her face, saw a ghost of a smile, and repeated, "Mama."

"Again."

"Maamma, maamma, maamma."

"Crazy papa."

"You are the mama, and mama will give papa a son."

Her eyes flew open at that, fierce, challenging, and amused. "How will papa arrange that, I wonder."

"Like this," I said as I rolled her onto her back and kissed and stroked her. But she was indifferent to me, willfully unresponsive. Nevertheless, I let my tongue play up and down her body. I visited all the sweet spots I had discovered since first we made love, for I knew her body to be my ally. Her body and I wanted the same thing. Soon, with or without El's blessing, her body opened herself to me, and when she was ready, and I was ready, and all my tiny sons inside me were ready, I began to tease her, going in, coming out, going slow, going fast, not going at all, eventually going all in a rush.

Somewhere in the middle of this, a bird, a crow, came crashing to the deck next to us. What I could make out, through the thick envelope that surrounded it, was a mass of shiny black feathers, a broken beak clattering against the deck and a smudge of blood that quickly boiled away. The whole bird, in fact, was being disassembled. Steam rose from the envelope, which emitted a piercing wail of warning. Henry spoke loudly into my ear, *Attention, Sam! In the name of safety, the militia isolation device orders you to move away from it at once.*

We were too excited to pay much mind. The envelope seemed to be doing its job. Nevertheless, we dutifully moved away; we rolled away belly to belly in a teamwork maneuver that was a delight in itself. A partition, ordered by Eleanor's cabinet no doubt, formed to separate us from the unfortunate bird. We were busy making a son and we weren't about to stop until we were through.

Later, when I brought out dinner and two glasses of visola on a tray, El sat at the patio table in her white terry robe looking at the small pile of elemental dust on the deck—carbon, sodium, calcium and whatnot—that had once been a bird. It was not at all unusual for birds to fly through the canopy, or for a tiny percentage of them to become infected outside. What *was* unusual was that, upon reentering the canopy, being tasted, found bad, and enveloped by a swarm of smartactives, so much of the bird should survive the fall in so recognizable a form, as this one had.

El smirked at me and said, "It might be Ms. Rickert, come back to haunt us."

We both laughed uneasily.

The next day I felt the urge to get some work done. It would be another two days before we could give the orphanage the go-ahead, and I was restless. Meanwhile, Eleanor had a task force meeting scheduled in the living room.

I had claimed an empty bedroom in the back for my work area. It about matched my Chicago studio in size and aspect. I had asked the building super, a typically dour reginald, to send up a man to remove all the furniture except for an armchair and a nightstand. The chair needed a pillow to support the small of my back, but otherwise it was adequate for long sitting sessions. I pulled the chair around to face a blank inner wall that Henry had told me was the north wall, placed the nightstand next to it, and brought in a carafe of strong coffee and some sweets from the kitchen. I made myself comfortable.

"Okay, Henry, take me to Chicago." The empty bedroom was instantly transformed into my studio, and I sat in front of my favorite window wall overlooking the Chicago skyline and lakefront from the 303rd floor of the Drexler Building. The sky was dark with storm clouds. Rain splattered against the window. There was nothing like a thunderstorm to stimulate my creativity.

"Henry, match Chicago's ionic dynamics here." As I sipped my coffee and watched lightning strike neighboring towers, the air in my room took on a freshly scrubbed ozone quality. I felt at rest and invigorated.

When I was ready, I turned the chair around to face my studio. It was just as I had left it month ago. There was the large, oak work table that dominated the east corner. Glass-topped and long-legged, it was a table you could work at without bending over. I used to stand at that table endlessly twenty and thirty years ago when I still lived in Chicago. Now it was piled high with prized junk: design trophies, hunks of polished gemstones from Mars and Jupiter, a scale model Japanese pagoda of cardboard and mica, a box full of my antique key collection, parcels wrapped in some of my most successful designs, and—the oldest objects in the room—a mason jar of paint brushes, like a bouquet of dried flowers.

I rose from my chair and wandered about my little domain, taking pleasure in my life's souvenirs. The cabinets, shelves, counters, and floor were as heavily laden as the table: an antelope skin spirit drum; an antique pendulum mantel clock the houseputer servos kept wound; holocubes of some of my former lovers and wives; bits of colored glass, tumbleweed, and driftwood in whose patterns and edges I had once found inspiration; and a whale vertebra used as a footstool. This room was more a museum now than a functional studio, and I was more its curator than a practicing artist.

I went to the south wall and looked into the corner. Henry's original container sat atop three more identical ones. "How's the paste?" I said.

"Sufficient for the time being. I'll let you know when we need more."

"More? This isn't enough? There's enough paste here now to run a major city."

"Eleanor Starke's cabinet is more powerful than a major city."

"Yes, well, let's get down to work." I returned to my armchair. The storm had passed the city and was retreating across the lake, turning the water midnight blue. "What have you got on the egg idea?"

Henry projected a richly ornate egg in the air before me. Gold leaf and silver wire, inlaid with once-precious gems, it was modeled after the Fabergé masterpieces favored by the last of the Romanoff Tsars. But instead of enclosing miniature clockwork automatons, these would be merely expensive wrapping for small gifts. You'd crack them open. You could keep the pieces, which would reassemble, or toss them into the soup bin for recycling credits.

"It's just as I told you last week," said Henry. "The public will hate it. I tested it against Simulated Us, the Donohue Standard, the Person in the Street, and Focus Rental." Henry filled the air around the egg with dynamic charts and graphs. "Nowhere are positive ratings higher than 7 percent, or negative ratings lower than 68 percent. Typical comments call it 'old-fashioned,' and 'vulgar.' Matrix analysis finds that people do not like to be reminded of their latent fertility. People resent . . ."

"Okay, okay," I said. "I get the picture." It was a dumb concept. I knew as much when I proposed it. But I was so enamored by my own soon-to-be-realized fertility, I had lost my head. I thought people would be drawn to this archetypal symbol of renewal, but Henry had been right all along, and now he had the data to prove it.

If the truth be told, I had not come up with a hit design in five years, and I was worried that maybe I never would again.

"It's just a dry spell," said Henry, sensing my mood. "You've had them before, even longer."

"I know, but this one is the worst."

"You say that every time."

To cheer me up, Henry began to play my wrapping paper portfolio, projecting my past masterpieces larger than life in the air.

I held patents for package applications in many fields, from emergency blankets and temporary skin, to military camouflage and video paint. But my own favorites, and probably the public's as well, were my novelty gift wraps. My first was a video wrapping paper that displayed the faces of loved ones (or celebrities if you had no loved ones) singing "Happy Birthday" to the music of the New York Pops. That dated back to 2025 when I was a molecular engineering student.

My first professional design was the old box-in-a-box routine, only my boxes didn't get smaller as you opened them, but larger, and in fact could fill the whole room until you chanced upon one of the secret commands, which were any variation of "stop" (whoa, enough, cut it out, etc.) or "help" (save me, I'm suffocating, get this thing off me, etc.).

Next came wrapping paper that screamed when you tore or cut it. That led to paper that resembled human skin. It molded itself perfectly and seamlessly (except for a belly button) around the gift and had a shelf life of fourteen days. You had to cut it to open the gift, and of course it bled. We sold mountains of that stuff.

The human skin led to my most enduring design, a perennial that was still common today, the orange peel. It too wrapped itself around any shape seamlessly (and had a navel). It was real, biological orange peel. When you cut or ripped it, it squirted citrus juice and smelled delightful.

I let Henry project these designs for me. I must say I was drunk with my own achievements. I gloried in them. They filled me with the most selfish wonder.

I was terribly good, and the whole world knew it.

Yet even after this healthy dose of self-love, I wasn't able to buckle down to anything new. I told Henry to order the kitchen to fix me some more coffee and some lunch.

On my way to the kitchen I passed the living room and saw that Eleanor was having difficulties of her own. Even with souped-up holoservers, the living room was a mess. There were dozens of people in there and, as best I could tell, just as many rooms superimposed over each other. People, especially important people, liked to bring their offices with them when they went to meetings. The result was a jumble of merging desks, lamps, and chairs. Walls sliced through each other at drunken angles. Windows issued cityscape views of New York, London, Washington, and Moscow (and others I didn't recognize) in various shades of day and weather. People, some of whom I knew from the news-nets, either sat at their desks in a rough, overlapping circle, or wandered through walls and furniture to kibitz with each other and with Eleanor's cabinet.

At least this is how it all appeared to me standing in the hallway, outside the room's holo anchors. To those inside, it might look like the Senate chambers. I watched for a while, safely out of holo range, until Eleanor noticed me. "Henry," I said, "ask her how many of these people are here in realbody." Eleanor raised a finger, one, and pointed to herself.

I smiled. She was the only one there who could see me. I continued to the kitchen and brought my lunch back to my studio. I still couldn't get started, so I asked Henry to report on my correspondence. He had answered over five hundred posts since our last session the previous week. Four-fifths of these concerned the baby. We were invited to appear—*with the baby*—on every major talk show and magazine. We were threatened with lawsuits by the Anti-Transubstantiation League. We were threatened with violence by several anonymous calls (who would surely be identified by El's security chief and prosecuted by her attorney general). A hundred seemingly ordinary people requested permission to visit us in realbody or holo during nap time, bath time, any time. Twice that number accused us of elitism. Three men and one woman named Sam Harger claimed that their fertility permit was mistakenly awarded to me. Dr. Armbruster's prediction was coming true and the baby hadn't even been converted yet.

This killed an hour. I still didn't feel creative, so I called it quits. I took a shower, shaved. Then I went, naked, to stand outside the entrance to the living room. When Eleanor saw me, her eyes went big, and she laughed. She held up five fingers, five minutes, and turned back to her meeting.

I went to my bedroom to wait for her. She spent her lunch break with me. When we made love that day and the next, I enjoyed a little fantasy I never told her about. I imagined that she was pregnant in the old-fashioned way, that her belly was enormous, melon-round and hard, and that as I moved inside her, as we moved together, we were teaching our son his first lesson in the art of human love.

On Thursday, the day of the conversion, we took a leisurely breakfast on the terrace of the New Foursquare Hotel in downtown Bloomington. A river of pedestrians, students and service people mostly, flowed past our little island of metal tables and brightly striped umbrellas. The day broke clear and blue and would be hot by noon. A gentle breeze tried to snatch away our menus. The Foursquare had the best kitchen in Bloomington, at least for desserts. Its pastry chef, Mr. Duvou, had built a reputation for the classics. That morning we (mostly me) were enjoying strawberry shortcake with whipped cream and coffee. Everything—the strawberries, the wheat for the cakes, the sugar, coffee beans, and cream—was grown, not assembled. The preparation was done lovingly and skillfully by hand. All the waitstaff were steves, who were highly sensitive to our wants and who, despite their ungainly height, bowed ever so low to take our order.

I moistened my finger with my tongue and made temporary anchor points where I touched the table and umbrella pole. We called Dr. Armbruster. She appeared in miniature, desk and all, on my place mat.

"It's a go, then?" she said.

"Yes," I said.

"Yes," said Eleanor, who took my hand.

"Congratulations, both of you. You are two of the luckiest people in the world."

We already knew that.

"Traits? Enhancements?" asked Dr. Armbruster.

We had studied all the options and decided to allow Nature and chance, not some well-meaning engineer, to roll our genes together into a new individual. "Random traits," we said, "and standard enhancements."

"That leaves gender," said Dr. Armbruster.

I looked at Eleanor, who smiled. "A boy," she said. "It definitely wants to be a boy."

"A boy it is," said Dr. Armbruster. "I'll get the lab on it immediately. The recombination should take about three hours. I'll monitor the progress and keep you apprised. We will infect the chassis around noon. Make an appointment for a week from today to come in and take possession of . . . your son. We like to throw a little birthing party. It's up to you to make media arrangements, if any.

"I'll call you in about an hour. And congratulations again!"

We were too nervous to do anything else, so we ate shortcake and drank coffee and didn't talk much. We mostly sat close and said meaningless things to ease the tension. Finally Dr. Armbruster, seated at her tiny desk, called back.

"The recombination work is about two-thirds done and is proceeding very smoothly. Early readings show a Pernell Organic Intelligence quotient of 3.93—very impressive, but probably no surprise to you. So far, we know that your son has Sam's eyes, chin, and skeleto-muscular frame, and Eleanor's hair, nose, and . . . eyebrows."

"I'm afraid my eyebrows are fairly dominant," said Eleanor.

"Apparently," said Dr. Armbruster.

"I'm mad about your eyebrows," I said.

"And I'm mad about your frame," Eleanor said.

We spent another hour there, taking two more updates from Dr. Armbruster. I ordered an iced bottle of champagne, and guests from other tables toasted us with coffee cups and visola glasses. I was slightly tipsy when we finally rose to leave. To my annoyance, I felt the prickly kiss of a militia slug at my ankle. I decided I'd better let it finish tasting me before I attempted to thread my way through the jumble of tables and chairs. The slug seemed to take an unusual length of time.

Eleanor, meanwhile, was impatient to go. "What is it?" she laughed. "Are you drunk?"

"Just a slug," I said. "It's about done." But it wasn't. Instead of dropping off, it elongated itself and looped around both of my ankles so that when I turned to join Eleanor, I tripped and fell into our table, which crashed into a neighboring one.

Everything happened at once. As I fell, the slippery shroud of an isolation envelope snaked up my body to my face and sealed itself above my head. But it did not cushion my fall; I banged my nose on the flagstone. Everything grew dim as the envelope coalesced, so that I could barely make out the tables and umbrellas and the crowd of people running past me like horror-show shadows. There was Eleanor's face, momentarily, peering in at me, and then gone. "Don't go!" I shouted. "Eleanor, help!" But she melted into the crowd on the pedway. I tried to get up, to crawl, but my arms and legs were tightly bound.

Henry said, *Sam, I'm being probed, and I've lost contact with Eleanor's system.*

"What's going on?" I screamed. "Tell them to make it stop." I, too, was being probed. At first my skin tingled as in a gelbath at a juve clinic. But these smartactives weren't polite and weren't about to take a leisurely three days to inspect my cells. They wanted in right away; they streamed through my pores, down my nasal passage and throat, up my urethra and anus and spread out to capture all of my organs. My skin burned. My heart stammered. My stomach clamped and sent a geyser of pink shortcake mush and champagne-curdled cream back up my throat. But with the envelope stretched across my face, there was nowhere for the vomit to go except as a thin layer down my throat and chest. The envelope treated it as organic matter attempting escape and quickly disassembled it, scalding me with the heat of its activity. I rolled frantically about trying to lessen the pain, blindly upsetting more tables. Shards of glass cut me without cutting the envelope, so thin it stretched, and my blood leaked from me and simmered away next to my skin.

Fernando Boa, said someone in Henry's voice in Spanish. *You are hereby placed under arrest for unlawful escape and flight from State of Oaxaca authorities. Do not resist. Any attempt to resist will result in your immediate execution.*

"My name is not Boa," I cried through a swollen throat. "It's Harger, Sam Harger!"

I squeezed my eyelids tight against the pain, but the actives cut right through them, coating my eyeballs and penetrating them to taste the vitreous humor inside. Brilliant flashes and explosions of light burst across my retinae as each rod and cone was inspected, and a dull, hurricane roar filled my head.

Henry shouted, *Shall I resist? I think I should resist.*

"NO!" I answered, "No, Henry!"

The real agony began then, as all up and down my body, my nerve cells were invaded. Attached to every muscle fiber, every blood vessel, every hair follicle, embedded in my skin, my joints, my intestines, they all began to fire at once. My brain rattled in my skull. My guts twisted inside out. I begged for unconsciousness.

Then, just as suddenly, the convulsions ceased, the

trillions of engines inside me abruptly quit. *I can do this*, Henry said. *I know how.*

"No, Henry," I croaked.

The envelope itself flickered, then fell from me like so much dust. I was in daylight and fresh air again. Soiled, bleeding, beat-up, and bloated, but whole. I was alone on a battlefield of smashed umbrellas and china shrapnel. I thought maybe I should crawl away from the envelope's dust, but the slug still shackled my ankles. "You shouldn't have done it, Henry," I said. "They won't like what you did."

Without warning, the neural storm slammed me again, worse than before. A new envelope issued from the slug. This one squeezed me, like a tube of oil paint, starting at my feet, crushing the bones and working up my legs.

"Please," I begged, "let me pass out."

I didn't pass out, but I went somewhere else, to another room, where I could still hear the storm raging on the other side of a thin wall. There was someone else in the room, a man I halfway recognized. He was well-muscled and of middle height, and his yellow hair was streaked with white. He wore the warmest of smiles on his coarse, round face.

"Don't worry," he said, referring to the storm beyond the wall, "it'll pass."

He had Henry's voice.

"You should have listened to me, Henry," I scolded. "Where did you learn to disobey me?"

"I know I don't count all that much," said the man. "I mean, I'm just a construct, not a living being. A servant, not a coequal. But I want to tell you how good it's been to know you."

I awoke lying on my side on a gurney in a ceramic room, my cheek resting in a small puddle of clear fluid. I was naked.

Every cell of me ached. A man in a militia uniform, a jerry, watched me sullenly. When I sat up, dizzy, nauseous, he held out a bundle of clean clothes. Not my clothes.

"Wha' happe' me?" My lips and tongue were twice their size.

"You had an unfortunate accident."

"Assiden'?"

The jerry pressed the clothes into my hands. "Just shut up and get dressed." He resumed his post next to the door and watched me fumble with the clothes. My feet were so swollen I could hardly pull the pants leg. over them. My hands trembled and could not grip. I could not keep my vision focused, and my head pulsed with pain. But all in all, I felt much better than I had a little while ago.

When, after what seemed like hours, I was dressed, the jerry said, "Captain wants to see ya."

I followed him down deserted ceramic corridors to a small office where sat a large, handsome young man in a neat blue unfiorm. "Sign here," he said, pushing a slate at me. "It's your terms of release."

Read this, Henry, I tongue with a bruised tongue. When Henry didn't answer I felt the pull of panic until I remembered that the slave processors inside my body that connected me to Henry's box in Chicago had certainly been destroyed. So I tried to read the document myself. It was loaded with legalese and interminable clauses, but I was able to glean from it that by signing it, I was forever releasing the National Militia from all liability for whatever treatment I had enjoyed at their hands.

"I will not sign this," I said.

"Suit yourself," said the captain, who took the slate from my hands. "You are hereby released from Custody, but you remain on probation until further notice. Ask the belt for details." He pointed to the belt holding up my borrowed trousers.

I lifted my shirt and looked at the belt. The device stitched to it was so small I had missed it, and its ports were disguised as grommets.

"Sergeant," the captain said to the jerry, "show Mr. Harger the door."

"Just like that?" I said.

"What do you want, a prize?"

It was dark out. I asked the belt they'd given me for the time, and it said in a flat, neuter voice, "The time is seven forty-nine and thirty-two seconds." I calculated I had been incarcerated—and unconscious—for about seven hours. On a hunch, I asked what day it was. "The date is Friday, 6 April 2092."

Friday. I had been out for a day and seven hours.

There was a tube station right outside the cop shop, naturally, and I managed to find a private car. I climbed in and eased my aching self into the cushioned seat. I considered calling Eleanor, but not with that belt. So I told it to take me home. It replied, "Address please."

My anger flared and I snapped, "The Williams Towers, stupid."

"City and state, please."

I was too tired for this. "Bloomington!"

"Bloomington in California, Idaho, Illinois, Iowa, Kansas, Kentucky, Maryland, Minnesota, Missouri, Nebraska, New York . . ."

"Hold it! Wait! Enough! Where the hell am I?"

"You're at the Western Regional Militia Headquarters, Utah."

How I longed for my Henry. He'd get me home safe with no hassle. He'd take care of me. "Bloomington," I said mildly, "Indiana."

The doors locked, the running lights came on, and the car rolled to the injection ramp. We coasted down, past the local grid, to the intercontinental tubes. The belt said, "Your travel time to the Williams Towers in Bloomington, Indiana, will be one hour, fifty-five minutes." When the car entered the slipstream, I was shoved against the seat by the force of acceleration. Henry would have known how sore I was and shunted us to the long ramp. Fortunately, I had a spare Henry belt in the apartment, so I wouldn't have to be without him for long. And after a few days, when I felt better, I'd again reinstall him inbody.

I tried to nap, but was too sick. My head kept swimming, and I had to keep my eyes open, or I would have vomited.

It was after 10:00 P.M. when I arrived under the Williams Towers, but the station was crowded with residents and guests. I felt everyone's eyes on me. Surely everyone knew of my arrest. They would have watched it on the nets, witnessed my naked fear as the shroud raced up my chest and face.

I walked briskly, looking straight ahead, to the row of elevators. I managed to claim one for myself, and as the doors closed I felt relief. But something was wrong; we weren't moving.

"Floor please," said my new belt in its bland voice.

"Fuck you!" I screamed. "Fuck you fuck you fuck you! Listen to me, you piece of shit, and see if you can get this right. I want you to call Henry, that's my system. Shake hands with him. Put him in charge of all your miserable functions. Do you hear me?"

"Certainly, sir. What is the Henry access code?"

"Code? Code? I don't know the code." That kind of detail had been Henry's job for over eighty years. I had stopped memorizing codes and ID numbers and addresses, anniversaries and birthdates long ago. "Just take me up! We'll stop at every floor above 200!" I shouted. "Wait. Hold it. Open the doors." I had the sudden, urgent need to urinate. I didn't think I could hold it long enough to reach the apartment, especially with the added pressure from the high-speed lift.

There were people waiting outside the elevator doors. I was sure they had heard me shouting. I stepped through them, a sick smile plastered to my face, the sweat rolling down my forehead, and I hurried to the men's room off the lobby.

I had to go so bad, that when I stood before the urinal and tried, I couldn't. I felt about to burst, but I was plugged up. I had to consciously calm myself, breathe deeply, relax. The stream, when it finally emerged, seemed to issue forever. How many quarts could my bladder hold? The urine was viscous and cloudy with a dull metallic sheen, as though mixed with aluminum dust. Whatever the militia had pumped into me would take days to excrete. At least there was no sign of bleeding, thank God. But it burned. And when I was finished and about to leave the rest room, I felt I had to go again.

Up on my floor, my belt valet couldn't open the door to the apartment, so I had to ask admittance. The door didn't recognize me, but Eleanor's cabinet gave it permission to open. The apartment smelled of strong disinfectant. "Eleanor, are you home?" It suddenly occurred to me that she might not be.

"In here," called Eleanor. I hurried to the living room, but Eleanor wasn't there. It was her sterile elder twin, her chief of staff, who sat on the couch. She was flanked by the attorney general, dressed in black, and the security chief, grinning his wolfish grin.

"What the hell is this," I said, "a fucking cabinet meeting? Where's Eleanor?"

In a businesslike manner, the chief of staff motioned to the armchair opposite the couch. "Won't you please join us, Sam. We have much to discuss."

"Discuss it among yourselves," I yelled. "Where's

Eleanor?" Now I was sure that she was gone. She had bolted from the cafe and kept going; she had left her three stooges behind to break the bad news to me.

"Eleanor's in her bedroom, but she . . ."

I didn't wait. I ran down the hallway. But the bedroom door was locked. "Door," I shouted, "unlock yourself."

"Access," replied the door, "has been extended to apartment residents only."

"That includes me, you idiot." I pounded the door with my fist. "Eleanor, let me in. It's me—Sam."

No reply.

I returned to the living room. "What the fuck is going on here?"

"Sam," said the elderly chief of staff. "Eleanor will see you in a few minutes, but not before . . ."

"Eleanor!" I yelled, turning around to look at each of the room's holoeyes. "I know you're watching. Come out; we need to talk, I want you, not these dummies."

"Sam, " said Eleanor behind me. But it wasn't Eleanor. Again I was fooled by her chief of staff who had crossed her arms like an angry El and bunched her eyebrows in an angry scowl. She mimicked my Eleanor so perfectly, I had to wonder if it wasn't El as a morphed holo. "Sam, please get a grip and sit down. We need to discuss your accident."

"My what? My accident? That's the same word the militia used. Well, it was no accident! It was an assault, a rape, a vicious attack. Not an accident!"

"Excuse me," said Eleanor's attorney general, "but we were using the word 'accident' in its legal sense. Both sides have provisionally agreed . . ."

I left the room without a word. I needed urgently to urinate again. Mercifully, the bathroom door opened to me. I knew I was behaving terribly, but I couldn't help myself. On the one hand I was relieved and grateful that Eleanor was there, that she hadn't left me—yet. On the other hand,

I was hurting and confused and angry. All I wanted was to hold her, be held by her. I needed her at that moment more than I had ever needed anyone in my life. I had no time for holos. But, it was reasonable that she should be frightened. Maybe she thought I was infectious. My behavior was doing nothing to reassure her. I had to control myself.

My urine burned even more than before. My mouth was cotton dry. I grabbed a glass and filled it with tap water. Surprised at how thirsty I was, I drank glassful after glassful. I washed my face in the sink. The cool water felt so good, I stripped off my militia-issue clothes and stepped into the shower. The water revived me, fortified me. Not wanting to put the clothes back on, I wrapped a towel around myself, went out, and told the holos to ask Eleanor to toss out some of my clothes for me. I promised I wouldn't try to force my way into the bedroom when she opened the door.

"All your clothes were confiscated by the militia," said the chief of staff, "but Fred will bring you something of his."

Before I could ask who Fred was, a big, squat-bodied russ came out of the back bedroom, the room I used for my trips to Chicago. He was dressed in a conservative business suit and carried a brown velvet robe over his arm.

"This is Fred," said the chief of staff. "Fred has been assigned to . . ."

"What?" I shouted. "El's afraid I'm going to throttle her holos? She thinks I would break down that door?"

"Eleanor thinks nothing of the kind," said the chief of staff. "Fred has been assigned by the Tri-Discipline Board."

"Well, I don't want him here. Send him away."

"I'm afraid," said the chief of staff, "that as long as Eleanor remains a governor, Fred stays. Neither she nor you have any say in the matter."

The russ, Fred, held out the robe to me, but I refused it

and said, "Just stay out of my way, Fred." I went to the bathroom and found one of Eleanor's terry robes in the linen closet. It was tight on me, but it would do.

Returning to the living room, I sat in the armchair facing the cabinet's couch. "Okay, what do you want?"

"That's more like it," said the chief of staff. "First, let's get you caught up on what's happened so far."

"By all means. Catch me up."

The chief of staff glanced at the attorney general who said, "Yesterday morning, Thursday, 5 April, at precisely 10:47:39, while loitering at the New Foursquare Cafe in downtown Bloomington, Indiana, you, Samson P. Harger, were routinely analyzed by a National Militia Random Testing Device, Metro Population Model 8903AL. You were found to be in noncompliance with the Sabotage and Espionage Acts of 2036, 2038, 2050, and 2090. As per procedures set forth in . . ."

"Please," I said, "in English."

The security chief said in his gravelly voice, "You were tasted by a slug, Mr. Harger, and found bad, real bad. So they bagged you."

"What was wrong with me?"

"Name it. You went off the scale. First, the DNA sequence in a sample of ten of your skin cells didn't match each other. Also, a known nastie was identified in your blood. Your marker genes didn't match your record in the National Registry. You *did* match the record of a known terrorist with an outstanding arrest warrant. You also matched the record of someone who died twenty-three years ago."

"That's ridiculous," I said. "How could the slug read all those things at once?"

"That's what the militia wanted to know. So they disassembled you."

"They! What?"

"Any one of those conditions gave them the authority

they needed. They didn't have the patience to read you slow and gentle like, so they pumped you so full of smartactives you filled a swimming pool."

"They. Completely?"

"All your biological functions were interrupted. You were legally dead for three minutes."

It took me a moment to grasp what he was saying. "So what did they discover?"

"Nothing," said the security chief, "zip, nada. Your cell survey came up normal. They couldn't even get the arresting slug, nor any other slug, to duplicate the initial readings."

"So the arresting slug was defective?"

"We've forced them to concede that the arresting slug may have been defective."

"So they reassembled me and let me go, and everything is okay?"

"Not quite. That particular model slug has never been implicated in a false reading. This would be the first time, according to the militia, and naturally they're not eager to admit that. Besides, they still had you on another serious charge."

"Which is?"

"That your initial reading constituted an unexplained anomaly."

"An unexplained anomaly? This is a crime?"

I excused myself for another visit to the bathroom. The urgency increased when I stood up from the armchair and was painful by the time I reached the toilet. This time the stream didn't burn me, but hissed and gave off some sort of vapor, like steam. I watched in horror as my situation became clear to me.

I marched back to the living room, stood in front of the three holos, rolled up a sleeve, and scratched and rubbed my arm, scraping off flakes of skin which cascaded to the floor, popping and flashing like a miniature fireworks display. "I've been seared!" I screamed at them. "You let them sear me!"

"Sit down," said the chief of staff. "Unfortunately, there's more."

I sat down, still holding my arm out. Beads of sweat dropped from my chin and boiled away on the robe in little puffs of steam.

"Eleanor feels it best to tell you everything now," said the chief of staff. "It's not pretty, so sit back and prepare yourself for more bad news."

I did as she suggested.

"They weren't about to let you go, you know. You had forfeited all of your civil rights. If you weren't the spouse of a Tri-Discipline Governor, you'd have simply disappeared. As it was, they proceeded to eradicate all traces of your DNA from the environment. They flooded this apartment first, removed every bit of hair, phlegm, mucus, skin, fingernail, toenail, semen, and blood that you have shed or deposited since moving in. They sent probes down the plumbing for trapped hair. They subjected Eleanor to a complete body douche. They scoured the halls, elevators, lobby, dining room, linen stores, laundry. They were most thorough. They have likewise visited your townhouse in Connecticut, the bungalow in Cozumel, the juve clinic, your hotel room on the Moon, the shuttle, and all your and Eleanor's domiciles all over the Protectorate. They are systematically following your trail backward for a period of thirty years."

"My Chicago studio?"

"Of course."

"Henry?"

"Gone."

"You mean isolation, right? They're interrogating him, right?"

The security chief said, "No, eradicated. He resisted. Gave 'em quite a fight, too. But no civilian job can withstand the weight of the National Militia. Not even us."

I didn't believe Henry was gone. He had so many secret backups. At this moment he was probably lying low in a half dozen parking loops all over the solar system.

But another thought occurred to me. "My son!"

The chief of staff said, "When your accident occurred, the chassis had not yet been infected with your and Eleanor's recombinant. Had it been, the militia would have disassembled it too. Eleanor prevented the procedure at the last moment and turned over all genetic records and material."

I tried sifting through this. My son was dead, or rather, never started. But at least Eleanor had saved the chassis. We could always try—no we couldn't. *I was seared!* My cells were locked. Any attempt to read or overwrite any of my cells would cause those cells to fry.

The attorney general said, "The chassis, however, had already been brought out of stasis and was considered viable. To allow it to develop with its original genetic complement, or to place it back into stasis, would have exposed it to legal claims by its progenitors. So Eleanor had it infected. It's undergoing conversion at this moment."

"Infected? Infected with what? Did she clone herself?"

The chief of staff laughed, "Heavens, no. She had it infected with the recombination of her genes and those of a simulated partner, a composite of several of her past consorts."

"Without my agreement?"

"You were deceased at the time. She was your surviving spouse."

"I was deceased for only three minutes! I was retrievably dead. Obviously, retrievable!"

"Alive you would have been a felon, and the fertility permit would have been annulled."

I closed my eyes and leaned back into the chair. "Okay," I said, "what else?" When no one answered, I said, "To sum up then, I have been seared, which means my genes are booby trapped. Which means I'm incapable of reproducing, or even of being rejuvenated. So my life expectancy has been reduced to . . . what? . . . another hundred years or so? Okay. My son is dead. Pulled apart before he was even started. Henry is gone, probably forever. My wife—no, my widow—is having a child with another man—men."

"Women actually," said the chief of staff.

"Whatever. Not by me. How long did all of this take?"

"About twenty minutes."

"A hell of a busy twenty minutes."

"To our way of thinking," said the attorney general, "a protracted interval of time. The important negotiation in your case occurred within the first five seconds of your demise."

"You're telling me that Eleanor was able to figure everything out and cook up her simulated partner in five seconds?"

"Eleanor has in readiness at all times a full set of contingency plans to cover every conceivable threat we can imagine. It pays, Mr. Harger, to plan for the worst."

"I guess it does." The idea that all during our time together, El was busy making these plans was too monstrous to believe. "So tell me about these negotiations."

"First, let me impress upon you," said the chief of staff, "the fact that Eleanor stuck by you. Few other Tri-Discipline officers would take such risks to fight for a spouse. Also, only someone in the position could have successfully prosecuted your case. The militia doesn't have to answer phone calls, you know.

"As to the details, the attorney general can fill you in later, but here's the agreement in a nutshell. Given the wild diagnosis of the arresting slug and the subsequent lack of substantiating evidence, we calculated the most probable cause to be a defect in the slug, not some as yet unheard of nastie in your body. Further, as a perfect system of any sort has never been demonstrated, we predicted there to be records of other failures buried deep in militia archives. Eleanor threatened to air these files publicly in a civil suit. To do so would have cost her a lifetime of political capital, her career, and possibly her life. But as she was able to convince the militia she was willing to proceed, they backed down. They agreed to revive you and place you on probation, the terms of which are stored in your belt system, which we see you have not yet reviewed. The major term is your searing. Searing effectively neutralizes the threat in case you *are* the victim of a new nastie. Also, as a sign of good faith, we disclosed the locations of all of Henry's hidy-holes."

"What?" I rose from my seat. "You gave them Henry?"

"Sit down, Mr. Harger," said the security chief.

But I didn't sit down. I began to pace. So this is how it works, I thought. This is the world I live in.

"Please realize, Sam," said the chief of staff, "they would have found him out anyway. No matter how clever you think you are, given time, all veils can be pierced."

I turned around to answer her, but she and her two colleagues were gone. I was alone in the room with the russ, Fred, who stood sheepishly next to the hall corridor. He cleared his throat and said, "Governor Starke will see you now."

II

It's been eight long months since my surprise visit to the cop shop. I've had plenty of time to sit and reflect on what's happened to me, to meditate on my victimhood.

Shortly after my accident, Eleanor and I moved into our new home, a sprawling old farmstead on the outskirts of Bloomington. We have more than enough room here, with barns and stables, a large garden, apple and pear orchards, tennis courts, swimming pool, and a dozen service people to run everything. It's really very beautiful, and the whole eighty acres is covered with its own canopy, inside and independent of the Bloomington canopy, a bubble inside a bubble. Just the place to raise the child of a Tri-Discipline governor.

The main house, built of blocks of local limestone, dates back to the last century. It's the home that Eleanor and I dreamed of owning. But now that we're here, I spend most of my time in the basement, for sunlight is hard on my seared skin. For that matter, rich food is hard on my gut, I bruise easily inside and out, I can't sleep a whole night through, all my joints ache for an hour or so when I rise, I have lost my sense of smell, and I've become hard of hearing. There is a constant taste of brass in my mouth and a dull throbbing in my skull. I go to bed nauseated and wake up nauseated. The doctor says my condition will improve in time as my body adjusts, but that my health is up to me now. No longer do I have resident molecular homeostats to constantly screen, flush and scrub my cells, nor muscle toners or far inhibitors. No longer can I go periodically to a juve clinic to correct the cellular errors of aging. Now I can and certainly will grow stouter, slower, weaker, balder, and older. Now the date of my death is decades, not millennia, away. This should come as no great shock, for this was the human condition when I was born. Yet, since my birth, the whole human race, it seems, has boarded a giant ocean liner and set sail for shores of immortality. I, however, have been unceremoniously tossed overboard.

So I spend my days sitting in the dim dampness of my basement corner, growing pasty white and fat (twenty pounds already), and plucking my eyebrows to watch them sizzle like fuses.

I am not pouting, and I am certainly not indulging in self-pity, as Eleanor accuses me. In fact, I am brooding. It's what artists do, we brood. To other, more active people, we appear selfish, obsessive, even narcissistic, which is why we prefer to brood in private.

But I'm not brooding about art or package design. I have quit that for good. I will never design again. That much I know. I'm not sure what I *will* do, but at least I know I've finished that part of my life. It was good; I enjoyed it. I climbed to the top of my field. But it's over.

I am brooding about my victimhood. My intuition tells me that if I understand it, I will know what to do with myself. So I pluck another eyebrow hair. The tiny bulb of muscle at the root ignites like an old fashioned match, a tiny point of light in my dark cave and, as though making a wish, I whisper, "Henry." The hair sizzles along its length until it burns my fingers, and I have to drop it. My fingertips are already charred from this game.

I miss Henry terribly. It's as though a whole chunk of my mind were missing. I never knew how deeply integrated I had woven him into my psyche, or where my thoughts stopped and his started. When I ask myself a question these days, no one answers.

I wonder why he did it, what made him think he could resist the militia. Can machine intelligence become cocky? Or did he knowingly sacrifice himself for me? Did he think he could held me escape? Or did he protect our privacy in the only way open to him, by destroying himself? The living archive of my life is gone, but at least it's not in the loving hands of the militia.

My little death has caused other headaches. My marriage ended. My estate went into receivership. My memberships, accounts, and privileges in hundreds of services and organizations were closed. News of my death spread around the globe at the speed of light, causing tens of thousands of data banks to toggle my status to "deceased," a position not designed to toggle back. Autobituaries, complete with footage of my mulching at the Foursquare Cafe, appeared on all the nets the same day. Every reference to me records both my dates of birth and death. (Interestingly, none of my obits or bios mention the fact that I was seared.) Whenever I try to use my voiceprint to pay a bill, alarms go off. El's attorney general has managed to reinstate most of my major accounts, but my demise is too firmly entrenched in the world's web to ever be fully corrected. The attorney general has, in fact, offered me a routine for my belt system to pursue these corrections on a continuous basis. She, as well as the rest of El's cabinet, has volunteered to educate my belt for me as soon as I install a personality bud in it. It will need a bud if I ever intend to leave the security of my dungeon. But I'm not ready for a new belt buddy.

I pluck another eyebrow hair, and by its tiny light I say, "Ellen."

We are living in an armed fortress. Eleanor says we can survive any form of attack here: conventional, nuclear, or molecular. She feels completely at ease here. This is where she comes to rest at the end of a long day, to glory in her patch of Earth, to adore her baby, Ellen. Even without the help of Mother's Medley, Eleanor's maternal instincts have all kicked in. She is mad with motherhood. Ellen is ever in her thoughts. If she could, El would spend all her time in the nursery in realbody, but the duties of a Tri-D Governor call her away. So she has programmed a realtime holo of Ellen to be visible continuously in the periphery of her vision, a private scene only she can see. No longer do the endless meetings and unavoidable luncheons capture her full attention. No longer is time spent in a tube car flitting from one corner of the Protectorate to another a total waste. Now she secretly watches the jennies feed the baby, bathe the baby, perambulate the baby around the duck pond. And she is always interfering with the jennies, correcting them, undercutting whatever place they may have won in the baby's affection. There are four jennies. Without the namebadges on their identical uniforms, I wouldn't be able to tell them apart. They have overlapping twelve-hour shifts, and they hand the baby off like a baton in a relay race.

I have my own retinue, a contingent of four russes: Fred, the one who showed up on the day of my little death, and three more. I am not a prisoner here, and their mission is to protect the compound, Governor Starke, and her infant daughter, not to watch me, but I have noticed that there is always one within striking distance, especially when I go near the nursery. Which I don't do very often. Ellen is a beautiful baby, but I have no desire to spend time with her, and the whole house seems to breathe easier when I stay down in my tomb.

Yesterday evening a jenny came down to announce dinner. I threw on some clothes and joined El in the solarium off the kitchen where lately she prefers to take all her meals. Outside the window wall, heavy snowflakes fell silently in the blue-grey dusk. El was watching Ellen explore a new toy on the carpet. When she turned to me, her face was radiant, but I had no radiance to return. Nevertheless, she took my hand and drew me to sit next to her.

"Here's daddy," she cooed, and Ellen warbled a happy greeting. I knew what was expected of me. I was supposed to adore the baby, gaze upon her plenitude and thus be filled with grace. I tried. I tried because I truly want everything to work out, because I love Eleanor and wish to be her partner in parenthood. So I watched Ellen and meditated on the marvel and mystery of life. El and I are no longer at the tail end of the long chain of humanity—I told myself—

flapping in the cold winds of evolution. Now we are grounded. We have forged a new link. We are no longer grasped only by the past, but we grasp the future. We have created the future in flesh.

When El turned again to me, I was ready, or thought I was. But she saw right through me to my stubborn core of indifference. Nevertheless, she encouraged me, prompted me with, "Isn't she beautiful?"

"Oh, yes," I replied.

"And smart."

"The smartest."

Later that evening, when the brilliant monstrance of her new religion was safely tucked away in the nursery under the sleepless eyes of the night jennies, Eleanor rebuked me. "Are you so selfish that you can't accept Ellen as your daughter? Does it have to be your seed or nothing? I know what happened to you was shitty and unfair, and I'm sorry. I really am. I wish to hell the slug got me instead. I don't know why it missed me. Maybe the next one will be more accurate. Will that make you happy?"

"No, El, don't talk like that. I can't help it. Give me time."

Eleanor reached over and put an arm around me. "I'm sorry," she said. "Forgive me. It's just that I want us to be happy, and I feel so guilty."

"Don't feel guilty. It's not your fault. I knew the risk involved in being with you. I'm an adult. I can adapt. And I do love Ellen. Before long she'll have her daddy wrapped around her little finger."

Eleanor was skeptical, but she wanted so much to believe me. That night she invited herself to my bedroom. We used to have an exceptional sex life. Sex for us was a form of play, competition, and truth-telling. It used to be fun. Now it's a job. The shaft of my penis is bruised by the normal bend and torque of even moderate lovemaking. My urethra is raw from the jets of scalding semen when I come. Of course I use special condoms and lubricants for the seared, without which I would blister El's vagina, but it's still not comfortable for either of us. El tries to downplay her discomfort by saying things like, "You're hot, baby," but she can't fool me. When we made love that night, I pulled out before ejaculating. El tried to draw me back inside, but I wouldn't go. She took my sheathed penis in her hands, but I said not to bother. I hadn't felt the need for a long time.

In the middle of the night, when I rose to go to my dungeon, Eleanor stirred and whispered, "Hate me if you must, but please don't blame the baby."

I ask my new belt how many eyebrow hairs an average person of my race, sex, and age has. The belt can access numerous encyclopedias to do simple research like this. *Five hundred fifty in each eyebrow*, it replies in its neuter voice. That's one thousand one hundred altogether, plenty of fuel to light my investigation. I pluck another and say, "Fred."

For Fred is a complete surprise to me. I had never formed a relationship with a clone before. They are service people. They are interchangeable. They wait on us in stores and restaurants. They clip our hair. They perform the menialities we cannot, or prefer not, to assign to machines. How can you tell one joan or jerome from another anyway? And what could you possibly talk about? Nice watering can you have there, kelly. What's the weather like up there, steve?

But Fred is different. From the start he's brought me fruit and cakes reputed to fortify tender digestive tracts, sunglasses, soothing skin creams, and a hat with a duckbill visor. He seems genuinely interested in me, even comes down to chat after his shift. I don't know why he's so generous. Perhaps he never recovered from the shock of first meeting me, freshly seared and implacably aggrieved.

Perhaps he recognizes that I'm the one around here most in need of his protection.

When I was ready to start sleeping with Eleanor again and I needed some of those special thermal condoms, my belt couldn't locate them on any of the shoppers, not even on the medical supply ones, so I asked Fred. He said he knew of a place and would bring me some. He returned the next day with a whole shopping bag of special pharmaceuticals for the cellular challenged: vitamin supplements, suppositories, plaque-fighting tooth soap, and knee and elbow braces. He brought 20 dozen packages of condoms, and he winked as he stacked them on the table. He brought more stuff he left in the bag.

I reached into the bag. There were bottles of cologne and perfume, sticks of waxy deodorant, air fresheners and odor eaters. "Do I stink?" I said.

"Like cat's piss, sir. No offense."

I lifted my hand to my nose, but I couldn't smell anything. Then I remembered the "stinkers" on the Moon shuttle, and I knew how I smelled. I wondered how Eleanor, during all those months, could have lived with me, eaten with me, and never mentioned it.

There was more in the bag: mouthwash and chewing gum. "My breath stinks too?"

In reply, Fred crossed his eyes and inflated his cheeks.

I thanked him for shopping for me, and especially for his frankness.

"Don't mention it, sir," he said. "I'm just glad to see you back in the saddle, if you catch my drift."

III

Two days ago was Ellen's first birthday. Unfortunately, Eleanor had to be away in Europe. Still, she arranged a little holo birthday party with her friends. Thirty-some people sat around, mesmerized by the baby, who had recently begun to walk. Only four of us, baby Ellen, a jenny, a russ, and I, were there in realbody. When I arrived and sat down, Ellen made a beeline for my lap. People laughed and said, "Daddy's girl."

I had the tundra dream again last night. I walked through the canopy lock right out into the white, frozen, endless tundra. The feeling was one of escape, relief, security.

My doctor gave me a complete physical last week. She said I had reached equilibrium with my condition. This was as good as it would get. Lately, I have been exercising. I have lost a little weight and feel somewhat stronger. But my joints ache something terrible and my doctor says they'll only get worse. She prescribed an old-time remedy: aspirin.

Fred left us two months ago. He and his wife succeeded in obtaining berths on a new station orbiting Mars. Their contracts are for five years with renewal options. Since arriving there, he's visited me in holo a couple times, says their best jump pilot is a stinker. And they have a stinker cartographer. Hint, hint.

Last week I finally purchased a personality bud for my belt system. It's having a rough time with me because I refuse to interact with it. I haven't even given it a name yet. I can't think of any suitable one. I call it "Hey, you," or "You, belt." Eleanor's chief of staff has repeated her offer to educate it for me, but I declined. In fact, I told her that if any of them breach its shell even once, I will abort it and start over with a new one.

Today at noon, we had a family crisis. The jenny on duty acquired a nosebleed while her backup was off running an errand. I was in the kitchen when I heard Ellen crying. In the nursery I found a hapless russ holding the kicking and screaming baby. The jenny called from the open bathroom door, "I'm coming. One minute, Ellie, I'm coming." When

Ellen saw me she reached for me with her fat little arms and howled.

"Give her to me," I ordered the russ. His face reflected his hesitation. "It's all right," I said.

"One moment, sir," he said and tongued for orders. "Okay, here." He gave me Ellen who wrapped her arms around my neck. "I'll just go and help Merrilee," he said, relieved, as he crossed to the bathroom. I sat down and put Ellen on my lap. She looked around, caught her breath, and resumed crying; only this time it was an easy, mournful wail.

"What is it?" I asked her. "What does Ellen want?" I reviewed what little I knew about babies. I felt her forehead, though I knew babies don't catch sick anymore. And with evercleans, they don't require constant changing. The remains of lunch sat on the tray, so she'd just eaten. A bellyache? Sleepy? Teething pains? Early on, Ellen was frequently feverish and irritable as her converted body sloughed off the remnants of the little boy chassis she'd overwritten. I wondered why during my year of brooding, I'd never grieved for him. Was it because he never had a soul? Because he never got beyond the purely data stage of recombination? Because he never owned a body? And what about Ellen, did she have her own soul, or did the original one stay through the conversion? And if it did, would it hate us for what we've done to its body?

Ellen cried, and the russ stuck his head out the bathroom every few moments to check on us. This angered me. What did they think I was going to do? Drop her? Strangle her? I knew they were watching me, all of them: the chief of staff, the security chief. They might even have awakened Eleanor in Hamburg or Paris where it was after midnight. No doubt they had a contingency plan for anything I might do.

"Don't worry, Ellie," I crooned. "Mama will be here in just a minute."

"Yes, I'm coming, I'm coming," said Eleanor's sleep-hoarse voice.

Ellen, startled, looked about, and when she didn't see her mother, bawled louder and more boldly. The jenny, holding a blood-soaked towel to her nose, peeked out of the bathroom.

I bounced Ellen on my knee. "Mama's coming, Mama's coming, but in the meantime, Sam's going to show you a trick. Wanna see a trick? Watch this." I pulled a strand of hair from my head. The bulb popped as it ignited, and the strand sizzled along its length. Ellen quieted in mid-fuss, and her eyes went wide. The russ burst out of the bathroom and sprinted toward us, but stopped and stared when he saw what I was doing. I said to him, "Take the jenny and leave us."

"Sorry, sir, I . . ." The russ paused, then cleared his throat. "Yes, sir, right away." He escorted the jenny, her head tilted back, from the suite.

"Thank you," I said to Eleanor.

"I'm here." We turned and found Eleanor seated next to us in an ornately carved, wooden chair. Ellen squealed with delight, but did not reach for her mother. Already by six months she had been able to distinguish between a holobody and a real one. Eleanor's eyes were heavy, and her hair mussed. She wore a long silk robe, one I'd never seen before, and her feet were bare. A sliver of jealousy pricked me when I realized she had probably been in bed with a lover. But what of it?

In a sweet voice, filled with the promise of soft hugs, Eleanor told us a story about a kooky caterpillar she'd seen that very day in a park in Paris. She used her hands on her lap to show us how it walked. Baby Ellen leaned back into my lap as she watched, and I found myself rocking her ever so gently. There was a squirrel with a bushy red tail involved in the story, and a lot of grown-up feet wearing very fashionable shoes, but I lost the gist of the story, so caught up was I in the voice that was telling it. El's voice spoke of an acorn who lost its cap and ladybugs coming to tea, but what it said was, I made you from the finest stuff. You are perfect. I will never let anyone hurt you. I love you always.

The voice shifted gradually, took an edge, and caused me the greatest sense of loss. It said, "And what about my big baby?"

"I'm okay," I said.

El told me about her day. Her voice spoke of schedules and meetings, a leader who lost his head, and diplomats coming to tea, but what it said was, You're a grown man who is capable of coping. You are important to me. I love it when you tease me and make me want you. It gives me great pleasure and takes me out of myself for a little while. Nothing is perfect, but we try. I will never hurt you. I love you always. Please don't leave me.

I opened my eyes. Ellen was a warm lump asleep on my lap, fist against cheek, lips slightly parted. I brushed her hair from her forehead with my sausage-like finger and traced the round curve of her cheek and chin. I must have examined her for quite a while, because when I looked up, Eleanor was waiting to catch my expression.

I said, "She has your eyebrows."

Eleanor laughed a powerful laugh. "Yes, my eyebrows," she laughed, "poor baby."

"No, they're her nicest feature."

"Yes, well, and what's happened to yours?"

"Nervous habit," I said. "I'm working on my chest hair now."

"In any case, you seem better."

"Yes, I believe I've turned the corner."

"Good, I've been so worried."

"In fact, I have just now thought of a name for my belt valet."

"Yes?" she said, relieved, interested.

"Skippy."

She laughed a belly laugh, "Skippy? Skippy?" Her face was lit with mirthful disbelief.

"Well, he's young," I said.

"Very young, apparently."

"Tomorrow I'm going to teach him how to hold a press conference." I didn't know I was going to say that until it was said.

"I see." Eleanor's voice hardened. "Thank you for warning me. What will it be about?"

"I'm sorry. That just came out. I guess it'll be a farewell. And a confession."

I could see the storm of calculation in Eleanor's face as her host of advisors whispered into her ear. Had I thrown them a curve? Come up with something unexpected? "What sort of confession?" she said. "What do you have to confess?"

"That I'm seared."

"That's not your fault, and no one will want to know anyway."

"Maybe not, but I've got to say it. I want people to know that I'm dying."

"We're *all* dying. Every living thing dies."

"Some faster than others."

"Sam, listen to me. I love you."

I knew that she did, her voice said so. "I love you too, but I don't belong here anymore."

"Yes, you do, Sam. This is your home."

I looked around me at the solid limestone wall, at the oak tree outside the window and the duck pond beyond. "It's very nice. I could have lived here, once."

"Sam, don't decide now. Wait till I return. Let's discuss it."

"Too late, I'm afraid."

She regarded me for several moments and said, "Where will you go?" By her question, I realized she had come to accept my departure, and I felt cheated. I had wanted more of a struggle. I had wanted an argument, enticements, tears, brave denial. But that wouldn't have been my El, my plan-for-everything Eleanor.

"Oh, I don't know," I said. "Just tramp around for a while, I guess. See what's what. Things have changed since the last time I looked." I stood up and held out the sleeping baby to El, who reached for her before we both remembered El was really in Europe. I placed Ellen in her crib and tucked her in. I kissed her cheek and quickly wiped it, before my kiss could burn her skin.

When I turned, El was standing, arms outstretched. She grazed my chest with her disembodied fingers. "Will you at least wait for me to give you a proper farewell? I can be there in four hours."

I hadn't intended to leave right away. I had just come up with the idea, after all. I needed to pack. I needed to arrange travel and accommodations. This could take days. But then I realized I was gone already and that I had everything I'd need: Skippy around my waist, my credit code, and the rotting stink of my body to announce me wherever I went.

She said, "At least stay in touch." A single tear slid down her face. "Don't be a stranger."

Too late for that too, dear El.

We were out of our minds with joy. Joy in full bloom and out of control, like weeds in our manicured lives.

WILLY IN THE NANO-LAB

Geoffrey A. Landis

A physicist engaged in doing solar cell research, Geoffrey A. Landis is a frequent contributor to Analog *and to* Asimov's Science Fiction, *and has also sold stories to markets such as* Interzone, Amazing *and* Pulphouse. *Landis is not a prolific writer, by the high-production standards of the genre, but he* is *popular. His story "A Walk in the Sun" won him a Nebula and a Hugo Award, his story "Ripples in the Dirac Sea" won him a Nebula Award, and his story "Elemental" was on the Final Hugo Ballot a few years back. His first book was the collection,* Myths, Legends, and True History. *He lives in Brook Park, Ohio.*

WILLY IN THE NANO-LAB

Willy made a nano-critter,
set it on his little sister.
It dissolved her into goo,
reassembled her as a kangaroo.

Little Willy, oh so clever,
put more nano-machines together.
Willy wasn't quite so smart:
they took Willy right apart.

It wasn't quite the thing to do;
dissolved his playroom into goo.
Now California's just goo that's gray
we didn't need it anyway.

—Geoffrey A. Landis

FURTHER READING

NOVELS:

Blood Music, Greg Bear
Queen of Angels, Greg Bear
Dispora, Greg Egan
Queen City Jazz, Kathleen Ann Goonan
Evolution's Shore, Ian McDonald
Necroville, Ian McDonald
Griffin's Egg, Michael Swanwick
Stations of the Tide, Michael Swanwick

ANTHOLOGIES:

Nanodreams, edited by Elton Elliott

COLLECTIONS:

Vacuum Diagrams, Stephen Baxter
Fractal Paisleys, Paul Di Filippo
Ribofunk, Paul Di Filippo
Axiomatic, Greg Egan
The Nanotech Chronicles, Michael F. Flynn

NON-FICTION:

Engines of Creation, K. Eric Drexler
Great Mambo Chicken and the Transhuman Condition, Ed Regis
Digital Delirium, edited by Arthur & Marilouise Kroker

SHORT STORIES

"Dogged Persistence," Kevin J. Anderson

"Statesmen," Poul Anderson
"Sins of the Mothers," Arlan Andrews
"Matter's End," Gregory Benford
"Down Under Crater Billy," Stephen Burns
"Death in the Promised Land," Pat Cadigan
"Life on the Moon," Tony Daniel
"Fidelity," Greg Egan
"The Mind's Place," Gregory Feeley
"Big Eater," Paul Di Filippo
"Distributed Mind," Paul Di Filippo
"Up the Lazy River," Paul Di Filippo
"The Blood Upon the Rose," Michael F. Flynn
"The Washer at the Ford," Michael F. Flynn
"The Day the Dam Broke," Kathleen Ann Goonan
"For White Hill," Joe Haldeman
"Dancing On Air," Nancy Kress
"The Days of Solomon Gursky," Ian McDonald
"Toward Kilamanjaro," Ian McDonald
"Getting to Know You," David Marusek
"On Sequia Time," Daniel Keyes Moran
"Procrustes," Larry Niven
"Whatever Gets You Through the Night," W.T. Quick
"Birth Day," Robert Reed
"Waging Good," Robert Reed
"The Bee's Kiss," Charles Sheffield
"Deep Safari," Charles Sheffield
"Les Fleurs Du Mal," Brian Stableford
"Reef Apes," Dave Smeds
"Suicidal Tendencies," Dave Smeds
"The Tree of Life," Brian Stableford
"The Gentle Seduction," Marc Stiegler
"Griffin's Egg," Michael Swanwick
"Nanoware Time," Ian Watson
"Flatline," Walter Jon Williams